THE DOOR

Magda Szabó was born in 1917 in Debrecen, Hungary. She began her literary career as a poet. In the 1950s she disappeared from the publishing scene for political reasons and made her living by teaching and translating from French and English. She began writing novels, and in 1978 was awarded the Kossuth Prize, the most prestigious literary award in Hungary. Magda Szabó died in 2007.

Len Rix's translations include three novels by Antal Szerb, including *Journey by Moonlight*, and one by Thomas Kadebó. In 2006 his version of *The Door* was shortlisted for the Independent Foreign Fiction Prize and was awarded the Oxford Weidenfeld Translation Prize.

D1387763

Magda Szabó

The Door

TRANSLATED BY
Len Rix

VINTAGE BOOKS
London

Published by Vintage

20

© Magda Szabó, 1987
Translation copyright © Len Rix 2005

Magda Szabó has asserted her right under the Copyright,
Designs and Patents Act 1988 to be identified as the author
of this work

First published with the title *Az Ajtó* by
Európa Könyvkiadó

First published in Great Britain in 2005 by
Harvill Secker

Vintage Books
Random House, 20 Vauxhall Bridge Road London, SW1V 2SA

www.vintage-books.co.uk

Addresses for companies within The Random House Group Limited, can be found at:
www.randomhouse.co.uk/offices.htm

The Random House Group Limited Reg. No. 954009

A CIP catalogue record for this book
is available from the British Library

This edition was published with the financial assistance of the
Translation Fund of the Hungarian Book Foundation

ISBN 978 0 09947 028 1

Typset by Palimpost Book Production Ltd,
Grangemouth, Stirlingshire

Penguin Random House is committed to a sustainable future for
our business, our readers and our planet. This book is made from
Forest Stewardship Council® certified paper.

Printed and bound in Great Britain by Clays Ltd, St Ives plc

THE DOOR

THE BOOK

THE DOOR

I seldom dream. When I do, I wake with a start, bathed in sweat. Then I lie back, waiting for my frantic heart to slow, and reflect on the overwhelming power of night's spell. As a child and young woman, I had no dreams, either good or bad, but in old age I am confronted repeatedly with horrors from my past, all the more dismaying because compressed and compacted, and more terrible than anything I have lived through. In fact nothing has ever happened to me of the kind that now drags me screaming from my sleep.

My dreams are always the same, down to the finest detail, a vision that returns again and again. In this never-changing dream I am standing in our entrance hall at the foot of the stairs, facing the steel frame and reinforced shatterproof window of the outer door, and I am struggling to turn the lock. Outside in the street is an ambulance. Through the glass I can make out the shimmering silhouettes of the paramedics, distorted to unnatural size, their swollen faces haloed like moons. The key turns, but my efforts are in vain: I cannot open the door. But I must let the rescuers in, or they'll be too late to save my patient. The lock refuses to budge, the door stands solid, as if welded to its steel frame. I shout for help, but none of the residents of our three-storey building responds; and they cannot because – I am suddenly aware – I'm mouthing vacantly, like a fish, and the horror of the dream reaches new depths as I realise that not only am I unable to open the door to the rescuers but I have also lost the power of speech.

It is at this point that I am woken by my own screaming. I switch on the light and try to control the desperate gasping for air which always seizes me after the dream. Around me stands the familiar furniture of our bedroom, and, over the bed itself, the family portraits, ikons in their high starched collars and braided coats, Hungarian Baroque and Beidermeier, my all-seeing, all-knowing ancestors. They alone are witness to the number of times I have raced down during the night to open the door to the rescuers and the ambulance; and they alone know how often I have stood there while the silence of the early-morning streets slowly gives way to the sounds of restlessly tossing trees and the cries of prowling cats that flood in through the open door, imagining what would happen if my struggle with the key proved in vain, and the lock failed to turn.

The portraits know everything, above all the thing I try hardest to forget. It is no dream. Once, just once in my life, not in the cerebral anaemia of sleep but in reality, a door did stand before me. That door opened. It was opened by someone who defended her solitude and impotent misery so fiercely that she would have kept that door shut though a flaming roof crackled over her head. I alone had the power to make her open that lock. In turning the key she put more trust in me than she ever did in God, and in that fateful moment I believed I was godlike – all-wise, judicious, benevolent and rational. We were both wrong: she who put her faith in me, and I who thought too well of myself.

Now, of course, none of that matters, because what happened is beyond remedy. So let them enter my dreams, the Kindly Ones, whenever they choose, with their high-heeled emergency-service buskins and tragic-mask faces beneath their safety helmets, to stand like a chorus with double-edged swords round my bed. Every night I turn out the light to wait for them, for the bell of this nameless horror to clang in my sleeping ear, for its ringing tones to lead me towards that dream-door that never opens.

My religion has no place for the sort of personal confession where we acknowledge through the mouth of a priest that we are sinners, that we deserve damnation for breaking the Commandments in every possible way, and are then granted absolution without need for explanation or details.

I shall provide that explanation, those details.

This book is written not for God, who knows the secrets of my heart, nor for the shades of the all-seeing dead who witness both my waking life and my dreams. I write for other people. Thus far I have lived my life with courage, and I hope to die that way, bravely and without lies. But for that to be, I must speak out. I killed Emerence. The fact that I was trying to save her rather than destroy her changes nothing.

THE CONTRACT

When we first met, I very much wanted to see her face, and it troubled me that she gave me no opportunity to do so. She stood before me like a statue, very still, not stiffly to attention but rather a little defeated-looking. Of her forehead I could see almost nothing. I didn't know then that the only time I would ever see her without a headscarf would be on her deathbed. Until that moment arrived she always went about veiled, like a devout Catholic or Jewess sitting shiva, someone whose faith forbade her from venturing too near the Lord with an uncovered head.

It was a summer's day, but by no means one to call for or even suggest any special need for protection, as we stood together in the garden, under a twilight sky tinged with violet. Among the roses, she seemed thoroughly out of place. One can tell instinctively what sort of flower a person would be if born a plant, and her genus certainly wasn't the rose, with its shameless carmine unfolding – the rose is no innocent. I felt immediately that Emerence could never be one, though I still knew nothing about her, or what she would one day become.

Her scarf projected forward, casting a shadow over her eyes, and it was only later that I discovered that their irises were blue. I would have liked to know the colour of her hair, but she kept it covered, as she would for as long as it remained synonymous with her inner self.

During that first early evening we lived through some

important moments. We each had to decide whether we could live and work together. My husband and I had been in our new home for only a couple of weeks. It was substantially larger than the previous one-room apartment which I had managed without help, not least because for ten years my writing career had been politically frozen. Now it was picking up again and here, in this new setting, I had become a full-time writer, with increased opportunities and countless responsibilities which either tied me to my desk or took me away from home. So here I stood in the garden, face to face with this silent old woman, since it had become clear that if someone didn't take over the housekeeping there would be little chance of my publishing the work I'd produced in my years of silence, or finding a voice for anything new I might have to say.

I had begun enquiring about domestic help the moment we finished moving our library-sized collection of books and our rickety old furniture. I pestered everyone I knew in the neighbourhood until finally a former classmate solved our problem. She told us there was an old woman who had worked for her brother for more years than she could remember, and whom she recommended wholeheartedly, assuming the person could find the time. She'd be better than a younger woman, being guaranteed not to set fire to the house with a cigarette, have boyfriend problems or steal; in fact she was more likely to bring us things if she took a liking to us, as she was a relentless giver of gifts. She had never had a husband or children, but a nephew visited her regularly, as did a police officer, and everyone in the neighbourhood liked her. My former classmate spoke of her with warmth and respect, and added that Emerence was a care-taker, someone with a bit of authority; she hoped the woman would take us on, because frankly, if she didn't warm to us, no amount of money would induce her to accept the job.

Things got off to a less than encouraging start. Emerence

had been rather brusque when asked to call round for a chat, so I tracked her down in the courtyard of the villa where she was caretaker. It was close by – so close I could see her flat from our balcony. She was washing a mountain of laundry with the most antiquated equipment, boiling bedlinen in a cauldron over a naked flame, in the already agonising heat, and lifting the sheets out with an immense wooden spoon. Fire glowed all around her. She was tall, big-boned, powerfully built for a person of her age, muscular rather than fat, and she radiated strength like a Valkyrie. Even the scarf on her head seemed to jut forward like a warrior's helmet. She had agreed to call, and so now we were standing here, in the garden in that twilight.

She listened in silence while I explained what her duties would be. Even as I spoke I was thinking that I had never believed those nineteenth-century novelists who compared a character's face to a lake. Now, as so often before, I felt ashamed to have dared question the classics. Emerence's face resembled nothing so much as a calm, unruffled, early-morning mirror of water. I had no idea how interested she might be in my offer. Her demeanour made it quite clear that she needed neither the job nor the money. However desperate I might be to employ her, that mirror-lake face, in the shadow of its ceremonial scarf, gave nothing away. I waited for what seemed ages. When she did finally respond, she didn't even raise her head. Her words were that perhaps we could talk about this later. One of her places of work was proving a disappointment. Both husband and wife were drinking too much, and the grown-up son was going to the dogs, so she wasn't going to keep them on. Assuming that someone could vouch for us, and assure her that neither of us were likely to brawl or get drunk, we might perhaps discuss the matter again. I stood there dumbfounded. This was the first time anyone had required references from us. "I don't wash just anyone's dirty linen," she said.

6

She had a pure, impressive, soprano voice. She must have been in the capital a long while – had I not at one point studied linguistics I would never have known from her accent that she came from our part of the country. Thinking the question would please her, I asked if she was from the Hajdú area; she just nodded, and agreed that she came from Nádori, or, to be more exact, from its sister village, Csabadul. Then she immediately changed the subject, in a way that made clear she had no wish to discuss the matter, she was in no mood to reminisce. It took me years to realise – as with so many other things – that she found my question pushy and prying.

Emerence had never studied Heraclitus, but she knew more about these things than I did. Whenever I could, I would rush back to my old village to seek out what had gone, what could never be brought back, the shadows that the family house had once cast on my face, my long-lost former home. And I found nothing, for where has the river wandered whose waters carried away the shards of my early life? Emerence knew better than to attempt the impossible. She was saving her strength for the time when she might actually do something about the past, though I would not understand what this meant until much later.

What I did gather that day, when she first pronounced those two names, Nádori and Csabadul, was that they were never to be mentioned, that they were for some reason taboo. Right, I thought, let's discuss the business in hand. Perhaps we could agree her hourly wage; that should mean something to her. But no, she didn't want to rush her decision. She would decide what we were to pay her when she had some idea of just how slovenly and disorderly we were, and how much work we'd be. She would set about getting references – not from the old school-mate, who would be prejudiced – and when she had, would give us her answer, even if it was no. I stared after her as she calmly strolled away, and there was a moment when I dallied with the thought that the old woman was so odd it might be better for all concerned if she turned us down. It wasn't too late – I could call out after her that the offer no longer stood. But I didn't.

A mere week later, Emerence reappeared. We had in the meantime bumped into her more than once in the street; but she had greeted us and passed on, as if she wanted neither to hurry the decision, nor slam a door shut before it had even opened. When she did at last call round, I noticed at once that she was dressed in all her finery. I instantly understood this language of clothes, and shifted about awkwardly in my scanty little sun-frock. She wore black – a finely-woven long-sleeved dress and gleaming patent-leather shoes. As if our previous discussion had never been interrupted, she announced that she would start the next day, and would be in a position later in the month to say what her wage was to be. As she spoke she stared stiffly at my naked shoulders. I took comfort in knowing that my husband would escape censure, sitting there, in thirty-degree heat, in his jacket and tie. Even in a heatwave he never wavered from the habits he had acquired in England before the war. The two of them beside me, thus attired, must have looked like a demonstration of dress code created for a primitive tribe, to which I belonged, inculcating the respect for external appearances considered appropriate to human dignity. If a single being in this world ever approached Emerence in his attitudes and values, that person was my husband. Naturally, for that reason, it was many years before they truly took to one other.

The old woman held out her hand to each of us in turn. Thereafter, she never touched me if she could avoid it. If I offered my hand, she would brush my fingers aside as if waving away a fly. She didn't enter our service that evening – that would have been unworthy, improper: she enlisted in it. As she was leaving, she said to my husband: "I wish the master good night." He stared after her. There was no man on the planet to whom this magnificent word might less apply. But that was how she addressed him until her dying day. It took a while for him to get used to his new title, and answer to it.

*

No formal agreement dictated the number of hours Emerence spent in our house, or the precise times of her arrival. We might conceivably see nothing of her all day. Then, at eleven at night, she would appear, not in the inner rooms, but in the kitchen or the pantry, which she would scrub until dawn. It might happen that for a day and a half we would be unable to use the bathroom because she had rugs soaking in the tub. Her capricious working hours were combined with awe-inspiring accomplishments. The old woman worked like a robot. She lifted unliftable furniture without the slightest regard for herself. There was something superhuman, almost alarming, in her physical strength and her capacity for work, all the more so because in fact she had no need to take so much on. Emerence obviously revelled in her work. She loved it. When she found herself with free time, she had no idea where to begin. Whatever she took on, she did to perfection, moving around the apartment in almost total silence – not because she was over-familiar or snooping; she simply avoided unnecessary conversation. She made demands, more than I had expected, but she also gave a lot. If I said we were having guests, or visitors turned up unannounced, she would ask if I needed help. Usually, I declined. I didn't want it known among my circle of friends that in my own home I was a person without a name. It was only for my husband that Emerence had found a title. I was neither "the lady writer" nor "madam". She didn't address me directly until she was able to place me in her scheme of things, until she had a clear sense of who I was and what title was appropriate for me. And in this too she was right. Until your attitude to a person is clear, any such defining term will be inaccurate.

Emerence, alas, was perfect in every respect; at times oppressively so. Her response to my timid words of gratitude was to make it clear that she didn't want constant approval. There was no need for praise; she was fully aware of what she had accomplished. She always wore grey, reserving black for holidays and special occasions. An apron, changed daily, protected her dress. Paper tissues she held in contempt, preferring snow-white linen handkerchiefs that crackled with starch. It came as a pleasant relief to discover that she did have some weaknesses after all. For example, she might stay silent half the day, for no apparent reason, no matter what I asked her. And I couldn't fail to notice that she was terrified of storms. The moment thunder and lightning approached she would drop whatever she was holding and, without a word of warning or explanation, rush back home to hide. "She's an old woman," I told my husband. "They don't come without manias." He shook his head. "This phobia of hers is both more and less than a mania," he said. "Clearly there is a reason for it, but it's not something she considers our business. When did she ever tell us anything significant about herself?" As I recall, she never had. Emerence wasn't much of a talker.

*

She'd been working for us for over a year when one day I had to ask her to take in a parcel for me, which was supposed to arrive that afternoon. My husband would be out examining and it was the only day on which the dentist could see me. I tacked a note on the door, telling the messenger who to seek out in our absence, and where. Then I ran over to her little flat. I had forgotten to mention it while she was tidying up. She'd just finished at our place and could only have been home a few minutes. There was no response to my knocking, but I could hear someone rummaging around inside, and the fact that the handle did not budge was hardly surprising. No-one had ever seen Emerence's door standing open. Even when she could (with great difficulty) be entreated to come out, the moment she was back inside she bolted everything up again. The whole neighbourhood was used to it.

I called for her to be quick. I was in a hurry and there was something I wanted her to do. At first my words were met with the same steady silence, but when I rattled the handle she shot out so fast I thought she was going to hit me. She came out, slamming the door behind her, and screamed at me not to pester her outside working hours. She wasn't paid for it. I stood there, scarlet down to my neck with humiliation. It was an extraordinary outburst, totally uncalled-for. Even if she did, for some strange reason, feel demeaned by my summoning her out of her private domain, she could have said so a little more quietly. I mumbled what I had come to ask her. She made no reply, but stood there glaring at me, as if I'd plunged a knife in her arm. Right. I bade her a polite farewell, went back home, phoned the dentist and cancelled the appointment. My husband had already left; I was the only one free to stay and wait for the parcel. I wasn't in the mood to read, I just dawdled around the flat. I kept wondering what I had done to deserve such a deliberately insulting and hurtful rejection. Besides, it was so untypical of the old woman. Her behaviour was usually so formal as to be almost embarrassing.

I was a long time on my own. To complete the ruin of my day, the package didn't arrive. I had waited in vain. My husband didn't return at his usual hour either, but stayed on with his students after the exam finished. I was leafing through a book of reproductions when I heard the key turn in the front door.

It wasn't followed by the usual words of greeting, so I knew it wasn't my husband. It was Emerence, the very last face I wanted to see on this evening of torment. By now, I thought, she will have calmed down, she's come to apologise. But she didn't even glance in. Not a word was said. I could hear her busy with something in the kitchen. Shortly afterwards, the door slammed and she'd gone.

When my husband arrived I darted out to fetch our usual supper of two glasses of yoghurt. In the fridge I found a cold platter of rose-pink chicken breasts that had been cut into slices and then reassembled with the skill of a surgeon. The next day I thanked Emerence for her conciliatory treat, and held out the newly washed plate. There was no "My pleasure, and good health to you." She denied all knowledge of the chicken and refused to take the plate back. I still have it today. Much later, when I telephoned to chase up the undelivered parcel, I discovered that I'd hung around the whole afternoon for nothing. The package was in the pantry, under the bottom shelf: she had brought it in with the chicken. She'd stood there waiting at our front door, given my message word for word to the courier, brought it in without telling me, and disappeared off home.

It was a major event in our lives. For a long time afterwards I thought her slightly insane and felt that we would have to make allowances for the idiosyncratic ways in which her mind functioned.

Many things served to strengthen this belief, not least the details provided by the local handyman who lived in the same villa as Emerence and was widely respected. He filled his spare time by doing odd jobs and collecting payments. I gathered that since he'd lived there – about a thousand years – not one of the residents had got beyond the porch that fronted Emerence's home. Guests, he said, were never invited in, and she took it very badly if anyone unexpectedly called to her to come out.

She kept her cat inside, and never let him out. You could sometimes hear the animal mewing, but you couldn't see what was in there. Every window was boarded over with shutters that were never opened. What else might she be hoarding in there, beside the cat? Even if she did have expensive things, locking them away like that was a very bad idea. Anyone might think she was hiding something of real value. It could lead to her being attacked. She never went out of the immediate neighbourhood, except perhaps for the funeral of someone she knew. She'd walk with them down that last road, but always scurry off home, as if in constant fear of danger. So there was no need to take offence if you weren't allowed in: her brother Józsi's son and the Lieutenant Colonel were also entertained on the porch, summer and winter alike. They had long accepted that entry was forbidden even to them. They laughed it off. They were used to it.

Hearing all this produced a rather alarming picture in my mind, and I became even more troubled. How could anyone live in such a shut-off way? And why wouldn't she let the animal out, if she had one? The villa had its own little patch of garden, with a fence around it. I thought, in truth, she must have been a little gone in the head. That idea lasted until one of her longstanding admirers, the laboratory technician's widow by the name of Adélka, revealed, in an epic narrative, that Emerence's first cat, a great hunter, had decimated the stock of a pigeon breeder, a tenant who had moved in during the war. The man found a radical solution. When Emerence explained that the cat was not a university professor amenable to reason, and that it was, unfortunately, in his nature to enjoy killing even when well-fed, the pigeon breeder wasted no breath suggesting she keep the beast under lock and key. He tracked the noble hunter down, grabbed hold of him and strung him up from the handle of Emerence's front door. Returning home, the old woman had to stand there, under her own porch roof, while he gave her a formal lecture: he had been forced, regrettably, to defend his family's only guaranteed livelihood, with the instruments of his choice.

Emerence said not a word. She released the cat from the wire, the 'instrument' the executioner had chosen over ordinary rope. The corpse was a shocking sight, its throat gaping wide. She buried it in the garden, where she had buried Mr Szloka, and that led to the man being later exhumed, which brought more slander on her name, because the cat-hangman called in the police. Fortunately the matter was smoothed over.

But none of this brought much joy to the pigeon-breeder. He could never get her involved in an argument; she looked straight through him; and on official matters she communicated through an intermediary, the handyman. However, the animals remained linked in some sort of dark bond. One after another the pigeons fell over, dead. So the police returned. The Lieutenant Colonel was then only a Second Lieutenant. The pigeon-breeder accused Emerence of poisoning the birds, but the autopsy found nothing in their stomachs. The local vet decided that they had died from an unknown bird virus. Other people had lost pigeons too, so there was nothing to be gained from pestering his neighbour and the police about it.

At this point the whole house ganged up against the cat-murderer. Mr and Mrs Brodarics, the most highly respected couple in the building, made a submission to the local council that the ceaseless coo-cooing at dawn was disturbing their sleep. The handyman declared that his balcony was constantly covered in droppings. The lady engineer complained that the birds triggered her allergies. The council didn't order the pigeon-breeder to destroy his stock, but they made it clear to him that people were disappointed, and wanted retribution, a proper punishment for the hanged cat.

Punishment duly arrived. The cat-murderer suffered a fresh disaster. His new consignment of birds perished as mysteriously as the old ones. Once again he tried to lay charges, only this time the Second Lieutenant didn't bother with an autopsy, he tore a strip off him for wasting police time. The hangman finally got the message. He hurled abuse at Emerence on her porch and, as his final act, despite a complete lack of incriminating evidence, did away with her new cat, before moving away to one of the leafier suburbs.

Even after his move, he continued to irritate the authorities with a stream of fresh charges against the caretaker. Emerence bore this persecution with such gentle serenity, and so much good humour, that both the council and the police came to like her very much. Not one of the allegations was taken seriously. They had come to realise that the old woman's character would always provoke anonymous accusations, the way magnetic mountains attract lightning. The police opened a special dossier on Emerence. In it they filed away the many and varied depositions, dismissing them with a wave of the hand. Each time a letter arrived, even the newest man on the job could recognise the pigeon-breeder's private lexicon, his rambling, baroque turn of phrase. Policemen regularly dropped in on her for a cup of coffee and a chat. As he rose steadily through the ranks, the future Lieutenant Colonel took each new recruit aside at the first opportunity and introduced him to her. Emerence prepared sausages, savoury scones, pancakes, whatever took his fancy. She reminded young men from the country of their old village, their own grandmothers, their distant families. They in turn never troubled her with the fact that the charges against her included murdering and robbing Jews during the war, spying for America, transmitting secret messages, regularly receiving stolen goods in her home and hoarding vast wealth.

Adélka's revelations eased my concern, especially after I had to call in at the police station about a lost certificate of identity. While I stood dictating my particulars the Lieutenant Colonel passed through the hall. Hearing my name, he had me sit with him while the new document was being made out. I thought the reason for his interest must be that he knew my work, but it turned out I was wrong. All he wanted to hear about was how Emerence was and what she was doing. He'd heard that she was still working for us, and was anxious to know whether her nephew's little girl was back home from hospital. I hadn't even known the child existed.

I think at the beginning I must have been rather afraid of Emerence. Although she looked after us for over twenty years, during the first five of them it would have taken precision instruments to measure the degree to which she permitted real communication between us. I make friends easily and chat away to complete strangers; Emerence imparted only what was essential. She finished her jobs quickly and carefully, always aware that she had countless other things to do and other calls to make. The twenty-four hours of her day were crammed full. And yet, even though she allowed no-one within her four walls, news raced to her door. The front porch of her flat was like a telex centre. Everything about everyone was reported there – death, scandal, glad tidings, catastrophe.

She delighted in providing for the sick. Almost every day I would meet her in the street, carrying a covered dish on a tray. I could always tell from its shape what she was holding. It was a large christening bowl. From it she served up food to anyone the local grapevine pronounced in need of a good meal. Emerence always knew exactly where she was needed. She inspired trust because people knew they could open their hearts to her without expecting her own confidences in return; they would get only commonplace remarks and well-known facts. Politics didn't interest her, the arts even less. She knew nothing about sport. She was aware of her neighbours' marital problems, but she never passed judgement. What she most enjoyed was studying the weather, since her visits to the cemetery depended entirely on her fears of a possible storm. She was terrified of them, as I have already said. The weather dictated not only what qualified as her social activities but, in autumn and winter, her every waking hour. Once the bitter cold arrived, everything was dominated by what fell from the sky. Her jobs included clearing the snow from almost all the larger houses around. She never had a moment to listen to the radio, except late at night or in the early hours, but she could tell what the next day would bring by walking down the street and looking at the stars to observe the brightness or fading of their fires, as her distant ancestors had done long before weather forecasts existed. She even used the names given them by her forefathers.

*

She was responsible for clearing the snow from eleven different buildings. On the job she was unrecognisable, her meticulously groomed person disguised as a sort of giant rag doll, toiling away in heavy rubber boots rather than her usual gleaming shoes. In a particularly severe winter you could imagine her permanently on the streets and never at home, and think that, unlike other mortals, she did not rest. This was indeed more or less the case. Emerence never actually lay down. After washing, she merely changed her clothes – her furniture did not include a bed. Instead she took short naps on a tiny couch, a so-called "lovers' seat". She claimed that the moment she lay down she became weak. Sitting gave her proper support for her aching back. Lying down, she felt dizzy. No, she didn't need a bed.

Of course, in the real snow storms she even went without the nap on the lovers' seat. By the time she'd finished at the fourth property, the driveway to the first was again thickly covered. She ran from one house to another in her huge boots, with a birch broom that was even bigger than she was. We became used to the fact that on days like these she wouldn't look in on us at all. I never raised this with her. Her unstated reasons were perfectly clear: we had a roof over our heads; she cleaned for us on a reasonably regular basis; we could wait until she had time again, when she would make it up to us. And anyway, a little bending and stretching would do me no harm at all.

Once the snow had finished asserting its authority, Emerence would reappear and impose miraculous order on the apartment. And without saying a word, she would leave a sweet pastry or pan of honey cakes on the kitchen table. These smuggled gifts of food carried the same message as the first we had received, the sliced chicken that followed her incomprehensible rudeness. "You have been good," the dish announced, as if we were schoolchildren (and not both on a diet!), "and good little boys and girls get their due reward."

I still don't know how she fitted so much living into one life. She almost never sat down. If she wasn't wielding a broom she would be bustling about somewhere with the christening bowl, or tracing the owner of some abandoned animal, or, if she failed in this quest, attempting to foist the poor waif on someone else. Mostly she succeeded, but if not, then the creature vanished from the neighbourhood, as if it had never nosed hungrily around the rubbish bins.

She worked long hours in a great many places, earning extremely well, but she refused to take tips in any form. Somehow I could understand that, but why she refused to accept presents was beyond me. The old woman was interested only in giving, and if anyone tried to surprise her with something, she never smiled, she flew into a rage. Over the years I tried, again and again, to make her gifts of various kinds, thinking that from me at least she might accept one. I never succeeded. She would inform me rudely that there was no extra charge for whatever she had done. Cut to the quick, I would put the envelope aside. My husband laughed at me. He told me to stop buttering her up and trying to change the way things were. She suited him very well, this fleeting shadow who, despite her ridiculous sense of timing and total disregard for normality, saw to all our needs, and wouldn't accept even a cup of coffee. Emerence was the ideal home help. If what she did wasn't enough, and if I had to have a deeply meaningful relationship with everyone I met, well, that was my problem. It wasn't easy for me to accept that, as with everyone else at that time, Emerence was determined keep us too at arm's length.

CHRIST'S BROTHERS AND SISTERS

The truth is, for many years we mattered very little to her. This changed suddenly, when my husband became ill, so ill that his life was in danger. Since the old woman had appeared to show no interest whatever in what happened to us, I was convinced that if I told her the full, terrifying truth it would impinge on her emotional life to the extent of a consolatory plate of food, at most. So I took my husband off to his operation for a pulmonary abscess without a word to her. No-one in our building or the wider neighbourhood knew where we were going, and this included Emerence. The pre-operative visits had all been made without her knowledge and she had no idea what was afoot.

When I finally arrived home, she was sitting in the armchair cleaning silver, with a tangled pile of teaspoons in her apron. The operation had lasted nearly six hours. Anyone who has sat staring at the emergency light over the door of a surgical theatre, knowing that the patient might never regain consciousness, will understand the state I was in when I stepped into the apartment. Emerence began by telling me that she'd been left out of the single most important event of my life; that I shared only transitory things with her, in the most general way. She was positively glaring at me. I'd shut her out, like a stranger, from all my terror of an operation that might well have proved fatal. No, she wasn't offended, she was furious. I replied that I'd never before known her show the slightest interest in us, so how was

I supposed to guess that what was happening now would affect her in any way? Meanwhile, no offence intended, but would she kindly leave me alone? I wanted an early night; it had been a difficult day and things weren't over yet.

She left immediately. I thought I had offended her so deeply that she was gone for ever. But about half an hour later I was startled out of a shallow, troubled dream by the sound of her moving about the flat, and then she appeared with a steaming goblet. It was a real work of art, made of thick, royal-blue glass, borne on an iron tray. A pair of hands were carved around it in the shape of an oval garland. On the woman's wrist was a bracelet, on the man's, lace trimming. Together they held a gold plaque inscribed *TOUJOURS*, in blue enamel lettering. I lifted it off its base and held it up to the light. It contained a dark, fuming liquid, smelling of cloves.

"Drink it!" she commanded.

I didn't want to drink. All I wanted was some peace and quiet.

"Drink," she repeated, as to a badly brought up, half-witted child. Then, when she saw me putting the cup down and refusing to open my mouth, she seized it and splashed some of the scalding mulled wine down my front. I screamed. She grabbed my hand and rapped the mug against my teeth. If I didn't want her to tip it all over me, I had to swallow it. And, despite being unbearably hot, it was wonderful. Five minutes later the trembling had gone. For the first time in her life, Emerence sat down beside me on the sofa, took the empty cup from my hands and waited for me to speak, to talk those unknown six hours, and whatever was still to come, out of my system.

But I couldn't talk, or begin to explain what I had been through, or in any way convey the horrors that had led up to it. Also, the wine was having an effect: I had downed it in a single gulp. I know I fell asleep because at one stage I woke suddenly to find the light on, as it had been when I returned home, but with the clock now reading two a.m. She must have uncovered our bed, because I was lying under a light blanket which she could only have taken from it. In her usual calm, everyday voice she stated that there was no point spending the night brooding about things. I should stop worrying. Everything would be fine – she could always sense death. None of the neighbourhood dogs had given any sign. No glass had been broken, either in her kitchen or in mine. If I didn't believe her, that was my right. Perhaps I'd rather turn to the Church? In that case she'd bring me a Bible. There was no obligation to speak to her at all.

At that moment I wasn't thinking of the mulled wine, or even her long vigil beside me. All I could feel was her mockery. Once again, her words had stung me. Wasn't it enough that every Sunday I went a roundabout way to church to avoid her comments? How, when she showed no desire to understand, could I explain to her what the act of worship meant to me; or how many unseen presences thronged the pews around me, who down the centuries had all shared my beliefs and prayed as I did; or how those sixty minutes of the service constituted the one hour when I could be sure of communing with my late father and mother? Emerence understood nothing of this. She rejected it. Like the leader of some primitive tribe she flew her standard – a sequinned evening dress – against the banner of the Lamb of God.

The old woman opposed the church with an almost sixteenth-century fanaticism; not only the priesthood, but God himself and all the biblical characters, with the single exception of Joseph, whom she revered for his occupation: her own father had been a carpenter. I once saw the house where she was born. From behind a hedge its warm glow radiated a simple dignity. The sturdy pillars of the veranda, under the twin-peaked roof, made you think at once of a baroque peasant dwelling and a Far-Eastern pagoda. Its design no doubt reflected the taste and personality of the late József Szeredás. The cow-trees, as Emerence called the now portly sycamores that surrounded the house, had put out huge branches and there was a flower garden in full bloom. At the time of my visit it was still the finest house in Nádori, the office and workshop of the carpenters' co-operative. Emerence's Voltairean anti-clericism didn't make sense. It was years before I understood its source. The problem troubled me deeply until I fitted all the pieces together with the help of another of her friends, Sutu the greengrocer, and the whole story fell into place.

Emerence's religious objections weren't the result of living through the years of siege that followed the ending of the Great War and the first peace, nor did they amount to a philosophical position taken amid the ashes of a world again reduced to rubble. They arose from a primitive desire for revenge over an aid parcel from Sweden. Her co-religionists had received a consignment from one of the churches in Scandinavia. Until then no-one had shown much interest in Emerence's beliefs, nor had they seen her at any of the services. She was always working, especially in her earlier years, when she regularly took in washing and dealt with the bulk of it on Sundays. While others went to pray, she fired up her little boiler and started soaping. The news duly reached her that fellow Christians abroad had sent gifts for the congregation. Her friend Polett had run straight to her with the news. When the distribution began in the chapel Emerence, having never shown her face in church before, suddenly appeared in her black Sunday best and stood waiting for her name to be called. People from the immediate neighbourhood knew who she was, but none of them thought for a moment that she was counting on receiving anything. The ladies in charge, who had acted as translators for the visiting Swedish mission, looked on in embarrassment at the gaunt figure standing there, blank-faced, waiting. They realised that even if she didn't attend church she was still a member of the congregation, but by then all the woollen and cotton garments had been shared out. All that remained at the bottom of the basket were some evening dresses, which some kind Swedish woman, weeding out her unwanted bits and pieces without considering the real situation here, had thought fit to include. They didn't want to send her away empty-handed. As it later emerged, they hoped she might be able to sell the garment at a theatre or community arts centre, or perhaps exchange it for something to eat. In no way did they intend the mockery Emerence felt, as she hurled the dress at the feet of their leader. From that day on, not work but a private vow kept her from church, even on those rare occasions when she did have an hour free. Henceforth, both God and the Church were iden-tified in her mind with those charitable ladies, and she never passed over an opportunity to take a dig at the worshipping classes. She didn't spare me either, whenever she caught me leaving the house half an hour before the Sunday service with the book of psalms in my hands.

When we first met, not knowing the story of the evening dress, I had invited her, in my well-intentioned ignorance, to go with me. She was not, she told me bluntly, one of your great ladies who trot along to church to parade themselves in green and blue paint. She wouldn't go even if she had no driveways to sweep. I stared at her in wonder, because from the very first it was apparent to me that she had a sister in the Scriptures, the biblical Martha. Her life too had been a ceaseless round of hard work and giving help to others. But what had made Emerence so like the saint? When I did finally learn the cause – the evening dress – I was profoundly shocked and demanded an explana-tion. She laughed in my face, which was most unlike her. Neither tears nor happy laughter had much part in her world.

She told me that she needed neither priest nor Church, and she never contributed. She'd seen enough of God's handiwork during the war. She had no quarrel with the carpenter and his son: they were ordinary working people. The son was taken in by politicians' lies. The moment he started to make trouble for the leaders, they had to get him involved in something, so that he would be executed. The person she felt most sorry for was his mother. She couldn't have had a single happy day. The strangest thing was, the first time she got a proper night's sleep must have been on Good Friday. Up till then she'd had nothing but worry over her son.

As she delivered this tirade about Christ as victim of political machinations and a trumped-up criminal charge, who finally stepped out of the life of his poor Virgin Mother after all her sleepless nights of heartbreak and worry, I fairly expected a bolt from above to strike her dead. She knew she had upset me, and she was glad. I held my head high and set off in the direction of the church. She followed me with a wicked stare. For the first time, I saw what a remarkable creature she was. She claimed no interest in politics and yet, by some mysterious everyday process, she had managed to absorb something of what we had all been through during those years after the war. And I thought too, someone should seek out the sort of priest who could reawaken in her what clearly was once there. Then I realised, she would only hurl insults at him. Emerence was a Christian, but the minister who might convince her of the fact didn't exist. Not one spangle remained of that evening dress, but the glitter of sequins was burned into her consciousness.

*

That night, of course, she only wanted to provoke me. But strangely, it calmed me down. If she sensed real trouble she wouldn't be teasing me, I thought, but, thank God, she was. She was having a bit of fun at my expense. I tried to get up, but she forbade it. If I was good, she would tell me a story, but I would have to stop wriggling and close my eyes. I nestled down. Emerence remained standing, leaning against the heater. I knew so little about her, only the rather shadowy picture I'd managed to piece together over the years from isolated scraps of information. It was practically nothing. On this most surreal of nights, with life and death waiting hand in hand in the wintry dawn, Emerence sought to quell my terrified thoughts by finally introducing herself.

"'You are Christ's sisters and brothers,' my mother used to say, because my father was a carpenter – a carpenter and cabinetmaker. His younger brother, my godfather, was a foreman-builder, but he died soon after my christening. He too was good with his hands, like all the Szeredás family. Our father was very knowledgeable, and a fine figure of a man. As for my mother, she was a fairy princess. Her golden hair trailed behind her on the floor; she could actually step on it. My grandfather was very proud of her. He wouldn't let her marry a peasant, and resented even a craftsman. He'd sent her to school and made my father promise he would never put her out to work. And he didn't. While my father was alive she just read books. But that didn't last very long, because, you see, when I was barely three the poor man died. It's strange, but my grandfather took violently against him for having the nerve to die, as if he'd deliberately wished it on himself to spite him.

"The coming of the war made everything a lot more difficult. I don't think Mother was in love with the foreman in the workshop at the start, but she couldn't run the place on her own, so she married him. My stepfather didn't care very much for books, but that wasn't the main problem. They were calling everyone up into the army, and the poor man was terrified that his turn would come. But he got on well with my mother, and he put up with us as well. He wasn't a bad man, although he made me leave school, and the headmaster was very upset about it, but I was needed to cook for the harvesters because Mother wasn't up to it, and I also looked after the twins. Our stepfather wasn't unkind to them, but this wasn't surprising. If you've ever seen two fairy-tale children, that's what they were. They were the living image of Mother. My little brother Józsi – you know his son, the one who comes to visit me – doesn't look like any of us. I never saw much of Józsi, because when my father died our grandfather Divék – Mother's father – made him go and live with him. He spent more time in Csabadul than with us in Nádori. My mother's remaining family live there to this day.

"When they took me out of school the headmaster made a terrible fuss. He said it was a dreadful shame, an utter waste. Stepfather told him that anyone who stuck his nose into another family's business was a troublemaker, and he'd better not try to turn me against the idea or he'd bash his head in. He'd married a widow with four children, and he might be called up at any moment: the woman couldn't cope with the work on her own. Did he think he was pleased that I'd also have to work? What was he supposed to do? He had no-one to help in the workshop, or, for that matter, on the land. There was a constant demand for farm produce, but now there wasn't even enough for the animals. Well, he said his piece to the headmaster and set me to work. He wasn't evil – you mustn't think that – just frightened. You must have seen what people are like, what they're capable of when they're afraid. I don't bear him any grudges, though he beat me often enough, because at first I wasn't much good. We had some land, but until then it had never been any concern of mine. I'd gone out to play, not to work. All the time, my stepfather was shaking and swearing, because call-up letters were flying around like birds.

"One evening, after I'd put the twins to bed and the house was at last quiet – Józsi was no longer at home but with my grandfather – Mother told him not to keep speaking of his fears because it would make them come true. In his terror he gabbled away: he feared the worst because he'd dreamed that if he was called up he would never see us again. And he didn't. He was the first conscript from Nádori to be killed.

"Mother had no idea where to begin with the workshop. There was a ban on the sale of wood, so there was no building going on and the men had disappeared. But in the early days she thought we'd be able to get by without a man – she was a farmer's daughter, she understood the land, somehow she would manage on her own. You should have seen how she struggled. I did all I possibly could to help – I wasn't a stupid child – but we were going nowhere. At nine years old I cooked for everyone and looked after the twins. When the news came of my step-father's death I realised she truly had loved him. Now she was in mourning for two men, my father and my stepfather, though my stepfather didn't even have a grave. She started to find life unbearable. Don't think it's only your sort who have feelings.

"She was weak, helpless, and very young. One day, when the little ones were being particularly difficult, something got into me too. I mean, I was still a child myself. She had hit me because I had spent my time playing instead of doing the chores she had given me, and I thought, 'I'll run away. I'll go and be with Józsi in Csabadul. Grandfather always looks after him so well. Even if he does give him things to do, it's not very much.' And I would take the twins with me. Mother could do what she liked, but we were clearing off. I could get there on foot, I thought. I knew which way it was; it was only the next village, after all.

"So off we went, early one fine morning, all three of us, me with a blond child on either hand. But we'd got only as far as the threshing yard when the twins wanted to sit down and eat, and then they demanded water. So I ran to the farmyard well with the tin mug I always wore on a string round my neck. I had found that small children are always wanting to drink, and I never went out without the mug, and certainly not if it was any distance. The well was close by, but not that close: what does a child know about near and far? Just as I got there a storm began. I'd never seen one break so quickly; we'd never had such thunder, or such a hurricane, in our part of the country. In seconds the sky was transformed. It wasn't black, as I'd seen it before, it was violet, and ablaze from end to end, as if fires had been lit between the clouds. Thunder rolled across, the noise almost burst my eardrums, but I filled the mug and ran back to where they had been, looking for those little blond heads, because when I'd looked back I hadn't seen them, only the lightning as it struck the tree beside them.

"By the time I had staggered over to where they were, smoke was pouring out everywhere. By then they were both dead, but I didn't realise it, because they looked like nothing you would consider human. Then the storm broke. The downpour clung to me like sweat. I stood there beside my little brother and sister, staring at the two black stumps. If they looked like anything at all it was charred logs of firewood, only smaller and more gnarled. I stood there stupidly, turning my face this way and that. Where were the little blond heads? Those strange things in front of me couldn't possibly be my siblings.

"So, are you surprised that my mother threw herself down the well? It was all she needed, a sight like this, and my hysterical screaming. I was screaming so loud that when the storm stopped I could be heard as far away as the main road, and of course the house. Mother ran out, barefoot and still in her nightgown. She hurled herself at me, and beat me. She had no idea I'd been running away from her tears and bad temper, her endless worrying and complaining. She didn't know what she was doing. In her despair, she wanted to hit out and destroy, to strike the nearest living thing as a way of striking at life itself. Then she saw the twins and realised why I had called her. For a second her face blazed, then she flashed past me and sped away in the rain, her wild hair trailing along the ground behind her, screeching like a bird.

"I saw what she was going to do, but I couldn't move. I stood there, next to the tree and the corpses. The thunder and lightning had stopped. If I'd run for help at that moment they might have saved her. Our house was right by the main road – the threshing yard was just beyond the garden – but I stood there as if bewitched, my mind blank. My brow was dripping wet, but my brain had gone numb. No-one could love the way I loved those two little ones. I stared at the stumps. I still couldn't make myself believe I had anything to do with them. I didn't cry for help. I stood there gaping, and then began to wonder vaguely what my mother was doing all that time at the bottom of the well. What was she up to? What could she possibly be doing? The poor woman had fled from me, from the terrible sight, from her fate. She'd had enough of everything. It's like that, sometimes. Suddenly you want to end it all.

"I gazed around for a short while, looking at this and that, then walked away at a calm, leisurely pace. There was no-one in the house, so no point in going there. I stood beside the main road and called out to the first person who passed by, to come and speak to my mother, because she'd gone into the well, and my brother and sister – the ones with the yellow hair – had disappeared from under the tree, and there was something black there instead. The neighbour had been strolling by, and now he ran to her, and in the end he sorted everything out. They left me with the headmaster while someone went for my grandfather. Grandfather took me away, but he didn't let me stay with him, only my little brother Józsi; and when the gentlemen came from Budapest looking for a maidservant, he handed me over at once. They took me away as soon as the funeral was over. I didn't understand a thing about the funeral, though I did see my loved ones again, because both coffins were open, my mother in one and the twins in the other. The sight of my mother there was just as puzzling as that of the twins. Their golden hair seemed to have melted away – there was nothing on their heads, in fact their heads were no longer there. They were so unlike actual children I couldn't cry or mourn for them. It was all too much. I could no longer take anything in.

"Do you know what I am saving up for? For a crypt. It'll be as big as the whole world, and there won't be another as beautiful anywhere. Every window will have different-coloured glass, and there'll be shelves in it, and a coffin on every shelf – my father, my mother, the twins, me, and, if Józsi's boy stays true to me, the other two places could be his. I started saving up for it even before the war, but then I needed the money for something else. They asked for it, for a good cause, so I gave it, it didn't matter. I saved up again. It was stolen, but I started again. I've always got money coming in. A certain person sends it to me from abroad. And then I've never in all my life been a day without work. There's enough now for the crypt. Every time I go to a funeral I look to see if there's a building like the one I'm planning; but there never is. Mine will be different from all the rest. You'll see, when the sun rises and sets, what wonderful bands of light it will throw through the coloured windows on to the coffins. My heirs will be able to build a crypt that everyone will stop and stand before. Do you believe me?"

VIOLA

It has always been important to me to lead a full emotional life: to have those who are closely connected to me show pleasure when we meet. Emerence's perfect indifference the next morning didn't exactly wound my pride, but was a disappointment after that surreal night, when she had stayed by my side and revealed her childhood self to me. I had slept free from care and anxiety, and by dawn I felt the world was a sane place after all. Not for a minute did I doubt that the operation would be a success, so completely had her words dissolved my fear. Before that night, her headscarf had concealed every important detail of her life; now she had become the central figure in a wild rural landscape, with the blazing sky behind her, charred corpses before her, and sheet lightning over the sweep of the farmyard well. I truly believed that at last something had been resolved between us, that Emerence would no longer be a stranger but a friend: my friend.

She was nowhere to be seen, either in the apartment when I awoke, or in the street when I set off for the hospital; but there was evidence of her handiwork in the section of pavement outside the front door swept clean of snow. Obviously, I told myself in the car, she was making her rounds of the other houses. I wasn't distressed, or heartbroken. I felt that only good news awaited me at the hospital, as indeed it did. I was out until lunchtime. Arriving home, rather hungry, I was sure she'd be sitting there in the apartment, awaiting my return. I was wrong.

I was faced with the disconcerting experience of walking into my own home, bearing news of life and death, and no-one to share it with. Our Neanderthal ancestor learned to weep the first time he stood in triumph over the bison he had dragged in and found no-one to tell of his adventures, or show his spoils to, or even his wounds. The apartment stood empty. I went into one room after another, looking for her, even calling out her name. I didn't want to believe that, on this of all days, when she didn't even know if my patient was alive or dead, she could be somewhere else. The snow had stopped falling. There could be nothing in the street requiring her attention. And yet she was nowhere to be found.

I went into the kitchen, suddenly no longer hungry, and began to warm up my lunch. Logic told me that I had no right to what I expected from the old woman, but logic can't screen out everything, certainly not such unexpected feelings of loss and sheer disappointment. She didn't clean for us at all that day. I found the blanket lying rumpled on the sofa, just as it had been when I had crawled out from under it. I tidied up the apartment. I even washed the floor. Then I went off to the hospital again, to even better news.

I returned with my confidence boosted, resolved that when I saw her again I would tell her nothing of what the doctors had said. I wasn't going to bore her with my private affairs. She obviously wasn't interested. And how could I even be sure she'd been telling the truth, on that evening of the mulled wine? I mean, the things she said were impossible, folk ballads in prose. Why on earth was I so obsessed with Emerence? Was I insane?

She finally looked in late that evening, and announced that more snow was promised, so she might not have time to clean tomorrow either, but she'd make it up to us when she could. Oh, and the master was better now, wasn't he? I wasn't interested in either her announcement or her inquiry. I made a show of leafing casually through my book, and said that my husband was as well as could be expected and she should feel free to go. Whereupon she did, wishing me a good and restful night. She didn't so much as clear up the empty yoghurt container I had forgotten to put in the rubbish bin, though she must have seen it. She didn't even bother to make up the fire. And she didn't come back later that night. There was no mulled wine, no fairy tale. It was two days before she appeared again. She cleaned thoroughly, and showed no further interest in the master. Obviously she knew by instinct that his condition was improving. She certainly wasn't one for needless conversation.

After this, she spent even less time at our place. Our lives were dictated by different things, mine by the hospital, hers by the snow. I had no visitors, and spent very little time in the apartment. Finally, towards Christmas, I brought my husband home. Emerence greeted him politely and wished him a full recovery. Such was her nature, we now qualified for the convalescent's free meal. I'd not been able to get my hands on the christening bowl when we met in the street: now was my chance to take a good look. Like the mulled wine goblet, it was a real work of art. Plumply-rounded, with two handles, it perched on its own little circular stand; the ceramic lid carried a flamboyantly executed Hungarian flag inscribed with the name and portrait of the great Kossuth. She had brought us a glistening chicken soup. She'd noticed me admiring the bowl the first time I'd seen it, she said: it was a very handy thing to have. She had been given it by one of her employers, Mrs Grossman, when the Jewish laws were in force. It wasn't used for christenings then but for seeds, but it would be a shame to use it as a flowerpot. And she had masses of porcelain and glass. The piece she'd brought the mulled wine in was also a legacy from Mrs Grossman.

A charming legacy too, I thought with disgust. I was already irritated by her return to her earlier, formal attitude, and the one thing I didn't need was the thought of her helping herself to the contents of someone's shattered and abandoned home. During those years leading up to the Second World War I had moved in privileged political circles, mixing with people who were substantially better informed than my Hungarian neighbours about what was going on around us. If I do finally write the history of that part of my life, my earliest years – the years people don't talk about very much – the subject will not be short of interest. I knew perfectly well what was inside those cattle trains, exactly who was being taken where and for what purpose. I would happily have returned the christening bowl, but couldn't have done so without stating my reasons, and I didn't want to upset my husband. At the time I was allowing him only carefully monitored doses of reality. The thought of being fed from some knick-knack that had belonged to a destitute stranger bound for the gas chamber would have made him leap out of bed, half-dead as he was. Emerence had obviously thought, like so many others at that time, if I don't take it, I'm giving it to someone else. So I allowed her to spoon the soup out, to the very last drop, and took my revenge by not mentioning that this was the first time he'd eaten anything with real appetite.

Emerence pottered about in the kitchen for ages. Though she had always rejected my acknowledgement in the past, I sensed that this time she did expect something. But I didn't even thank her. I set the empty bowl down before her and went back to the bedroom. I could feel her eyes on my back, and it pleased me that at last she was the one who couldn't understand why I was offended. I was triumphant, aloof, rather contemptuous. I was sure I had discovered the reason no-one was allowed into her home. The handyman's suspicions were justified. Behind that locked door there might well be objects of real value, treasures looted from those under sentence of death. It would certainly be a bad idea to show them off. What if someone were to recognise something – then she'd see where it all led, the pointlessness of all that busy looting back then. She couldn't even sell her plunder without risk of discovery. What a picture! The poor Grossmans didn't even have a grave and she was saving up for the Taj Mahal! And she didn't open the door because she was keeping a cat in there! She would even keep an animal prisoner for an alibi. Not bad thinking – all that was missing from the story was any mention of the Grossman dowry.

She had more pride than I did. If she was in any way surprised, she didn't once ask why the air around us had so suddenly cooled. As I have mentioned, my husband was rather reserved, especially with her, and even though he had never said as much, the old woman's presence had, for years, made him visibly uncomfortable. Emerence vibrated like a new element that might be harnessed for good or bad. It was simply not possible to shut her out of our married life. But at least she no longer brought us gifts. I no longer felt, as I had before, that she was in charge. I believed I had discovered her secret. I didn't even think she was particularly clever because, if she'd had any intelligence, and used it, after '45 she would have been given every opportunity to educate herself. If she'd made the effort to study after the war she could have been an ambassador by now, or a government minister. But she had no use for culture. All she thought about was how much she could hoard, while doling out charity from a stolen christening bowl, and stupefy me, in the small hours of an anxious morning, with the sort of tale she must have heard from a fairground entertainer or found in a trashy novel in her grandfather's attic. Storms and lightning, a well, all those crashing discords – it was too much. Now her political indifference and her hatred of the Church made better sense – much wiser to steer clear of all groups. Budapest was a large place: there may well have been surviving Grossman relatives; anyone might hear the story of the permanently locked apartment, and start to think, and put two and two together, as I had. And why would such a person go to church anyway? What sort of thing would they believe in?

It was a hard winter. Emerence was inundated with work. My husband's illness filled my every waking minute. The old woman and I seldom bumped into each other. Was it surprising that we almost never embarked on a real conversation?

Then I found a dog.

My husband was now able to go out again, and was starting to be his old self, though he still needed my constant care. It wasn't the first time in our thirty-five years of marriage that he'd miraculously clawed his way out of the jaws of death, emerging rejuvenated and victorious – and at the very last moment. In all aspects of his life, winning was supremely important to him.

It was Christmas day, and the two of us had been to the clinic to collect a prescription, and were making our slow way home in a twilight thick with drizzle, when we noticed a puppy buried up to his neck in snow under the line of trees. It was a form of execution you saw in war films about prison camps in the Far East. The victim would be buried up to his ears, with sand covering his mouth so he could communicate only through his nose. He couldn't cry out, so he whimpered. This dog was whimpering too. Whoever had counted on someone coming to his rescue was a clever psychologist. Who could pass by a living creature in the jaws of death, on the night of Christ's birth? It was one of those moments against whose power my animal-hating husband was defenceless. He certainly did not want a stranger in our home, least of all a dog, which would demand not only food but also affection; and yet he helped me dig it out of the freezing snow. We had no plan to keep it; we imagined someone else would probably give it a home. The creature promised nothing but trouble. But it couldn't stay where it was. It would be dead by the morning. It wasn't in need so much of food as a vet.

"Well, there's an unusual present for you," said my husband, as I buttoned the little dog inside my coat. The terrified black face peered out from under my fur collar, sniffing the air as we went, while from under the coat itself came a steady trickle of melting snow from its legs and belly. "You don't often get a real Christmas surprise."

Emerence meanwhile had completed a major clean of our apartment, and every room was sparkling. Strolling back with the puppy, we had been debating where he should be housed, and had decided on my late mother's room, with its beautiful antique furniture, a room we didn't even bother to heat. "I hope he likes the eighteenth century," my husband said. "Dogs only chew things until they're about two. After that, they stop all by themselves." I made no reply. He was right, but what else could we do, even if the poor creature snuggling into my neck was likely to destroy the whole lot? And thus we made our way, like some mysterious and very minor religious sect on its Christmas Eve procession, its one black relic borne on my neck.

Never before then, or later, when she would have given her very life for me, did I witness such an outpouring of maternal passion from Emerence as when she saw what, or rather who, we'd brought home. We found her tidying up in the kitchen and laying out the Christmas pastries on a platter. She immediately threw down the knife and snatched the dog from my hands. She seized a duster, gave the puppy a thorough rubbing down, then placed it gently on the worktop to see if it could walk. The animal flopped down helplessly on its skinny backside. It was still frozen stiff from the snow and, in its fright, instantly made a mess. Emerence threw a sheet of newspaper over the evidence, and then searched with me in the built-in cupboard for the smallest of our fluffy bath towels. Until that moment I hadn't realised she had any idea where our things were kept — she'd always insisted that I put them away myself, so terrified was she of taking something that wasn't hers. But she obviously knew where these things at least were in our cupboards. She might not touch anything, but she made a note, double-checked, and remembered. Other people were not allowed secrets.

I gave her the terry towel, she wrapped the puppy with great care, as if it were a baby, and walked up and down the hall, murmuring in its ear. I went in to use the telephone. There was no time to waste if we were to save the animal's life. The television was on, and everything was Christmas. The lights, music and smells of the season filled the air. I had put almost everything of my past behind me, but the stardust atmosphere of Christmas lingered on, made manifest in the child in glory in the arms of the Virgin. To all this Emerence was blind and deaf. She walked up and down the hall with the little dog, wheezing out some old song in her rasping voice, in her own cock-eyed, upside-down, and intensely moving celebration of Christ's birth. With the tightly swaddled black puppy in her arms, she rocked back and forth, a caricature of motherhood, an absurd Madonna.

God knows how long this would have gone on, if someone from the house next door hadn't rung the bell to call her back immediately. A pipe had burst and had to be dealt with. Mr Brodarics had already phoned the workmen, but she had to get back quickly and turn off the mains. With a face of thunder she pushed the dog into my arms and set off to wrestle with the tap and mop up water. But every fifteen minutes she came back to check how the animal was doing. Meanwhile, our friend the vet had been wheedled away from the sparklers and had taken charge of the dog. Emerence listened to his diagnosis with visible scepticism. She considered every kind of doctor foolish and ignorant. She couldn't stand them. She didn't believe in their medicines or their inoculations. Injections, she maintained, were given only to make money, and stories of rabid foxes and cats were spread so that doctors could earn more.

The struggle to save the dog's life went on for weeks. The old woman cleaned up the traces of diarrhoea without comment. When I was out, contrary to all her most passionate convictions, she pushed medicines into the dog and held it while they gave it antibiotic injections. Meanwhile, we offered it to all and sundry, but no-one wanted it. We gave it a fine French name, which Emerence uttered not once, and which the dog ignored. But day by day it grew, and as it gained health it began to reveal, like all mongrels, every charming and agreeable quality. And at last it was completely well. It proved to be far more intelligent than any of the pedigree dogs owned by our friends. It wasn't very pretty – too many breeds had gone into its making – but everyone who saw it, and noted the extraordinary light in its dark eyes, sensed immediately that its level of intelligence was almost human. By the time we had at last accepted that nobody would take it, we had come to love it. We bought all the usual paraphernalia, including a sleeping basket which it chewed to pieces within a fortnight, scattering shreds of wickerwork all over the apartment. When it did feel like sleeping, it ignored the blankets and pillows, and lay down in the doorway on its ever thickening coat of gently curling hair. It rapidly acquired a vocabulary for everything it needed, and became a member of the family who could be left out of nothing, an individual in its own right. My husband tolerated it, even fondled it if it did anything unusually clever or funny; I loved it; Emerence adored it.

But the memory of the christening bowl and the mulled wine

goblet was still fresh, with all their associations. Of course one had to respect those animal-lovers who had watched without regret or protest as the sealed cattle-wagons rolled into the distance – the malicious rumours that there were people locked inside were so obviously lies. But I noted with a certain irony the enthusiasm with which she told stories of how geese, ducks and hens were drawn to her. It couldn't have been easy to take your intimate friends, whom you had tamed so swiftly they would take the grain from your own mouth and leap up trustingly beside you on the lovers' seat, and slit their throats when the time came to cook them.

For as long as I felt that Emerence's attachment to the dog was based on her passionate need to serve, it was all very pleasing, but when I realised that she had become his real mistress I was furious. The dog had quite different standards for each of us, behaving in three distinct ways. Towards me, he was familiar and friendly; with my husband he was quiet and almost correct; but the moment the old woman appeared he hurled himself at the door and greeted her with tears of joy. Emerence was forever explaining things to him, in a specially raised voice, with precise articulation, as if teaching an infant who was just beginning to speak. She made no secret of what she was teaching him; she repeated the same message over and over again, like a poem, and she didn't care in the least how we took it. "With your mistress, you can do whatever you like. You can jump on her, and lick her face and hands. You can sleep beside her on the sofa. Your mistress will let you do this because she loves you. The master is silent as water, and you don't know what lies beneath, so don't ever disturb the water, my dear little dog, don't ever annoy the master, because your place here is to serve. But you're in a good home, as good as any could be, for a dog in an apartment." As for herself, she never gave orders, the animal understood her wishes without the need for words.

By this time she had even given him a name. She called him Viola. The fact that he was a male dog didn't bother Emerence. Occasionally she didn't so much teach as train. "Sit down, Viola. Until you sit, no sugar. Sit down. SIT DOWN!"

When I first realised how she was rewarding him I reminded her, rather sharply, that the vet had said dogs were not to be given sugar. "The vet's an idiot," she replied, patting Viola's shoulder firmly. "Sit, boy, sit. If he sits, he gets something nice, something sweet. Sugar, the animal gets sugar. Sit, Viola, sit." And Viola sat, at first for the sugar, later by conditioned reflex and for nothing, as soon as he heard the trigger word.

Occasionally the old woman would ask if she could take him to guard her house, as she'd be out all day clearing snow. My husband consented willingly; at least then the dog wouldn't be hurling himself about and barking. I asked if she wasn't worried about her cat, as I'd heard she had one in the flat, but she said she wasn't at all concerned. She'd teach him to get on with other animals without harming them. Viola could be taught to do anything. If the dog did anything naughty she beat him horribly, despite my express prohibition and her own over-whelming love for him. Not once in the fourteen years of his life did he receive a beating from me. But then Emerence was his real mistress.

I would love to have witnessed the creature's first moments in the old woman's domain, that empire never before revealed to anyone, but the bar to entry remained. I gathered from the fleas he brought home that he had met the cat, and that thence-forth we could expect the pleasure of their company too. The first encounter can't have been uneventful. There was a wound on his nose and a deep scratch on his ear, and his general demeanour indicated that there had indeed been a battle in which he was the loser. Emerence had used drastic means to instil in him that "we don't annoy the cat". He didn't take it as a tragedy.

He came home with his chubby adolescent jowls pushing against Emerence's knee every step of the way. After that there seemed to be no trouble. Whenever I took him for a walk I couldn't help noticing his behaviour. As the stray cats fled under balconies for refuge, he gazed on benignly, without a hint of anger or dismay, clearly baffled by their reaction when he meant them no harm.

Viola guarded Emerence's home all through the winter. I put a stop to it only after a certain Saturday night, when he came home drunk. When she brought him home, I couldn't believe my eyes. The dog was reeling, his belly was like a barrel, he was panting heavily and rolling his eyes. I couldn't even pick him up because he kept toppling over. I crouched down to examine him. He hiccuped, and I smelt the beer. "Emerence, the dog's drunk!" I gasped.

"We had a little drink," she replied calmly. "It won't kill him. He was thirsty. It did him good."

I stood up. "You're out of your mind, and you're not to take him again. That's final. After all we did to save his life, we're not going to kill him by turning him into an alcoholic."

"Because a little bit of beer is going to kill him," she said, with a bitterness that surprised me. "Oh yes, I'm sure, I shared the roast duck and the beer with him because he begged me – *he* asked for it – what was I supposed to do? He can tell me everything – he almost spoke. He absolutely loved the food and drink. He isn't just any old dog. So he'll die, will he – because he had dinner with me, because he didn't, with the greatest respect, fancy the rubbish you people give him, diet food, to be eaten only at certain times, never in the dining room and never from your hand – though the only real food is what he takes from your hand, not from a bowl? I'm the one who's killing him, the one who brings him up, talks to him, teaches him right and wrong." She was speaking with deadly seriousness, like a teacher whose most sacred feelings had been wounded. "Or perhaps it was you who taught him to sit, and stand up, and run and fetch a ball, and say thank you. All you two do is hide yourselves away at home like a pair of statues. You don't even talk to each other, you bang away on your typewriters in separate rooms. Well, you keep Viola, then. You'll see how far you get."

The statement over – with matters of importance Emerence didn't say things, she made an announcement – she turned on her heel and left. Viola collapsed and began to snore. He was so drunk he didn't even notice that he'd been abandoned.

The problems didn't begin immediately, only the next morning, when Emerence failed to come for him. She had always served him his breakfast, given him his walk and then taken him away with her. He controlled himself and made no messes, but from six-fifteen he was whining so loudly I was forced to get up. It was a while before I realised there was no point in waiting for Emerence. She was like Jehovah: she punished for generations.

The whole shameful scene finally came to a head outside her flat, when the dog insisted on going in, as he did every morning. I had never understood why it was better for him to be shut up with her than at home with me, where he had so much more room to flop around in. Anyway, when he realised that hauling on the leash was getting him nowhere he became mutinous, tugged furiously and then bounded along, with me in tow. He was a strong dog, I a fearful pedestrian on an icy street. Mounds of snow covered the pavement, each a potential hazard. I was terrified of falling and breaking something, but I couldn't let go in case he ran under a car.

That morning I was given a lesson in where the two of them went for their walk. Viola ran me through Emerence's district. Half-blinded by the falling snow and gasping for breath, with Viola setting the pace, I was hauled to each of the eleven houses where she cleaned, hurtling from one to the next in a mindless Peer Gynt dash. Finally he tugged so hard he managed to pull me over. But we had reached his destination. We'd found the person he was looking for. Emerence was standing with her back to us, so he jumped up at her from behind, nearly knocking her over as well. However she was strong – ten times stronger than I have ever been. She turned, saw me kneeling there in the snow, and instantly realised what had happened. First she yanked the dog firmly by the stray end of the leash; then, whenever he started to whine, she hit him. I hauled myself to my feet, feeling thoroughly sorry for the animal.

"Sit, you wicked creature," she shouted, as if to another person. "This is not the way to behave, you scoundrel." Viola stared at her in amazement. Emerence looked him in the eye, like a lion tamer. "If you want your mistress to let you come again you will have to promise her that you won't get drunk, because your mistress is right, only she didn't stop to think that nobody celebrates my birthday, or that you are the only one who knows when it is, because you're the only one I've told. I haven't told my brother József's boy, or Sutu, or Adélka, or Polett, and the Lieutenant Colonel has forgotten when it is. But that's not how we behave when we sober up – like hooligans. Instead, we ask permission. Now get up, Viola!"

So far the dog had been crouching on his stomach, weeping. He hadn't moved a muscle during the beating, or made the slightest attempt to escape. Now he picked himself up. "Say you're sorry!" I had no idea he knew how to take an oath, but it seems he did. He placed his left paw against his heart and with the right, like a patriotic statue, pointed to the sky. "Say it, Viola!" she directed, and Viola barked. "Again!" Again he barked, keeping his eyes fixed on his tamer to see how well he was doing. Instinct told him that his future depended on it. "Now promise that you'll be a good boy," I heard her say, and

Viola put out his paw towards her. "Not to me, I already know; to your mistress." Viola turned to where I stood, and like those pictures of St Francis and the wolf, looking guilty and a little sly, he offered me his right front paw. I didn't take it, I was in so much pain from my knee, and so utterly furious with them both.

Seeing his entreaties were useless he tried a new ploy. Without instruction he saluted me, then again put his left paw on his heart. I gave up. Once again they had defeated me, and we all three knew it. "Don't worry about him," said Emerence. "Today he'll have lunch with me. I'll bring him home this evening. And wash your leg – it's bleeding. I hope you'll be all right."

The order came only through her eyes, and a slight movement of the head, but Viola understood. With clear articulation, he barked at me twice, thanking me. Emerence attached the lead to the fence and resumed her sweeping. I had been dismissed. Slowly I made my way home, alone, through the thickly falling snow.

FRIENDS AND NEIGHBOURS

With the addition of Viola to the family, our circle of acquaintances widened. Until then we had been in regular contact only with friends; now, if only superficially, we got to know the entire neighbourhood. Emerence walked the dog in the morning, at midday and in the evening, but there were times when she couldn't do the midday session because of some unexpected extra work, and then it was left to us. Either my husband saw to it or I did it myself, but Viola always led the way. He generally began by hauling his leash to Emerence's flat, where he would have to be taken right up to the door to make quite sure that she wasn't hiding inside. But his nose would soon tell him that she wasn't playing a trick, she really wasn't at home, and we were able to continue. Sometimes she was at home, but caught up in some task for which she had no need of his assistance. On these occasions we had to wait outside with the dog, shamefaced, until his whining and scratching finally produced her, muttering curses and ordering him not to pester her. Sometimes she wouldn't just smack him, she told him off like an over-insistent guest, shouting things like: "Why are you dragging me out? We were together this morning and we'll see each other again tonight!" Or she would pat him on the neck a few times, stuff something sweet in his mouth, play out the whole performance with him to its end, and only then chase him back into the street.

If we didn't find her at home, we had to look for her outside one of her houses. If she was found, the entire front porch ritual would be played out in the open air, and more than once Emerence took Viola through the performance with my husband or myself as the reluctant focus. This way we made the acquaintance of several of our neighbours whom we would not otherwise have met.

Whenever Emerence had company – this was only in good weather, at those times of the year when she put benches outside her door and it was possible to sit and chat – Viola would be ordered to find his food and water bowls, which the old woman hid in different places, while the guests watched his tricks in amazement. I was often struck by how readily everyone accepted her declaration of a Forbidden City, where they could be received only on the porch. Local acquaintances, close friends and even blood relations such as her brother József's boy, all found that the closed-door rule applied equally to them.

The reception area to which access was permitted was rectangular in shape and quite spacious, with the doors of the larder, shower and lumber room opening on to it. As it was clearly a sacred place, the Forbidden City, I guessed, must have been grandly furnished with the Grossman family's belongings. The porch itself was always spotlessly clean. So long as the season permitted, the old woman washed the stone floor twice a day. There, if she had a free hour or two during the day, she would play the hostess at a table placed between two benches. I often saw her, either through the hedge as I walked past or from my window, serving tea or coffee to guests of varying ages and social classes. She would pour out refreshments into fine porcelain cups, with the smooth, confident actions of someone who had done it a thousand times, and who had learned how to conduct herself at table from someone of importance. I remember attending the opening night of Shaw's *Man and Superman*, in which a famous actress played Blanche.

Throughout the performance I kept wondering who the lovely young artiste had reminded me of in the tea-serving scene. Then I realised. It was Emerence, entertaining guests at the entrance to her forbidden domain.

At one time a number of prominent people lived in the neighbourhood, and a policeman would regularly walk our street. Later the politicians moved away, or died, and as they disappeared so too, one by one, did the surveillance men. By the time Emerence came to work for us the only person in uniform appearing with any regularity on our street was the Lieutenant Colonel. For many years I puzzled over their relationship, and why it didn't bother the friendly officer that entry was denied him, when she might be hiding anything in her home. Later I discovered that he had been inside, and knew its secrets. In addition to the accusations of pigeon poisoning and desecration of graves, politically-motivated and totally libellous "information" had been received. The police had to see, if only once, what needed to be hidden and kept secret, and was of such value that no human eye might ever gaze upon it. Emerence, grumbling and muttering, opened up her entire premises to the Lieutenant Colonel – then still a Second Lieutenant – when he dutifully called with his canine assistant, but all they found was an unshapely cat (the third she had owned since moving in) who, as soon as he saw the dog, fled to the top of the kitchen cupboard. There was no secret transmitter, no escaped convict, no stolen goods, only a dazzlingly clean dining area and a room fitted out with a stunningly beautiful set of furniture under covers, in which no-one appeared to be living, since there were no personal belongings to be seen. And in fact the friendship between Emerence and the officer began with an argument. As soon as she had shut the door behind them she started shouting. Was there a law that stated that she had to open her home to everybody who happened to be passing, and let them in if they felt like ringing the bell? Why didn't they go and look instead for the bandit who kept filing reports about her? In fact the real insult was the honour of regular visits by the police. First it was the dead pigeons, then the business of the dead cat, now they were looking for weapons or the source of an epidemic. She'd had all she could take of the police. Enough was enough.

The force had by now assumed a defensive, conciliatory stance. The Second Lieutenant was deploying all his eloquence to calm her down, but Emerence's voice rose louder and louder. She told him that the politicians who lived locally carried guns. They had nothing better to do so they shot crows. The police, sure enough, gave them every protection, and then came to snoop around her place with a dog. She hoped the sky would fall on the lot of them! On them, mind you, not on the poor dog. It wasn't his fault if he was misused. She wasn't angry with the dog, just the Second Lieutenant. And then the force's cup of bitter humiliation was filled to overflowing. Instead of digging up a second corpse or any other incriminating object buried in the garden, the officiating dog, in breach of every regulation, allowed Emerence to stroke his head, wagged his tail anxiously, and then – the climax of shame – abandoned duty to gaze up at her with baffled, loving eyes. The whine he let out was a coded plea to his superior, begging forgiveness and explaining that he couldn't help it, a will stronger than any other had forced him to the feet of this strange woman. The Second Lieutenant roared with laughter. Emerence's face of thunder slowly began to clear, and she stopped shouting. Somehow, for the first time, they became aware of each other. The police officer rarely went into homes where people were so totally unafraid of him, and it was the first time Emerence had met a public official with a private sense of humour and a positive attitude. So each made a note of the other. The investigator apologised and left, but later returned with his wife. Their rare and beautiful friendship held strong even after the young woman unexpectedly died. The Lieutenant Colonel told me subsequently that Emerence had helped him through a very difficult time.

Ever since our days had fallen under the timetable coordinated by Viola and the old woman, I had come increasingly to doubt my earlier suspicions about the provenance of the christening bowl and the cup. After all, if the Lieutenant Colonel had become a regular visitor, and had himself examined what she had in there, he must have made checks on how she had come by it. If he hadn't arrested her, then it could well be that I was mistaken, and that the family had left her their belongings in return for something she had done for them. At that time, help often took such strange forms.

Meanwhile the number of our acquaintances continued to grow, and Viola and Emerence got to know more and more people, who began to greet us too. Emerence's three long-standing friends now stopped more often to exchange a few words with me. These were Sutu, who ran a fruit and vegetable stall, Polett, who did ironing, and Adélka, the widow of a laboratory technician. One summer afternoon, when the four of them were taking coffee with some temptingly aromatic pastries, Emerence beckoned me over to join them. I was out walking Viola and could hardly snub her and her friends, but the question was decided when the dog hauled me in and began to beg at the table. He crowned this achievement by refusing to leave when I was ready to go home, which made me very angry.

That evening, when the old woman arrived to walk him before he went to bed, I asked her if she would like to have him permanently with her. Our original intention had only ever been to give him a refuge, not a home. If she had him, she wouldn't have to keep her door locked, because the dog would need only a word from her to see any intruder off.

While I was speaking, the old woman stroked the dog's neck with so much tenderness and affection you would have thought she was caressing a flower or a new-born babe; but all the while she shook her head. It wasn't possible. If she were allowed to, she would have got a dog for herself years ago. But according to her lease she could only keep an animal inside the dwelling – and then only a chicken or perhaps a goose – while it was being prepared for the table, and she was almost never at home. A dog needed freedom, somewhere to move about, a garden; he wasn't a criminal in need of punishment. Being locked up wasn't easy for a cat, so you had to think what it would be for an animal like Viola – so full of curiosity, so eager to make friends and explore everything. That dog wasn't born to be a slave, even if he was happy to guard the house. And anyway, old people shouldn't keep dogs, because sooner or later they'd be orphaned and then what happened? They were kicked out and left to stray. But if it upset me that Viola was so fond of her, she could put a stop to it. You could alienate animals as well as people.

I felt that she was evading responsibility and got very angry with her. If she didn't want to have him, why entice him to her? Only later – very much later – when I began to consider the warning signs, did it occur to me that no-one had ever taken on board the fact that one day she would die. I too had always felt that, somehow, she would be with us as long as we lived; that, with Nature itself, she would be renewed with the spring; and that her refusal to conform was not limited to banning entry to her locked-up house but applied to everything, even to death itself. But just then, I thought she was lying. I made Viola pay for my own weakness and banned him from the television room. The dog loved the TV screen. He would flick his head from left to right as the ball flew, and prick up his ears at birdsong and the sounds in wildlife documentaries. He even recognised things he'd never experienced himself: no-one had ever taken him up János Hill. By the end of the week I felt utterly ashamed. I couldn't blame him for something he wasn't responsible for; and even if he was, I didn't have the right. So I accepted it. I acknowledged that the old woman and the dog belonged together. I was too sleepy in the morning, too busy at midday, and too tired in the evening to give him attention or take him for walks with any regularity. My husband was often unwell, and we made frequent trips abroad. Viola needed Emerence: that's how it was. In every practical sense, he was her dog.

I then began to wonder why she had brought up the question of her age at this point, for the first time. It had never entered our conversation before. Emerence lifted unbelievable weights, she ran upstairs with the heaviest parcels and suitcases; she had the strength of a mythological hero. And never once had she mentioned how old she was. We'd only worked it out from what she had revealed about her life, that she was three when her father died, and nine when her stepfather was called up, and then almost immediately killed, in 1914. If she was nine in 1914, then she must have been born in 1905. She was shockingly, appallingly old. So it was only logical that she would give thought to the time when she finally collapsed. Others, those to whom she hadn't entrusted these facts, could only guess at her age. When that terrible, never-to-be-forgotten day did arrive it was only possible to bury her with the help, yet again, of the Lieutenant Colonel. In all the drawers hauled out for decontamination there was not a single document confirming her identity. Quite possibly she was the only person in the country who had completely shut the authorities out of her life, the moment she could. But back in the early days the Lieutenant Colonel had seen some papers of hers, and had actually leafed through her old employment book, which was used at the time as proof of identity. Later, for some reason we would now never understand, she must have destroyed everything. She hated passports, certificates, even tram tickets. We also had to set aside the nonsense she had scrawled about herself, in great crabbed letters, among several eccentric entries in the tenants' book we found when sorting through her things – that she had been born at Segesvár on 15 March 1848. It was the sort of frivolous, flippant remark that was typical of the way she retaliated against intrusive questions. Emerence's little acts of revenge were savage but nicely varied.

Sutu had been a teenager when Emerence arrived in the street, and she told us later that, neither before or immediately after the war, would Emerence have been able to get occupancy of the place, or even move home, without papers. Even so, she had taken over the caretaker's flat in the villa, bringing the legendary furniture with her. The owner himself had installed her, before leaving for the West. So there must have been documents relating both to her and her permanent companion. He was the cause of her starting to lock everything up, this unfriendly friend. She wouldn't let anyone in, she watched over him jealously – as if anyone would want him! – and of course he wasn't well. He had papers exempting him from service. He hardly ever went out. He wasn't fit for the army or for work and, according to Emerence, he was riddled with arthritis. She always got involved with this type, both animals and people. Wrecks interested her. It was the same with Mr Szloka, right up to his death. He too wasn't the full measure of a man, and to crown everything he had no family.

Sutu's tale contained so many disturbing elements that I made her repeat it, twice, until it sank in. It implied that Emerence had lived with someone, both during the siege and before it, so from the start she didn't just have a cat but a lodger (or whatever) as well. Furthermore, her circle of admirers included this Mr Szloka, who could neither escape nor fend for himself in his total abandonment because he had such a severe heart condition. He couldn't even do aircraft alert duty, and then he died suddenly at the most inconvenient moment. It was a confused and difficult time. The siege had begun, and Emerence ran in vain from Pontius to Pilate, looking for someone to dispose of the body. She tried everyone, but it was the start of a national holiday. No-one would take responsibility, and the result was that they had to get rid of the poor fellow themselves. Emerence agreed to bury Mr Szloka in the garden in return for his bicycle. Later the bicycle went missing, probably taken by her "friend", because he too vanished, Sutu had no idea where. Emerence buried Mr Szloka under the dahlias, and he mouldered quietly away until the council finally exhumed him in the summer of '46.

Up until then the occupants of the house had changed constantly, and included every sort of nationality. Emerence washed for the Germans and then for the Russians. Then the world returned to normal and people once again lived in peace. Malicious reports began to be made about her, not about the alleged pigeon poisoning or political slanders, but accusations of interfering with corpses, because she had buried the hanged cat in Mr Szloka's grave. However when she explained to the Lieutenant Colonel that this cat had been her entire family, he told her he'd teach these good neighbours who made extra work for the police a bit of respect. He'd have them sent on community service to help clean up Vérmező Park. There were at least as many rotting horses there as there were people, and they would be required to separate what was left of them, and then bury the humans in sacred ground and the animals where they could. Didn't they have anything better to worry about when the country was struggling to get on its feet again after total collapse? How he envied them! If they kept dragging up these cat stories, he'd investigate the piece of human trash who couldn't stand Emerence Szeredás' cat so he'd strung it up, in his murdering Fascist way, rather than come to an understanding with its owner. There were laws against cruelty to animals.

*

One day, Emerence did not arrive to walk the dog. There was no reason for her absence, but I saw nothing of her all day. It was autumn, still a long way off the first snowfall, yet she failed to appear. I walked the dog myself, through a soft, gentle rain. Viola looked for her at home in the morning, but his sensitive nostrils told him she wasn't behind the closed door, so we went to each of her houses in turn. He even led me down to the market, but his dejected behaviour continued to signal that she was nowhere around, perhaps not even in the district. She wasn't anywhere Viola knew about.

Back home, he cowered miserably while I set about the cleaning. Whenever she failed to turn up people asked for her at our flat, and the doorbell rang constantly. Everyone who knew her was concerned. What had happened? She hadn't swept the leaves off the pavement; the rubbish bin wasn't outside the front door; she hadn't brought the finished laundry; the night before she hadn't been to babysit; she hadn't even done the shopping. I opened and closed that door non-stop. Viola howled, bared his teeth, refused to eat, and waited.

THE MURANO MIRROR

It was late evening when Emerence finally turned up and took Viola for his walk. His cries of relief defied imagination. On their return, she tapped on my door and asked me if I would go home with her. There was something she had to discuss with me that she didn't want the master to hear. We could have gone into any of the rooms, but she insisted I go with her. So off the three of us went, Emerence, me, and Viola dancing along ahead of us. At that time of night there was no need to put him on a leash to stop him bounding up to other dogs and getting into fights. Once on the porch, Emerence offered me a seat at the table, which was covered with a spotless nylon cloth. I sat down, and was hit by the usual dense, heavy smell, a nauseating blend of chlorine, cleaning fluids and some sort of air freshener. The rest of the house was silent, and no lights shone in the windows. It wasn't yet the witching hour, and by day the thought would never have struck me, but now, with just the three of us on the porch, I suddenly began to sense something of the presence, or presences, that inhabited Emerence's home. Some sound was audible in the deep silence, a low, soft sound. Viola crouched down by the gap beneath the door and began to snuffle noisily. When he wanted to get in somewhere, he produced this special signal, rather like a human groan or heavy, painful breathing.

It was an extraordinary evening however one looked at it, not harmonious, but filled rather with a sense of foreboding. In normal circumstances I tend not to analyse my situation, but

I found myself reflecting that I knew almost nothing about Emerence, beyond her general mania and her deftly evasive answers to my questions.

"Sometime in the next few days I'm having a visitor," she began. It was the voice of someone emerging from anaesthesia, speaking with the exaggerated precision of a wandering mind striving for clarity. "You know I never let anyone into my home, but I can't make this visitor sit where you are now. It's impossible."

Experience had taught me never to cross-examine her, she'd only take fright and reveal even less. If she was expecting the sort of guest who couldn't be entertained on her porch, let alone taken inside, then it wasn't just anybody. Could it be the two golden-haired siblings who were burnt to cinders? But perhaps they never existed except as characters in a story. Or even God himself, in whom Emerence did not believe, because he had given her an evening gown instead of woollen cast-offs? This person must be even more important than either her "little brother Józsi's son" or the Lieutenant Colonel.

"Would you allow me to entertain this person in your flat? Other people would gossip about it, but not you. We'd act as if the person was your guest. The master is out working that afternoon. If you ask him, he'll agree to anything. Will you do it? You know I'll make it up to you."

I stared at her. "You want to receive a guest in our home?" The question was superfluous. Emerence had planned everything down to the last detail. Of course that was what she wanted.

"But you must do all you can to make the person think I live there, with you. I'll bring everything, the cups, coffee, drinks. You won't have to provide anything, just the space. Say yes. I will repay you. By the time the master gets home, we'll be gone. Wednesday at four o'clock. Is that all right?"

In the doorway Viola gave a deep sigh. Outside, it was drizzling softly. The international situation had been normalised for some years, so Emerence's guest could have been the French President himself without her fearing political consequences. The fact that she couldn't receive him here on her own doorstep did little to deepen the mystery in which she wrapped herself like a shawl. I shrugged my shoulders. Yes, this person could come. I only hoped I wouldn't have to hang around waiting – she'd already asked me to be at home so she wouldn't be alone with the visitor.

Walking home, I asked myself how I was going to get my husband to agree to it. He loathed anything that was not straightforward, especially situations that were open-ended, uncertain, ill-defined. But instead of raising objections, or putting his foot down, he laughed. He found something bizarre in the idea. It stirred his writer's imagination. Emerence and the visitor she wanted to entertain here! Perhaps she was looking for a husband. Maybe the visitor was replying to a lonely hearts ad, and Emerence, who never opened the door to her own home, was bringing him here to look him over? Let him come! He was almost sorry he wouldn't be there himself. He wasn't worried about leaving us in the apartment with a perfect stranger. Viola would tear anyone who attacked us limb from limb. Hearing his name, the dog gave my husband's hand an enthusiastic lick and rolled over for us to rub his belly. It was difficult to get used to the fact that he understood everything.

On the appointed day, Emerence was like a madwoman restraining herself with an iron will. Viola, who picked up everyone else's mood, was also far from normal. The old woman brought plates and bowls of every sort, all on covered trays. This infuriated me and I asked her why she was parading her things down the street if the banquet required such secrecy? She wasn't a leper, and clearly neither was her guest, so why couldn't they use our plates and forks? There was the side-board – she could take whatever she wanted. She could lay the table with my mother's best crockery and silver. Did she think I'd mind?

She didn't thank me, but she took note. She never forgot a gesture, friendly or otherwise. She replied that she wasn't trying to hide anything, she just didn't want the person to see that she lived alone, without any family around her; and she didn't wish to explain why she never opened her door, or why she lived the way she did.

As she was laying the table in my mother's room, I suddenly decided to say something that I had been meaning to for ages. She was setting out the cold meat and salad – she could bring a touch of magic even to the laying out of food – and I asked her if she had ever considered the idea of speaking to a medical expert about her symptoms: shutting the world out of her home couldn't be called rational behaviour. Doctors would have a name for this compulsion, or whatever it was; it was obviously curable. "A doctor," she said, fixing her eyes on me as she polished the long-stemmed champagne glasses she kept for special occasions. "I'm not ill, and the way I live doesn't hurt anyone. Anyway, you know I can't stand doctors. Let me be. I don't like it when you lecture me. If I ask for something and you give it, do it without preaching a sermon, otherwise there's no point."

I left her, went into the bedroom and put on a record so as not to hear what I couldn't see. By then I had had quite enough of this arrangement. One day, I thought, Emerence would get us into real trouble. She was clearly off her head. Who was she bringing here? If I hadn't known the dog was there I would have been really worried. And why on earth did she need cham-pagne glasses for this clandestine meeting? I didn't like my own secrets. I liked other people's even less.

The music that flooded out from the record screened every-thing. Two rooms stood between mine and my mother's, where she had laid out her feast. I'd read, or rather leafed through, about fifty pages when I began to be suspicious. Emerence had indicated that she wanted me to meet the stranger, but where was this guest? And what was going on all this time, in total silence? Even Viola was quiet. Had the person arrived? Almost an hour had passed since the appointed time, when finally I heard him bark. I thought, how practical of her to wait for her visitor to arrive with cold meat rather than hot food, with all its problems – at least it would stay fresh. I continued listening to the music. Suddenly the door burst open, Viola bounded in and danced in agitation about the bed: he was very clearly telling me something. This was very odd. If her guest was afraid of dogs Emerence would have sent him into one of the outer rooms, not further into the apartment. So what were they up to, to make the old woman no longer want him around?

I found out soon enough. Seconds after the dog appeared, so did she. Her face gave nothing away – she certainly knew how to behave like a deaf mute. By now Viola was sprawling beside me on his stomach at the head of our bed. Emerence didn't even see him. She announced that the caller hadn't been the one she was expecting. That person wasn't coming. The handyman had run over from the villa to say that the hotel where the visitor was to stay had got his phone number and left a message with him for Emerence. The visit had been cancelled at the last minute, for business reasons, and she wasn't even coming to Budapest, though if the trip were to happen at some future date she would send word nearer the time.

So I had missed all my official engagements for a visitor who, in the end, failed to appear. Well, I didn't see anything tragic in that, apart from the fact that Emerence had laid out a small fortune for nothing. But the old woman went out of the room like a typhoon, slamming the door behind her. I heard her screaming at the top of her voice at the dog (who had slunk out after her), so loudly that I felt obliged to go and see what she thought she was doing with him. After all, he hadn't done anything. From my mother's room came a loud clattering sound, and, for the first time ever, I was shocked by Emerence's language. Curses and obscene insults were pouring from her mouth. I pushed the door open, then stopped dead. It wasn't the dog she was abusing, it was someone else. Viola was sitting at the table, in my mother's chair, eating. Emerence had pulled the platter in front of him, he had grabbed a slice of roast meat and was wolfing it down. He had one paw planted on the place mat, the other scrabbling for a grip on the Murano mirror tray — on which I had never, in all my life, not even on the greatest occasions, placed anything — while the five-branched silver candelabra rocked unsteadily back and forth. Every so often Viola would drop a mouthful and scramble after it, leaving greasy paw prints on the tray. I don't think I have ever been so angry.

"Get off, Viola! Get down! My mother's mirror! Her porcelain! What's going on here, Emerence? Have you gone mad?"

I had never before heard Emerence cry, and I never would again. But now she wept openly. I didn't know what to do, because the dog never obeyed me at crucial moments unless she repeated my command. He calmly carried on eating, while Emerence stood sobbing on the other side of the table. Viola gave her regular sympathetic glances, but ate on regardless, unable to resist the delicacies. There was no denying that Emerence had taught him how to behave at table. He might have been an actor in a play, so almost perfect was the way he ate, sitting on his haunches, the way humans do, with both front paws leaning on the table. It was just that he wasn't eating from a plate, and he was helping himself with his mouth rather than his paws. The picture was so absurd, and made me so furious, I was lost for words. Our own dog, sitting and eating at my mother's table, laid out for a feast in her very room, was refusing to obey me. Every now and then he cast a sidelong glance at a large cake that stood on the sideboard, visibly calculating how he would get it down; and all the while Emerence wept inconsolably. The dish was now almost empty, but from what was left of the food I could tell it hadn't been cheap. The hoped for guest must have been highly regarded. I felt the anger continuing to rise in me, and was on the point of exploding, when Emerence suddenly wiped the tears from her face and dabbed her eyes with the back of her hand. Then, like someone coming round from sedation, she shuddered violently, then hurled herself at the happily munching dog and beat him all over with the handle of the serving fork. She called him everything – an ungrateful monster, a shameless liar, a heartless capitalist. Viola squealed, jumped down from the chair and lay on the rug, for her inscrutable judgement to be carried out upon him. He never ran when she beat him, never tried to protect himself. The horror, with all its unreality, was dreamlike. Viola cowered and trembled under the blows, so terrified he couldn't even swallow the last mouthful. It fell from his jaws on to my mother's favourite rug. The way Emerence went after him with the serving fork, I thought she was going to stab him. It all happened in a flash. I was so frightened I began to scream. But just then the old woman crouched down beside the dog, lifted up his head and kissed him between the ears. Viola whined with relief, and licked the hand that had beaten him.

No, I thought, this was too much. She could find another audience for her outbursts. I turned on my heel and requested that she kindly remove the debris from my mother's room and, if it wasn't too much to ask, refrain from casting us in supporting rôles, or use our home as a theatre for these impossible episodes in her private life. I didn't quite say it like this, I put it in terms she could understand. She understood.

From the bedroom, I could hear her moving around. I couldn't know what she was actually doing, but I discovered later that she had been putting things in the fridge: the sweets, the champagne and the untouched platter of mixed roast meats, all for us. The dish Viola had eaten from was emptied into his food box. The animal didn't move a muscle. Finally all was silent. I thought she had gone, but she was getting ready, and was attaching Viola's collar and lead. Always, when she had upset him, she instituted an especially long walk; she would do this even if it meant giving up her ironing or preparing dough. When she called out to let me know they would be going in the direction of the woods, she was her usual self, standing with the dog in the doorway, offering her apology. I never heard anyone do so with so much dignity, and so little servility or self-reproach. I felt ever afterwards that she had been mocking me, as if it wasn't her but I who was in the wrong. Of course no explanation followed, and off she went.

That evening, when I described Emerence's afternoon to my husband, he just waved his hand. I brought that sort of thing on myself, I heard him say – I took everything and everyone so seriously, and I was for ever getting myself mixed up in other people's business. She should have received her secret visitor on her porch club – this wonderful person who was so much more important than the Lieutenant Colonel, for whom only my mother's room was good enough. She'd cooked and baked until she dropped, and it was all to no end, because the guest hadn't come. I would have to give her back whatever she'd packed in the fridge. He had no wish to eat the failed visitor's leftovers. He wasn't Viola.

I felt he was right, but also that he wasn't. I did what he wanted, and piled the tray with as much as I could carry, to take back. I too was angry with the old woman, but I had also seen in her eyes that whatever it was that had happened that afternoon, had been the worst of horrors. And I had heard her sobbing. In the few hours that had elapsed since her departure I had calmed down enough for a new suspicion to stir in me. Perhaps there was a deeper issue here than nursing our mutual grievances. What I had seen, as Viola sat eating, might not have been the idyll it seemed. The banquet might have expressed a deeper level of feeling, something more properly mythological. When I thought about it, the pair of them at that table weren't at all like a mistress giving her good little dog his reward, they were more like figures from a Greek myth, taking part in some horrific celebration. The roast meat the animal had snatched was only a semblance. It was more than food, it was a meal not for human witness, a tangle of viscera, a species of human sacrifice – as if Emerence were feeding the actual person to the dog, along with all her fond memories and feelings. The person who hadn't come that afternoon, who had merely sent a message, had wounded that most important part of Emerence about which she would never speak, not to anyone. Viola was the unwitting Jason. Beneath Medea-Emerence's headscarf glowed the fires of the underworld.

So I wasn't at all happy about having to return the food, and even less pleased that she had treated us to the remains. I'm a countrywoman too. I have the same country sensibilities. I knew I would give her deep offence. But there was no more unequivocal way of letting her know she had overstepped the mark.

The tray was heavy, and I had difficulty opening the front door. People stared as I carried it across the street. Emerence was nowhere to be seen, but from behind her door came unmistakable sounds of movement. I could hear her talking, apparently in discussion with her cat, explaining things the way she did with Viola. I called out that I was sorry, but I couldn't keep the leftovers from her banquet, so I was returning them; they were on the porch table; she could come out and get them. Emerence squeezed herself through the narrow gap of the open door, to stop the cat coming out and her visitor peering in. She was in her everyday clothes, no longer dressed up. She said not a word, but reached into the little lobby where she stored things, brought out a huge saucepan and scraped everything into it. She mashed the cake in with the meat and the salad, and marched off to her bathroom, where I heard her spooning it into the toilet and flushing it away. Viola was beside himself, but she gave him none of it, and wouldn't allow him near her. It was as if she had never known him. She even kicked him away.

Once again I was afraid of Emerence, truly afraid. I tightened my grip on Viola's leash, though I knew that if she did suddenly launch a hysterical attack, the animal would defend her rather than me. Next, she disposed of the drinks, taking the bottles by the neck and hurling them against the doorframe. The champagne exploded, and the dog began to howl in terror. She threw the bottles in the rubbish bin, and swilled the porch down with the spilt wine and champagne. It smelt like a tavern. During that quarter-hour chance brought Sutu, Adélka and Polett along, but the moment they spotted us each turned away. They couldn't follow what was going on, but none of us inspired confidence – Emerence silently spreading the blood-red wine across the stone floor, the dog howling and me standing there like a statue – the further away from us the better. They didn't hang about.

By now I was convinced that what had taken place over my mother's table that afternoon had indeed been a murder. Emerence had used the feast to symbolically settle her account with the guest. Some years later I actually got to know the sacrificial victim, a slim, attractive young woman stumbling along beside me in that tumultuous All Souls' Day procession. She may have known how to cope with greater challenges than visiting Emerence's last resting place, but she could hardly have picked a more inconvenient time to conduct her business in Budapest, or indeed to visit the cemetery. She laid her bouquet in the fairy-tale crypt, quite unaware (only I ever knew) that it would make no difference — that very night, the long-stemmed roses in their cellophane wrapping would be stolen. She told me she was sorry she wasn't able to come that day. She could have got to see Emerence, but she was a businesswoman, and since her father and uncle who lived abroad had retired she'd been running the factory, and her promised visit had happened when the European deals which would have brought her to Budapest were put on hold. There was no point in coming just to visit the old woman. That would have to wait for another time, when she could deal with the business meeting and the visit to Emerence both at once. New York wasn't exactly a stone's throw away.

She was having dinner with us. It was only what I found in the fridge, not quite Emerence's festive outlay, with candles admiring their reflections in the Murano mirror. I told her how deeply the old woman had been upset by her failure to arrive. It surprised her. She didn't understand how a mere change of date could cause so much pain. It was the sort of thing that happened all the time in business. But earlier, at the cemetery, I had noticed a kind of damp, unpleasant chill blowing around us. It was as if the old woman were refusing to accept the candle she'd lit for her. As she reached the grave the wind gusted, the birches shook the drops from their branches on to her neck, and every candle flame died the moment it flared into life, as if Emerence were blowing it back in her face with the full force of her lungs. And on countless other occasions after her death it was as if Emerence turned on her ghostly heel and put two fingers up at our guilty consciences, and our attempts to approach her. Each time it was as if yet another undisclosed facet of her million secrets glittered before us.

The most distressing thing of all was that, if they had managed to meet, Emerence might well have both understood and accepted her visitor's explanation, that she hadn't meant to hurt or insult; that she wasn't some immature adolescent who set all those feverish preparations at nothing. She was no longer an infant, but a full-grown businesswoman striking a balance between her commercial and personal life; someone who, as an adult, could accurately reconstruct the feelings once aroused by her total dependence on Emerence, and who realised how much she and her family were indebted to their one-time servant.

But there were no tearful reminiscences, as she shared our low-calorie supper. She was sorry that she never met the old woman. It would have been like seeing her for the first time, because Emerence, for her, had been a faceless person. She was very small at the time, and however fond she might have been, she had quite forgotten her. I wondered what this well-disposed young person would have said were she told that Emerence, her common sense dethroned for fifteen minutes by blind rage at the rejection of her love, had figuratively killed her, by throwing the meat – symbolising her, the child she had once saved, now found utterly unworthy – to the dog, and ordering him to eat it.

That whole evening with Emerence seems far away now, horribly far away. What I felt when I got home that night was that I had done something that in the end wasn't right, something demeaning. I should never have allowed Emerence to invite a stranger into our home. It had been wrong to help her cultivate the impression, in anybody, that she lived with family and not alone, thus helping to deepen the impenetrable mystery that surrounded her. But once I had done so, it was quite wrong to throw back in her face something she didn't want to see, and had made us a gift of. What stupid pride takes us over at times like that! Perhaps she might have got through this crisis – though I had no idea what it was really about – more easily if she could feel that at least something useful had come from all her work. The dishes she had prepared were such as you seldom saw, even on the menus of great hotels. It had been quite wrong to throw things back in her face. That day someone had badly hurt the old woman, with reason or not I couldn't say. Perhaps it all had a simple, logical explanation. Emerence didn't view things as I did. There were many things she grasped in a flash which others could never see, but just as many that she didn't understand. So why had I, too, hit out at her? When I thought about the way she beat Viola, and yet the dog hadn't taken it badly. That animal understood everything. It absorbed information through so many secret antennae, so many mysterious channels.

We were lying in bed, and my husband had been asleep for some time. I was in a bad mood, unable to relax or doze off, so I got dressed again. Viola, who was in the third room, by my mother's bed, gave a low grunt as I started to move, but didn't whine. He scratched quietly at the door, as if not wanting to wake my husband. Good. Let's go together, my boy, I thought. I know it isn't far, but I don't like wandering around at night on my own.

And off we went, like the heroes of my childhood adventures in the *Aeneid*, indeed like the youthful *pius pater Aeneas* himself, in *Book Six*. Perhaps this was the moment in our relationship – and our lives – when things finally came to a head. *Ibant obscuri sola sub nocte per umbram / perque domos Ditis vacuas.* In the pitch blackness we moved very slowly, Viola and I. The gate was shut. I rang Emerence's bell, and waited for her to appear. It was long past midnight, but I could see that the porch light was still on, and Emerence wouldn't retire before putting it out. She came out almost immediately, and we stood on either side of the bars. Panting heavily, Viola placed his foot on the stone step.

"Is the master ill?" she asked. Her voice was business-like, dry, politely subdued. The house lay sleeping.

"He's fine. I'd like to come in."

She let me through and shut the gate behind us. She had come out of her flat but, even at this hour, the door had been carefully closed. Viola hunched down on the doorstep, sniffing for the cat through the narrow gap around the architrave. I wanted to say something fine and conciliatory, such as that I had no idea what was happening, or had happened earlier, but I was truly sorry that, when she was so upset that afternoon, I hadn't been more understanding; and that, even though I had no idea what had so distressed her, I did feel for her. But nothing came to mind. I only know what I have to do on paper. In real life, I have difficulty finding the right words.

"I'm hungry," I said at last. "Have you anything left to eat?"

The smile that – against every logical expectation – lit up her face, was like the sun breaking through steel-grey clouds. It occurred to me, for the first time, how rarely she did smile. First, she disappeared into the bathroom, and I heard the splashing of water as she washed her hands (she never touched food without doing so), then she flung open the pantry door. It seemed she kept not only food on its shelves but also linen. Viola would have followed her but I caught hold of the leash, and the old woman ordered him to stay where he was, so he lay down again. She returned with a yellow damask tablecloth, plates, cutlery and, not the remains of the joint from which she had laden the visitor's tray, but a quite different roast, steeped in strong spices.

It was unbelievably tasty. I tucked in heartily, and Viola got the bone. She also offered me wine, not commercially bottled but straight from the demijohn, and I drank that too. I don't much like alcohol, but on that night of all nights I had to accept whatever I was given, or my visit would be pointless. I had no idea who I represented at the table, but I knew that I was standing in for someone else, for the visitor who had failed to come, the person for whom she had gone to so much trouble. I did my best to personify a stranger of whom I knew nothing. Together we massaged Viola's ears and played with his paws, and, when I was ready to leave, Emerence escorted me home, as if we were going all the way to Kőbánya on foot, in slippers and dressing gown. We spoke only about the dog, as if he were the most important thing – his bearing, his handsome build, his quick understanding. Neither of us mentioned the failed guest. When we reached our apartment, Emerence handed me the leash, waited while I stepped into the garden, then slowly, with precise enunciation, as if she were taking a vow, whispered after me – on this Virgilian night, with its mixture of real and surreal elements – that she would never forget what I had done.

My husband didn't stir as I slipped into bed beside him, but I had much difficulty getting Viola to go back to his place, so excited was he by all that had happened that day. At last he too fell asleep, not in my mother's room but in the bathroom doorway. I knew when he had finally calmed down, because he snored like a man.

JUNK CLEARANCE

I believe it was from this moment that Emerence truly loved me, loved me without reservation, gravely almost, like someone deeply conscious of the obligations of love, who knows it to be a dangerous passion, fraught with risk. Early in the morning of Mother's Day that year, she burst into our bedroom. My startled husband had difficulty rousing himself from his drugged sleep, so I got up, and gazed in amazement at her standing in the fresh light flooding in through the open window. She was again in her best clothes, leading Viola to my bed on his leash. On his head was a cheap felt hat with a curving rim; it was jet-black, with a newly cut rose blazing in its band; his collar was interwoven with a garland of flowers. And from then on she appeared at dawn each Mother's Day with the dog, singing the old holiday greeting on his behalf:

> Thank you, Lord, for I am loved,
> and fed and have a downy bed;
> and thank you Teachers, Mum and Dad:
> God grant good harvest in the field.

This little verse, which she would have recited on public occasions to her teachers in a rudimentary school, sometime between the 1905 Russian Revolution and the outbreak of the First World War, rang out in her unwavering voice beside our bed, year after year. Viola always did his best to rub himself free of the little hat from God knows where, but this wasn't permitted. And each year the old woman finished with the same coda: *I, the boy-child, thank you for everything. The rose in my hat is for my lady mistress.*

There was indeed a rose in his hat every Mother's Day. Ever since, I have been unable to see a black felt hat without calling up this memory of the two of them: it is dawn, the air is fresh and fragrant; Emerence is in all her finery, our dog has a garland around his neck, and his ears are flattened down under the rim of the hat. In Bluebeard's Castle, the parts of the day were clearly defined; and Emerence too had claimed her eternal time of day on Earth. Every dawn is hers, with its special light, and gentle mists rising from the lawn.

This ritual got on my husband's nerves so intensely that on the eve of Mother's Day he avoided going to bed. He either dozed in the armchair, in his dressing gown, or took himself off to my mother's room, closing the door behind him. What made the dawn visit intolerable for him was being caught still in bed, undressed. But I also think it irked him that Emerence had so much affection for me, and expressed it in such an eccentric way.

For there was nothing offhand or casual in the way Emerence loved me. It was as if she'd learned it from the Bible, which she'd never held in her hands, or had drawn closer to the Apostles during her three years of schooling. Emerence didn't know the words of St Paul, but she lived them. I don't believe there was anyone – apart from those four pillars supporting the arch of my life, my two parents, my husband and my foster-brother Agancsos – capable of giving me such unqualified and unconditional love. Her feelings made me think of Viola, wandering so forlornly through the labyrinth of his private emotions, except that Viola wasn't my dog, but hers. No matter where she was working, if it occurred to her that I might need anything she would instantly drop whatever she was doing, and relax only when she was satisfied that I wanted for nothing; at which point she would rush off again. Every evening she prepared dishes she knew I would enjoy, and she appeared with other things as well, gifts that were both unexpected and undeserved.

Then one day they organised a general clearance of household junk in our district. Emerence systematically scoured the streets, picking up everything that was either of interest or designed for some unusual purpose. She washed her booty carefully, repaired it and smuggled it into our home. This was before the wave of nostalgia hit the nation; but Emerence, with the surest of touches, was going about collecting items which later came to be considered of value. One morning I found in the library: a painting in a damaged frame, later discovered to be of some worth; one half of a pair of patent-leather boots; a stuffed falcon clinging to a branch; a pot for heating water adorned with a ducal coronet; and the make-up box of a former actress – we'd been woken by the heavy perfume emanating from it. It was a traumatic start to the day. Viola was howling – he had done the rounds rummaging with Emerence and had a good sniff of everything, but when they'd got back he'd been shut up in my mother's room so he wouldn't be a nuisance while the collection, planned as a surprise, was prepared, cleaned yet again, and put in place. It also included a garden gnome and the somewhat tattered statue of a brown dog. It was Viola's restlessness that finally got us out of bed that morning. What made the scene really explosive was that it was my husband, and not me, who was first out of the bedroom. The dog was yelping outside the door, wanting to come in. Emerence, with her well-bred delicacy over the giving of gifts, had laid out the treasures and disappeared. My husband had an absolute fit when he went into his study (which was lined with bookshelves from floor to ceiling) and found the garden gnome, next to the single boot, leering at him from the rug in front of his collection of English classics. Emerence had pushed *Ulysses* back on the shelf to make way for the crowned water heater, which she had filled with plastic flowers. The falcon was perched over the fireplace.

Hearing his (for once) unmodulated tones, I rushed in. Never before had I heard my husband express himself with such force, or realised what blind fury lay hibernating beneath his habitual calm. He did not confine himself to an analysis of what might reasonably wake a man in his own house. The argument assumed a wider philosophical scope. What was the point of living if such things were possible – if a godless garden gnome could take over his rug, next to half of a pair of cavalry boots with spurs shaped like eagle's wings? In his rage he leaped from one topic to another. It was a dreadful morning. I didn't know what to do. I tried in vain to explain to him that the old woman expressed herself through means determined by her own interests. Everything there – he had to accept – was motivated by love. This was her peculiar way of demonstrating her feelings. Her choices were an expression of her individual point of view. There was no need to jump around from topic to topic, and no need to shout! It was horrible to listen to. I would sort it all out myself.

My husband dashed out of the house. In truth, I felt sorry for him. I had never before, not once, seen him quite so upset, or so entirely at a loss. Later, when he was at last able to make nervous jokes about it, he told me that Emerence had been outside, sweeping the street. She greeted him, and as he shot past her, she smiled at him as if he were a badly brought-up child who, at his age, ought to know how to say hello nicely, but if he didn't, well, so be it. One had to remember that he would learn in time. Generally, Emerence regarded our relationship as a complete mystery. She didn't understand why I had involved myself in it, but since that was how things were, she accepted it, just as I had accepted that she would never open her door. If that's how the master was, what was one to do? There was no such thing as a sane man.

Among the gifts there was only one intended for him, which I had failed to notice at first among all the junk. It was a truly beautiful leather-bound edition of *Torquato Tasso*. I hid it among the rest of the books. I couldn't at first think what to do with the other things: the gnome, for example, who carried a lamp and sported a tattered green apron and a tassel on the peak of his cap. I had arranged our kitchen rather idiosyncratically, with bits and pieces inherited from my great-grandmother. It had everything: a flour tin, a tool for shaping pasta into snails, a sausage-making machine, a hanging scale with some old weights, and a Peugeot coffee grinder, by then a listed industrial relic. The dwarf fitted snugly into a space under the sink. I fished out the ducal water heater (its little bucket would be just the thing for my scouring powder) and into the actress's make-up box I stuffed my own cosmetics.

But there remained the unresolved problems of the painting, the riding boot and the falcon. The falcon I entrusted to Viola, with excellent results. Within minutes of my letting him out of my mother's room the dog had gnawed it to pieces, leaving only fragments. I hoped the embalming chemicals wouldn't harm him, but the bird looked so very old that the poison can have been doing little for it. It had shed half its feathers, and some rodent had taken a bite out of it, so its wooden perch instantly broke off. I tapped the painting out of its frame. On its stretcher a ravaged-looking young woman stood beside a seething black ocean, staring at the foam with morbid intent. Behind her stood a mansion, and a row of cypresses plunging down a steep slope. I hung the painting on the inside of the translucent window in the kitchen door and stood the boot in the entrance hall. We had no umbrella stand, and I thought it would do as one, since Emerence had polished it so beautifully. The madwoman on the kitchen door, the antique coffee-grinder, the garden gnome by the sink next to the tub of lard, inscribed, in huge letters, *She who loves her husband cooks with lard*, which had bedecked my aunt's kitchen – so extreme was the overall impression created by the apartment that our visitors reacted in one of two ways. Either they were paralysed with amazement, or they were overcome with laughter. Even the walls of our kitchen were something else. Instead of wallpaper or paint, we had oilcloth covered in squirrels, geese and other poultry. Most of our visitors were artists. For them, the place was a familiar world of gentle lunacy. My ultra-correct relatives, with no fantasy life of their own, I had written off long ago. The only real opposition I might have encountered would have been from Emerence. It would have been quite reasonable for her to resist my having turned the kitchen and entrance hall into a madhouse. But from the first she took pleasure in being able to move around among the décor and props of this eccentric private theatre. She had a real feeling for the strange world of E.T.A. Hoffman. Emerence loved anything out of the ordinary. She considered it among the great events of her life when she asked for, and was given, an old-fashioned dressmaker's dummy left me by my mother. She carried it home in triumph, like a sacred relic. I tried in vain to understand why she filled her house with such fantastically useless objects, and then never opened her door to anyone. In any case I was stunned by the honour she had done me by asking for something. As I said, Emerence as a rule never accepted anything. Later, only very much later, in one of the most surreal moments I have ever experienced, I wandered amidst the ruins of Emerence's life, and discovered, there in her garden, standing on the lawn, the faceless dressmaker's dummy designed for my mother's exquisite figure. Just before

77

they sprinkled it with petrol and set fire to it, I caught sight of Emerence's ikonostasis. We were all there, pinned to the fabric over the doll's ribcage: the Grossman family, my husband, Viola, the Lieutenant Colonel, the nephew, the baker, the lawyer's son, and herself, the young Emerence, with radiant golden hair, in her maid's uniform and little crested cap, holding a baby in her arms.

*

Emerence's passion for strange objects wasn't anything new. What surprised me that morning was that she had been collecting not for herself but for me. I didn't dare offend her, nor did I wish to, but with the dog with the chipped ear, there was nowhere to begin. It was a desperate sight, an error of judgement perpetrated by a dilettante with a disturbed view of the world. I stowed it away behind the pestle and mortar. I knew that if my husband found it he would throw it in the bin. That little dog was a step too far.

By the time Emerence arrived, I was already sitting at work by my typewriter, alone.

"Did you see what those idiots threw away?" she asked. "I took the lot. There wasn't a thing left for anyone else. Weren't you thrilled?"

How could I not have been thrilled? I'd rarely known such a harmonious morning! I made no reply, but carried on banging at the typewriter, stunted embryos of meaningless sentences emerging under my exasperated fingers. She went through all the rooms, one by one, to see where I had placed everything. She objected to the gnome and the painting being assigned to the kitchen. Why hide such rare things away? She hit Viola on the head for destroying the falcon — the poor thing couldn't tell her that I had put its tempting corpse right under his nose. So far I had got off lightly, but what most interested her was where I had put her beautiful little dog. I told her I had hidden it because it wasn't fit to be seen. She stood on the other side of my desk and shouted at me:

"So, have you become so much of a slave you're too scared to do anything for yourself? Just because the master doesn't like animals, you can't even have statues of them, they're banned? Do you think this horrible shell is any prettier? But you keep it on your desk and you're not ashamed to store your invitations and calling cards in it. Dogs no, shells yes? Get it out of my sight, or one of these days I'll smash it to pieces. I loathe the touch of it."

She snatched up the shell. It was a nautilus, on a base of coral. It once sat on Maria Rickl's console, and was left to my mother when the Kismester apartment was divided up. Emanating disgust, Emerence carried it off to the kitchen, with all the invitations and calling cards, parked it between the semolina and the icing sugar, and in its place set down the dog with the tattered ear. This was going too far. I had accepted Emerence's presence both in the places and the events of my life, but she wasn't going to take over the way I arranged my surroundings.

"Emerence," I said, with more than usual seriousness, "kindly take the little statue back to the street where you found it, or, if you don't want to throw it away, put it where I had it, out of sight. It's a piece of commercial junk. It's damaged; it's in appalling taste, and it cannot remain here. It's not only the master who can't stand it. I can't either. It's not a work of art. It's kitsch."

Her blue eyes blazed at me. For the first time I saw in them, not interest, affection or concern, but undisguised contempt.

"What is this kitsch?" she asked. "What does it mean? Explain it to me."

I wracked my brain for a way to explain to her the vices of the innocent, ill-proportioned, cheaply-made little dog.

"Kitsch is when a thing is in some way false, created to provide trivial, superficial pleasure. Kitsch is something imitative, fake, a substitute for the real thing."

"This dog is fake?" she asked, with rising indignation. "A fraud? Well, hasn't it got everything – ears, paws, a tail? But it's all right for you to keep a brass lion's head on your desk. You think it's wonderful, and your visitors gush over it, and make knocking noises with it, like idiots, though it doesn't even have a neck – nothing – just a head, but they go bang bang with it on the stationery cupboard. So the lion, which doesn't even have a body, is not a fake, but the dog, that's got everything a dog has, is? Why are you telling me such lies? Just tell me straight that you don't want any presents from me, and that's that. So what if the top of the ear is chipped? You'll take a bit of pottery your friend from Athens dug up on some island and stick it behind glass. Do you have the nerve to tell me that filthy black thing is *complete*? At least, don't lie to yourself. Admit it. You're scared of the master. I can understand that. But don't try to hide your cowardice by calling things kitsch."

The shocking thing was, she had hit on something that was in a way true. I did find the statue repulsive, but that wasn't the real reason I had stuck it behind the mortar. It was as she said. I was afraid of, or rather for, my husband. The entire contents of the Heraklion museum wouldn't have been worth causing him a return of his bad times – so I had gabbled away like a left-wing art critic. Emerence maintained a sarcastic silence. Then she buried the dog deep in the bag she always carried, and set off. On her way out through the hall she noticed the boot, standing in shadow against the wall. She seized it, and scattered the umbrellas at my feet. She was so angry she turned scarlet, and shouted at me:

"Are you out of your mind? Do you think sane people keep umbrellas in a boot? Do you think I brought it here to be used as a box? That I'm so stupid I don't know what's right and proper?"

She yanked open the hall cupboard, took a screwdriver from the toolbox and set to work on the boot. She stood with her back to me, facing the light, cursing me without pause. It was an unusual experience for me. I was never scolded as a child. My parents' method of punishment was more refined. They hurt me with silence, not words. It upset me more if I was made to feel I didn't deserve to be spoken to, asked questions or given explanations. Emerence tucked the boot under her arm, as if she were intending to take it home with her, and flung the spur she had removed down on the table top.

"Because you're blind and stupid and a coward," she continued. "God knows what I love about you, but whatever it is, you don't deserve it. Maybe, as you get older, you'll acquire a bit of taste. And a bit of courage."

And out she went, leaving the spur on the table. I picked it up. My husband might appear at any moment, and I didn't want any further upset. The large centrepiece glinted blood-red. I stood, dumbstruck, holding a tiny piece of pure craftsmanship, blackened as it was with age, in which someone had set a garnet. Emerence, having thoroughly cleaned everything before bringing it to the flat, must have noticed what was on it. It was the reason she had given it to us – obviously not only a single boot, but a precious stone she'd found in the centre of the silver spur. A goldsmith might make it into a piece of jewellery. The stone was flawless, wonderful.

Once again, as I gazed at the winking, blood-red garnet, all I felt was deep shame. I was about to run after the old woman, but then the thought returned: I had to break her habit of demonstrating her attachment to me by these undisciplined, insane means. I know now, what I didn't then, that affection can't always be expressed in calm, orderly, articulate ways; and that one cannot prescribe the form it should take for anyone else.

My husband returned, bearing a large pile of newspapers. He had walked his anger off, and come back to a peaceful apartment. He searched each room to see if the offensive items had been removed. The kitchen was a surprise, but by then he had pretty much calmed down, and he realised that that area was beyond help or hurt. Ever since we'd moved in, my playful nature had been collecting the most impossible objects – it would have made no difference if we'd suspended a stuffed whale from the ceiling, like something in my great-grandparents' vast emporium. The madly staring woman and the ducal water heater merely added to the general air of an occupational therapy museum made to look like a kitchen-diner. Luckily he failed to spot the gnome lurking in the shadow of the U-bend. At last order was restored. And once again I had misread the calm before the storm. I was enjoying it, even though Viola's head was drooping miserably. His listless demeanour should have warned me that something was brewing.

By midday it was clear that I would have to walk the dog. Emerence obviously intended to punish me. Fine. I would take him myself. Viola's behaviour was demonic; he almost wrenched my wrist from its socket. For some reason a police convoy was moving down the avenue, so we couldn't go on the grass, and the pavements still bore the remains of the junk clearance. Viola wanted to sniff everything and honour it with his calling card. At one point I caught sight of Emerence in the far distance. She was bending over to pick up a brightly painted box. I turned my back on her and dragged the furious Viola home.

That evening it wasn't Emerence who came but her brother's boy, the one who visited her regularly if not often, and his beautician wife with the tiny hands. We had known them some time, as Emerence had brought them over to be introduced. "My little brother Józsi's boy" was a kindly, good-hearted man, amused and not offended by his exclusion from Emerence's domain. The old woman was very fond of these young people, though she was forever demanding to know why they didn't have more children. They were saving up for a house, and for long package holidays abroad, and there was no place for a new baby in their lives. Emerence showed her disapproval, but was always giving them sums of money, both large and small, for their travels, or to replace their car. She had a lot of money, and someone sent her a monthly remittance of some kind from abroad. I once asked her who this person was. She replied it was none of my business. And of course it wasn't.

But that evening there was a seriousness beneath the nephew's laughing manner. His aunt had asked him to tell us we should look for help elsewhere. She was leaving us. She would work out the remaining ten days to the first of the month to give us time to find a replacement.

My husband shrugged. The morning's surprises hadn't exactly deepened their friendship. But I found it inconceivable that the message could be serious, that never again would I see her in our home, coming and going at all hours of the day. She'll be back, I told myself. She's sulking because she didn't like my lecture on kitsch. She'll come again, surely, if not for my sake then for Viola's. But the nephew wasn't hopeful.

"Please don't take what she says lightly," he went on. "She never jokes. If she makes an announcement she doesn't go back on it. Now that she's decided, she'll never come to your home again. She didn't tell me what had upset her, but I long ago gave up trying to fathom her, or influence her. It's impossible. She understands nothing of the modern world, and she takes almost everything the wrong way. When I wanted to explain the importance of land reform to her, she slapped me and screamed that she wasn't interested in what happened in '45; it was nothing to do with her; she'd got nothing out of the changes. So, please, never attempt to persuade her of anything. She nearly drove the propaganda people mad, she was the only one who wouldn't pledge a penny to the Loan for Peace. It pains me to think what scenes the Lieutenant Colonel saved her from at the time. By the way, she also kicked me out today. She sent me over with orders to get lost as soon as I had delivered the message – she didn't want to see me again for a good long while."

"We're not going to plead with her," said my husband. "She's a free citizen. In any case, I'm the one who offended her, by not letting her turn my home into a flea market with her tasteless rubbish."

The nephew thought for a while before he spoke.

"Her taste is impeccable, doctor." He gazed steadily at my husband. "I thought you would have noticed that. It's just that when she goes looking for presents for the two of you she doesn't buy for grown-ups. She chooses for two young children."

My mind went back to when she had last set the table, both the food itself and the way she presented it on the plates. It was true her taste was impeccable. And perhaps it was also true that when it came to me and my husband, she chose for a child. Maybe it hadn't been the gemstone in the spur that had caught her eye, she might have thought a handsome boot was just the thing for a little boy of two. And, as I'd brought Viola home, I'd be thrilled by a plaster dog.

The nephew went on to talk about his aunt's intention to make a will. This task was now in the hands of the Lieutenant Colonel. After what had happened that morning she wasn't likely to be asking us for help, and he couldn't contribute because he was an interested party – she had told him she was leaving him her money. The amount she'd set aside should be quite large. After all, she lived rent-free; somebody, he didn't know when, had provided her with enough clothing, bedlinen and even furniture for a lifetime. The only money she spent was on food. She even gathered her own fuel from the row of trees at the edge of the wood. The furniture had probably been damaged by her cat, but they already had some nice things, so they weren't relying on it. The money they did need, for the house they wanted to build. But they hoped the old lady would live another thousand years, there were so few good, honest people like her in the world, though – as his present visit to us showed – she was unpredictable and hot-tempered as well.

He took his leave, and asked us, despite what had happened, to give him a call if ever we noticed that she needed help, or if she fell ill, though that had never happened in his lifetime. The old lady had never been sick, even though she did more work than five younger people put together. Whatever had happened, we weren't to hold it against her. She was a good woman.

It wasn't a question of holding anything against her. My husband, though he didn't boast about it, felt a sort of grim satisfaction; but I was plunged into gloom. We'd grown used to the absolute order prevailing in our home. Both of us, though me chiefly, had been able to take on more work because it had become ingrained in us that there was always someone there to straighten us out. My first concern wasn't that the pattern of our lives would collapse, that for weeks I'd be unable to settle down to write, or that I'd never manage the housework. It was rather that I knew Emerence was genuinely fond of us – even, with reservations, of my husband – so how could we have given such offence, and against which of her private and rigid codes of conduct? Clearly she wouldn't be punishing us to this extent for rejecting the little dog with the chipped ear.

As for Viola, it was as if he'd gone insane. He soon realised that there was nothing to be done, he would have to be satisfied with us, and from then on he sprawled about as if he'd been poisoned. How he understood the significance of "Józsi's boy's" few words was yet another of his secrets. My husband began to analyse the situation. When all was said and done, what had taken place was unacceptable. Emerence couldn't object to our desire to surround ourselves with things chosen according to our own taste. If she continued to make an issue of it, we'd have to get along without her. I felt tired, so tired it no longer felt real; though I had no right or reason to feel so utterly weary. Nothing had occurred that should have caused such exhaustion. I found lunch waiting in the fridge, just as before. I hadn't been able to write a single line, but then the ebb and flow of writing involves, even on good days, being in a state of grace. The situation had drained my energy. Cheerfulness keeps you fresh, its opposite exhausts. Now I was miserable, but not because I had to look for another help. The problem was simpler. I had finally accepted that it wasn't just Emerence who was attached to me, with the sort of feelings normally reserved for family, but that I, too, loved her.

Anyone with a good eye would have seen that my unfailing, unvarying sociability was a cover for the appalling fact that I am capable of nothing more than friendship, and truly attached only to the number of people I might count on one hand. Since my mother's death, Emerence had been the one living soul I had allowed to get close to me, and I was discovering this now, when I had lost her over a plaster dog with a chipped ear.

It was a difficult evening, though my husband did his best to make things easier. He took Viola out, which I knew would be pure torture for him. Viola hauled him about and refused to obey; he always misbehaved when he had to go out with him. My husband even sat with me and watched TV, though he only liked listening to the radio. He tried all he could to be of help. Neither of us mentioned Emerence; we were each deep in our own silence about her. My husband needed to feel he had somehow won — it rejuvenated him, gave him new strength; it even improved his health. The day Emerence declared war was for him a day of victory. As he sat there, I could almost see the triumphal garland on his head. Viola went off to lie down, ignoring all our overtures; his drooping tail indicated sorrow — real sorrow. We went out to sit on the terrace, and he padded off to my mother's room where he collapsed theatrically, as if he had been wounded.

It was now the second evening of the junk clearance. At such times there was always a lot of coming and going after dark, and from our balcony we used to watch the people collecting. Something was clearly up with Emerence, because the brigade of workers normally under her command were busily stooping and bending away without her. The old woman had a loyal band of visitors, admirers and protégées, but among them were a select few who enjoyed special favours. These were Sutu, whose corner stand supplied the street with fruit and vegetables, Adélka, the laboratory technician's widow, and Polett, an elderly spinster with a slight hunchback who took in ironing. According to Emerence, Polett had at one time been in service as a governess, had later taught languages, and had generally seen better days before falling on hard times. Apparently the soldiers had robbed her of everything, and after the war there was no call for either governesses or language teachers. The family she had worked for had fled to the West, abandoning her without so much as her last month's pay. The poor old girl must have had a troubled destiny. She almost always looked hungry, even though the neighbours were forever asking her to take in their ironing, so she wasn't entirely without income. And she really could speak French. Her regular visits for coffee were reflected in Emerence's ever-widening vocabulary. Among the old woman's many and varied talents was that she never forgot what she had once heard, and she would use foreign expressions with great accuracy.

But on that evening only Sutu, Adélka and Polett, each with her own huge bag, were out there bending and lifting in the gathering dark. So far as Emerence was concerned this was prime hunting time, but she was nowhere to be seen. I could always identify her, in even the deepest shadow, by her movements — she bobbed up and down between the discarded items like a modern-day Dorothy Kanizai scouring the battlefields of defeat for signs of life among the wounded.

This time, it wasn't Viola who resolved the crisis, with his primitive but effective resources. Now, probably for the first time, I felt the full force of Emerence's power. The old woman made not the slightest move in our direction, but by some form of radar she reduced the animal to paralysis. Willpower can be projected in a great many ways, but this was the most indirect. Emerence adored Viola, and she set out to get him back by banishing him. Life continued to trundle along. I rushed around looking for help. A totally unsuitable person called Annie appeared from nowhere, and lasted a few days. Her main activity during that time was to throw herself into the bathtub after half an hour's work, juggle with the soap while shrieking at the water, then stroll around the flat as naked as the day she was born, under the pretext of cooling off. Annie's visitation can only have been brought upon us by Emerence's dark powers, because someone had known I was here on my own. I had taken care not to mention it to anyone in the street or immediate neighbourhood, and yet Annie had appeared out of the blue, with impressive references, at a time when I was up to my neck in unfinished business. I took her on trial, but her guest appearance lasted no more than a week, not because of the bathroom scenes but because of Viola. He growled whenever he saw her, as he did at anyone who went near the vacuum cleaner or duster.

Emerence had vanished from our lives, but she paralysed everything around us. She was like a character in an epic poem who dissolves into thin air. We never ran into her. She knew the pattern of our lives and obviously took care that whenever we were out, or might go out, she stayed out of sight as much as she could. When I was forced to turn down a third literary commission for lack of time, my husband, after a criminally unsuccessful dinner, announced, in his calm, undramatic way, that the dog with the chipped ear was costing us more than a few words of propitiation were worth. There was no point in denying that we couldn't manage without Emerence. We'd have to put the statue in some conspicuous place, and hide it when guests came. Unfinished novels shouldn't have to wait around for a thing like that. We couldn't get on with our work, myself even less than him, because the flat was my responsibility. We would have to submit to Emerence's terms.

I didn't take Viola with me to the Papal Palace, nor did he wish to come. The paralysing spell must have still been in force; he didn't stand up, he just glanced at me with that utterly human expression, as if wondering whether I really had the courage to go, and pondering the real reason behind my decision. Was I looking to secure conditions of creative calm for us, or did I feel that I owed it to Emerence's dignity as a human being?

She wasn't out on the porch; those days she never was. First, I knocked on the door, without result, then I went round the side and tapped on the shutters.

"Emerence, will you come out? We need to talk."

I thought she might be putting off the moment, but she had already opened the door, and was standing in front of it. Her mood was serious, almost sombre.

"Have you come to apologise?" she asked. There was no trace of anger in her voice.

Once again, this was too much. I had to choose my words

very carefully, so that we could both keep within the bounds of reason.

"No. Our tastes are different, but that doesn't matter. We didn't mean to hurt your feelings. If you wish, the plaster dog can stay. But we can't manage without you. Will you come back?"

"You'll keep the plaster dog?"

There was a confident certainty in her voice. It was that of a statesman laying out his terms.

"Yes," I answered.

"Where will you put him?"

"Wherever you like."

"Even in the master's study?"

"As I said, wherever you like."

And so we set out.

Viola showed absolutely no response; not until Emerence reached the bottom of the stairwell and softly spoke his name. Then I thought he was going to break the door down. She wished my husband a polite "good evening", and once again offered him her hand, as if enlisting for the second time. She petted Viola, who by now was delirious with joy, then glanced around. The little dog was on the kitchen table. The door was ajar and she spotted it straight away. Seeing it, she looked at us, then at the statue again, then back at us; and her face lit up with one of those unforgettable smiles she reserved for very special occasions. She picked up the little dog, dusted it carefully, and hurled it to the floor. Nobody spoke. No word or sound would have fitted the moment. She stood there among the fragments, like a queen.

And for years we lived, not just in peace and calm, but joyously, in Odessa.

My husband and Emerence put up with each other, but gradually, and somewhat to their mutual surprise, this turned to liking. At first this was because they shared a devotion both to Viola and me from which they had no hope of ever being free; later they gained an understanding of each other's signals. My husband mastered the semantics of Emerence's non-verbal communication, and she came to accept as normal things which had once defied comprehension, such as an idle existence in which we might go half a day in silence, with one of us staring at the poplars at the bottom of the garden, doing nothing that the eye could see, while maintaining that this was work. Yet I believe we three lived in real harmony, truly glad to be alive. Strangers visiting for the first time thought that Emerence, pottering about in the kitchen, was my aunt or godmother. I let that pass, because it was impossible to explain the precise nature of our relationship, or its sheer intensity; how, though she was so different from either of our mothers, she was like a new-found mother to us both. The old woman never cross-examined either of us, nor we her. She told us as much about herself as she saw fit, but generally she said little, like a real mother whose past has become immaterial in her total concern for the future of her children.

As the years went by Viola became more serious, but his performing skills also blossomed. He could open the door using the handle and bring newspapers or slippers to order; and he now congratulated my husband as well as me on birthdays and name days. Emerence laid down the rules for each of us. The master was given the greatest degree of personal freedom, next came Viola, and lastly me. I was often summoned to coffee, when some need arose in her circle of devotees. Adélka in particular liked to discuss her problems with me. She was the sort of woman who, having been given advice, would then talk it over with three or four other friends. When she did this, Emerence came close to beating her. Sutu and Polett had less to say. Polett in particular became more and more taciturn. She was rapidly losing weight; and then suddenly she stepped out of our lives.

Sutu came running over with the news of the suicide. She bought her merchandise in the market at daybreak, and so she was up before everyone else in the street except Emerence. She couldn't have appeared at a worse time. I opened the door reluctantly, and her news made me sad and upset. By then I had come to know Polett well. Emerence's coffee meetings had brought us together, and I felt that we all had a part in her death. There must have been hints of what she intended, which we had failed to notice. Sutu wanted to know how she should tell Emerence. They had lunched together only the day before. Emerence was closer than anyone to Polett, and knew things about her that she would never have revealed to Sutu. No, she couldn't tell her. I would have to do it. She had to be there when the police arrived, because unluckily for her, she had been the one who found the poor woman. Look how considerate Polett had been, even in the way she ended it all! She didn't make things more difficult by disappearing. She didn't even go inside, she hanged herself in the garden, from the walnut tree, so we wouldn't have to break down the door. The most interesting thing was that she had pulled a hat over her head, obviously not wanting to give anyone a fright; but she was still a horrible sight, hanging there, with her Sunday hat on (we'd seen it thousands of times, the one with the pretty brass buttons) pulled down to her neck. Adélka already had the news, it had made her ill; but now Sutu had to rush off, she couldn't keep her stall shut all this time. I should get over to Emerence quickly. If the old woman didn't find out in good time she'd be permanently offended; and as I might have discovered, when she was angry, it was terrible.

Tell Emerence anything? Bring her news? She knew everything.

When I got there she was out on her porch, shelling peas. Once again her face was like a mirror, turned towards the bowl, totally impassive and yet paler than usual, though she couldn't have ever been rosy-cheeked, even as a girl. Had I come about Polett? From her tone she might have been inquiring whether Viola had been for a walk. She'd seen her at dawn, when the dog gave the sign. She went out when she heard it. Had it not woken us? No. My husband was asleep, but I had pricked up my ears, because Viola was making a real racket – he'd howled for a while after midnight, and I had marvelled at the number of different noises this dog could make. Viola had been announcing a death, the old woman went on, in the same colourless voice, so she thought she'd go and look for the dead person. She scoured the neighbourhood; somewhere a light in a window would tell the sad story. She suspected old Mrs Böőr – for weeks she'd been like a woman whose grave had already been measured up – but there were no lights on anywhere. So she looked in the garden. It was pure chance that she found Polett. If she hadn't left the front door of her little house open, Emerence wouldn't have gone in. Polett was always nervous in that shack of a home, and never slept with the door ajar, so she immediately thought something had happened to her. But the house was empty. She switched on the light and saw there was no-one on the divan and the blankets hadn't been disturbed. She set off again to look for her. And then she saw her in the garden, under the tree. In the moonlight, the brown hat on her head appeared jet black.

I stared at Emerence, unable to speak. It wasn't her lack of sadness, it was her display of complete unconcern with which she had taken the news. "We never actually discussed the hat," she went on, as she rolled the peas in her fingers. "She didn't tell me she would wear it. All we agreed on was the dress, and how she would be buried. She didn't have a black slip, so I gave her one. She looked rather odd with that hat pulled down to her neck. Her shoes had fallen off. Did they find them?"

I felt compelled to ask, all the same. "So you knew what she was going to do?"

"How could I not have known?" she answered, as she gave the peas a stir, and considered whether she had done enough for everyone. "We even agreed that she wouldn't use poison. When I worked for that detective inspector, the one who always did the suicide cases, he told me most of the ones who poisoned themselves were found outside their front doors, as if they'd had second thoughts. The moment they began to choke, they wanted out. It's a very painful way to die, poisoning, except of course for the rich. They've other means at their disposal, which the local doctor won't prescribe. But there's nothing better than a hanging. It's simple and straight-forward. I've seen enough of them here in Pest," she went on. "When the Whites were in power, it was the Whites doing it, and when it was the Reds' turn, they did the same, and the speeches they made before killing them were the same, and the legs of the victims kicked out in exactly the same way, no matter which colour had strung them up. Hanging's not bad. It's more pleasant than a bullet. Shooting doesn't always work, and then you watch each time they take aim, however many times it takes, and in the end, if you don't die straightaway, they have to come over and beat you to death or shoot you in the back of the head. I know those executions. I've seen enough of them."

The last time I had felt as I did on that June day, was at Mycenae, at the grave of Agamemnon.

As Emerence ran her gnarled fingers through the peas, my thoughts went back not just across time, but over place and into history. I saw Emerence the child before the death of her father; her water nymph of a mother; the stepfather who never returned from Galicia; the twins who turned into charred logs in that wild circle of land beside the well. I saw the young girl who had become (from what I'd just heard) maidservant to a detective inspector, and probably to more than one, since the employer who strung up Reds was probably not the same one who arrested the Whites.

I asked: once she realised what Polett had in mind, had she tried to talk her out of it?

"The thought never occurred to me," she said. "Won't you sit down? Sit and help me shell the peas. There aren't enough for the four of us. If people want to go, then let them. Why should they linger? We made sure she had enough to eat; nobody tried to burgle her home; they let her live in that little pigsty for nothing; I even arranged for her to have company. But obviously we weren't enough, not Sutu, not Adélka, not me. We listened sympathetically to all her nonsense, even if we couldn't understand because she spoke French. We knew that, most of the time – even in a foreign language – her cackling amounted to the same old thing. She was lonely. Who isn't lonely, I'd like to know? And that includes people who do have someone but just haven't noticed.

"I brought her a kitten – they were allowed in her building – but she got in a rage, saying it wasn't company. I don't know what would have been good enough for her if neither we nor the animal were. One of its eyes was blue and the other green, and it could look at you with those two odd eyes in such a way, it didn't even have to miaow, you knew what it wanted. But that wasn't enough for Polett. It wasn't human — as if we aren't animals too, only less perfect. They can't inform on us, or tell lies about us, and if they steal it's for a reason, because they can't go into a shop or a restaurant. I begged her to take it in. I mean, even if it wasn't the answer to her loneliness, it was an orphan — some horrible person had thrown it out. On its own, with nowhere to live, it would have died. And it was so tiny. But no, no, no. She needed a human being. Fine, I told her, then go and buy one in the market; around here there's only us and the cat.

"Well, now she's found a friend, she's got a hoe handle for company, she isn't alone. Was it Sutu who sent you here? Or that bird-brained Adélka? They were so stupid, the two of them. Neither of them noticed that she was heading this way. It's true she never told them, but she didn't have to tell me, or Viola. We just knew. I didn't take her hat off; I didn't see her face. You might take a look for me, to see whether she had an easy death. I'm not going. I still haven't forgiven her. She's welcome to hang herself. We three made a real fuss of her. Viola liked her too. We sat and listened to her wailing. I took her a pet, she refused it. Well, if she wanted to go, why shouldn't she? There was nothing for her here. She always had a sore stomach. She couldn't take work in any more — though she ironed better than any of us — you should have seen what she could do at an ironing board. Right, that's the peas done. Are you going or staying? If you see Sutu, send her over. Tell her that as soon as she closes up she's to come and help me. Today I'm bottling cherries for the winter."

The two lions on the gate of Mycenae stirred; each grew a living eye, one green, one blue, and they began quietly to miaow. I rose unsteadily to leave, praying that I wouldn't meet Sutu. I began to turn over in my mind what I should say to her. Emerence wouldn't hide from her the things she had told me.

I would have to try and persuade her, at the very least, not to mention it to the police. What would they think, if it got out that Emerence had let Polett go to her death, had even given the poor woman practical advice, knowing what she intended?

Emerence had turned her attention to the cherries, and was hauling out the same cauldron in which she had been boiling sheets the day we first met. I stopped where I was.

"Emerence," I began cautiously, "shouldn't we discuss what we're going to tell the police? Sutu might blurt out something silly."

"Now you're being silly," she waved away my concerns. "You don't think anyone's going to waste breath on Polett? Who is interested in an old woman who hangs herself, and even tells us why she did it in a letter? Do you think I didn't make her write a suicide note? Everything has to be done properly, even death. I talked through everything with her – her clothes, the letter. I'm only sorry I can't stop her being pawed by those animals at the post-mortem. No man ever saw her. The first will be that chief dissectionist. Her virgin body won't be anything new to him. He knows all about dead bodies. I used to work for one of them myself."

Agamemnon's grave deepened. She'd never mentioned the dissectionist.

"People who don't know you wouldn't believe how clueless you are," she continued, "though I tell you again and again. You think life goes on for ever, and that it would be worth having if it did. You think there'll always be someone to cook and clean for you, a plate full of food, paper to scribble on, the master to love you; and everyone will live for eternity, like a fairy tale; and the only problem you might encounter is bad things written about you in the papers, which I'm sure is a terrible disgrace, but then why did you choose such a low trade, where any bandit can pour shit over you? God knows how you got yourself a name. You're not very bright, and you know nothing about people. Not even Polett, you see; and yet how often did you drink coffee with her? I'm the one who understands people."

The stream of cherries tumbled into the cauldron. By now we were in the world of myth – the pitted cherries separating out, the juice beginning to flow like blood from a wound, and Emerence, calmness personified, standing over the cauldron in her black apron, her eyes in shadow under the hooded headscarf.

"I loved Polett. How could you not have seen that? But it wasn't enough. Sutu did too, but it still wasn't enough. And even that stupid Adélka respected her. We three loved her. Compared with her, we're pretty well off, we've got jobs – in Adélka's case a pension – and we all chipped in, so she wouldn't be short when she wasn't earning. She got food, firewood, dinners. We looked after her. But she wanted something else, something more, I don't know what. She didn't even want the kitten, although I would have fed it too. That was the limit. Why did she never stop whining? If someone can't be helped, then they don't want help. If she'd had enough of life, no-one had the right to hold her back. I told her exactly what she should write for the police and she copied it down: 'I, Polett Dobri, spinster, because of sickness, old age and above all loneliness, have of my own free will ended my life. I leave my belongings to be disposed of by my friends Etel "Sutu" Vámos; Adél, widow of András Kürt; and Emerence Szeredás.' It was all quite clear. I brought her iron back with me the same night, so we wouldn't argue over it. After that, what could they ask about?"

The Polett business, like every other difficulty involving Emerence and her circle, was taken care of by the Lieutenant Colonel. He told me the computer files later revealed that Paulette Hortense D'Aubry had been born in Budapest in 1908.

Her father was a legal translator; her mother, Katalin Kemenes, a woman of no formal education whose last occupation had been ironing. No religious affiliation was recorded, though Emerence swore she was Reform. The reverend minister was less than delighted when asked to preside at the burial. He said that Polett, like Emerence, had never once called on him, and God was not pleased when people decided for themselves when their hour had come. Fortunately he didn't hear Emerence's comments. The old woman recalled her own experience with the charitable ladies. Polett had also been present at the distribution, but had got even less than Emerence, with her sequinned evening dress. The ladies had it in for her, she was too high-flown and besides, like Emerence, they never saw her at worship. This was true, because while they were at prayer, Polett was doing their ironing, Sundays and every other day. She used a coal-heated iron, because in those days the electricity in the area wasn't working fully — they provided current only at certain times — and Polett's head was almost lifted off by the steam. No doubt that was what they meant when they described her mental state as "high-flown".

*

In those days I still clung stubbornly to the pattern of life I had as a girl. On major festivals I would even go to church twice, as I had done whether at home or away at boarding school. If Emerence caught sight of me at these times she would stare contemptuously as I scuttled off down the street like a guilty schoolgirl to avoid the same unvarying harangue, that people who went to church had nothing better to do. Apart from everything else, this wasn't true, because the fact was I never had time for anything. Every night I had to make up those hours spent away from my typewriter. Writing isn't an easy taskmaster. Sentences left unfinished never continue as well as they had begun. New ideas bend the main arch of the text, and it never again sits perfectly true.

Anyway, I managed to persuade the priest that Polett was an elderly soul with an unblemished reputation. He might at least eulogise her richly since she was being given a pauper's burial. As it was, anyone making that last journey with her to the Farkasrét cemetery would have been pretty surprised by Emerence's final farewell. Instead of adding a wreath to the few modest flowers, she set a pot of flowering geraniums tied with a cream-white funeral ribbon in pride of place beneath the urn. It bore the message: *Here loneliness ends. May you rest in peace. Emerence.* The urn was of the cheapest sort, the grave badly sited, the mourners few, and the service quickly over. We went off to visit the graves of people we knew, but Emerence stayed there, in front of the little plaque, while they sealed up the urn. Some time later, as we strolled towards the exit, we met her again. She had obviously just concluded her own private obsequies. Her eyes were full of tears, her lips swollen. I'd never seen her so utterly crushed.

That evening, she came for Viola. The dog was as depressed as she was. There was none of his usual jumping around for joy at a walk. When she brought him back she sent him off to his blanket, and he went to sleep without protest. I was sorting out a cupboard, but turned to face her when she called out:

"Have you ever killed an animal?"

I said I had never killed anything.

"You will. You'll put Viola down. You'll have him injected, when the time comes. Try to understand. When the sands run out for someone, don't stop them going. You can't give them anything to replace life. Do you think I didn't love Polett? That it meant nothing to me when she'd had enough and wanted out? It's just that, as well as love, you also have to know how to kill. It won't do you any harm to remember that. Ask your God — since you're on such good terms with him — what Polett told him when they finally met."

I shook my head. Why was she always getting at me? This was hardly the time for silly banter.

"I loved Polett," she repeated. "I don't know why I bother telling you what I just have. You're so stupid you haven't understood me yet again. If I hadn't loved her, I would have stopped her. When I shout at people they listen. She avoided me because she knew that if she disobeyed me she'd be in trouble. Do you think anyone else told me stories about Paris, and the cemetery where they always take flowers for some woman; and the place where the Emperor is buried so that you have to look down to see him? Who else but Polett could tell me things like that, while she still saw some point in living? How else could I have thanked her for teaching me so many things? When I saw that she was beyond help, I had to give her the courage to have the last word herself, rather than someone else, or the ever-increasing misery, the pain in her spine, and the constant humiliation.

"Sutu never really liked her. She looked down on her, because of all that had happened to her. I haven't told you about this — it hardly matters now, poor thing — but one of her ancestors was some sort of thief or criminal, who finished up on the scaffold. The whole family were on the run. They emigrated, and that's how they ended up in Hungary. Polett wasn't ashamed of it, she talked about it openly. Only, Adélka kept on and on about what sort of people they were. I don't know what she's got to be so proud of — her father did time for a stabbing, and for breaking and entering. They didn't string him up, but he wasn't that much better than Polett's relation. When she heard that he'd had his head cut off, Adélka just laughed. But she's stupid as a pumpkin, and she didn't like Polett's stories either. She's killed enough chickens, she should have grasped that if you do it right the head comes off straightaway – you don't have to hack it off. Polett swore that her ancestor wasn't a criminal, it was just politics that brought him here. They got caught up in it and carried away. I believed her, and so did Sutu, because there really are people like that. How many innocent people have been killed here in Hungary? When I was only a girl, engaged to the baker, they didn't just cut his head off, they tore him limb from limb. You don't believe me? Well don't, then. The mob ripped him apart. He hadn't done anything wrong. All he did was open the shop after the commanding officer ordered him not to sell bread to anyone but the soldiers. But he felt sorry for the people, so he shared out the bread, but they didn't believe him when he said it was all gone, so they dragged him out and killed him. They tore him apart, like a loaf of bread. When the mob sorts you out, it takes a while. It's a slow death.

"Well, I'm off now. I wanted to tell you this. If I had a bed, I'd lie down on it tonight, for once. But ever since they got the young people out, and Éva was rescued, and the Grossman grandparents drank cyanide and I found them dead in their bed, I've only been able to sleep in an armchair or in the lovers' seat. So, g'night. Don't give Viola anything more to eat. He's scoffed quite enough already."

I sat out on the balcony overlooking the garden, gazing at the flowers and the sky. In the fragrant evening, time stood still, the silence was absolute. Polett the Huguenot. The baker Emerence was to marry. Gradually they settled into my consciousness, alongside the unknown Grossman grandparents, whose nerves could no longer take Hitler. The chickens at the foot of the guillotine, watching how death happens. A pervading smell of yeast.

Emerence never referred to the baker again, but years later I saw his picture on the dressmaker's dummy. It took me a while to work out who it was.

POLITICS

Emerence never spoke of Polett again. It was as if she had never existed. She, on the other hand, spent more time with us than ever. I think she would have preferred to be only with us, and with us all the time. The bond between us – produced by forces almost impossible to define – was in every way like love, though it required endless concessions for us to accept each other. In her eyes, any work that didn't involve bodily strength and use of the hands was loafing, little better than a conjuring trick. I had always recognised physical achievements, but had never rated them above mental ones, and if ever in the course of my life the philosophy of Jean Giono had prevailed too strongly, those years of the Personality Cult would have freed me from its influence. Books formed the basis of my world, my unit of measure was the printed word, but I didn't think of it as the one salvation, as she considered her standard to be. Without consciously arriving at the concept herself, or being aware of and using the phrase "anti-intellectual", she was the thing itself, an anti-intellectual. Her feelings allowed her to admit a few exceptions, but her idea of a professional person was of a ruling class of gentlemen in suits. As far as she was concerned, anyone who didn't finish a job with his own hands, but had someone else do it instead, qualified for the term. This applied equally to the past as to the present, when fresh upheavals in the social order were creating an upper echelon of the rich and powerful. Her own father, who at the turn of the century had been a well-to-do craftsman, she thought of as working with his hands because she had a fixed image of him surrounded by wood shavings, despite the fact that he owned a house and land, a store of valuable timber and expensive tools. Not for the world would the old woman have uttered that shameful word, "bourgeois", but she was the embodiment of what it stood for. The countless places she had worked in had taught her fine manners but had done nothing for her mental outlook. In her eyes, men who didn't handle tools, however important their function – the Lieutenant Colonel was an exception, he kept order – were all parasites; and their women, whatever fine phrases they might embroider their speech with, just empty mouths needing to be fed.

At first, I was included among them. Emerence looked with suspicion on every piece of paper, every brochure, every book or writing desk. It wasn't that she didn't know Marx; she never read anything, not even a newspaper. I believe she tried to look down on us too, as chronically work-shy, but living alongside us somehow undermined her, something softened her hostility the moment she crossed our doorstep. She seemed to have persuaded herself that what we were pounding away on was a machine of sorts, and that there was some small merit in the way we earned our bread.

This anti-intellectualism hadn't prevented her from seizing job opportunities that arose out of political changes which gave her line of work a rarity value and guaranteed her complete security. From each of her employers she had learned something, without altering her opinion of any of them. She glanced at our books for only as long as it took to dust them. Things she'd learned by rote in her three years of elementary school had long vanished from her head, under the laval flow of time, and one verse remained, the Mother's Day greeting. Her literary instruction, since that moment at the farmyard well, had been shaped by her various employers, and by life itself. The decades of her life in Hungary had exposed her only to the rhetoric she so hated, and which had drained away any interest she might have had in poetry. By the time she might have heard something different, she had lost the desire to enrich her mind. They had torn the baker to pieces during the Aster Revolution and then, as she told me later, the hero of her great love had vanished before her eyes and his worthless successor had robbed her. Emerence never knew that in some ways she had reached the same position as Captain Butler in *Gone with the Wind*. Like the unscrupulous hero of that novel, she had no wish to lay her heart on the line, not for anyone or anything. After the Second World War a limitless horizon lay open before her. She could have cut herself as large a slice as she wanted. She had a good, coolly analytical mind, and her logic was flawless. But she had no wish to cultivate or advance herself, or work for the collective good, whether by obeying directives or joining in campaigns. She made her own decisions about what steps she would take and why, how far she would take them, and for whom. So she remained in the sphere of christening bowls and multicoloured cats. She never read the papers, or listened to the news, and the word "politics" was banned from her world. No tears came to her eyes, and no self-conscious quaverings filled her voice if she chanced to utter the word "Hungary".

Emerence was the sole inhabitant of her empire-of-one, more absolute than the Pope in Rome. At times her total indifference to the wider public life led to some lively scenes between us, and a stranger who witnessed us might have thought we were performing a cabaret. On one such occasion, though my family goes back to the Árpáds, I was endeavouring – driven almost to tears with rage – to persuade her of the significance of everything that had happened in Hungary since the war, the redistribution of land, and how the working class – her class, not mine – now had endless opportunities opening up for them. Emerence replied that she knew the peasant mentality; her own family were peasants. They didn't care a straw who bought their eggs and their cream so long as it made them rich. The worker would fight for his rights only until he became the boss. She wasn't interested in the proletarian masses (she didn't use the word, but she described the thing), and above all she hated the idle, lying gentry. Priests were liars; doctors ignorant and money-grabbing; lawyers didn't care who they represented, victim or criminal; engineers calculated in advance how to keep back a pile of bricks for their own houses; and the huge plants, factories and institutes of learning were all filled with crooks.

By now we were really shouting at each other; myself, like Robespierre, representing the power of the people – although it was in those years that they were doing their best to drive me to the point where I could no longer work, and send me to the ghetto I'd been assigned to with my husband (who had himself been so harassed and humiliated he couldn't work at all) in hopes I might decide just to go away, either by changing what I did or the way I lived, or by leaving the country; though it was only my rage that kept me on my feet, rage because I had always known that the people harassing me were concerned only with their own shabby little careers; but I clung to the thought that the country was still writhing in the pangs of birth, it couldn't help the fact that such dishonourable midwives had been sent to its bedside, or that it had brought forth a world of Sparafuciles, placing power in hands so filthy they would have been cut off in St László's day because their owners were worse than thieves, people who decade after decade had robbed the country of all credit.

Despite her years, Emerence too had all those opportunities, or at least she did have at the time of the Great Change; but she had nothing but scorn for the twists and turns of history, and told the party "educators" to their faces that she didn't want speeches from anyone, on any subject. The place for sermons was in church; she'd been set to work as a cook when still a child, and no-one asked her then if she minded; by the age of thirteen she was a menial in Budapest, so her visitor could go straight back where he'd come from, and he could start by getting off her porch; she worked for her living with her hands, not her mouth, like the propagandists, and she didn't have time to listen to rubbish. When the real crackdown came, it was a miracle that she wasn't locked up. There was something monstrous, deformed, in the contempt she heaped on every-thing. Those propagandists must have lived through the most agonising moments of their lives when Emerence acquainted them with her political philosophy. In her view Horthy, Hitler, Rákosi and Charles IV were all exactly the same. The fact was that whoever happened to be in power gave the orders, and anyone giving orders, whoever it was, whenever, and whatever the order, did it in the name of some incomprehensible gobbledegook. Whoever was on top, however promising, and whether he was on top in her own interests or not, they were all the same, all oppressors. In Emerence's world there were two kinds of people, those who swept and those who didn't, and everything flowed from that. It made no difference under which slogans or flags they staged national holidays. There was no force that could overcome Emerence. The propagandist, shocked to the depths of his heart, gave her a wide berth there-after. She couldn't be fended off or stopped in her tracks; he couldn't take a familiar or friendly line with her, or even make simple conversation. She was fearless, enchantingly and wickedly clever, brazenly impudent. No-one ever managed to persuade her that even if one granted the absurd distinction she insisted on, that merit depended on whether one swept or not, it was up to her alone whether she wanted to join those who didn't sweep themselves but got others to sweep for them, because now, in 1945, the state was offering her that choice. Her final trump card, if all else failed, was to play the poor old lady for whom things of this world had become too much, and stare dreamily into space, as if it had all come too late for her. The hopeful young activist would insist: "All roads are still open to you, my dear madam. You come from peasant stock; how could it be too late for you? They'll take you off to study, or send someone here to explain where you should present yourself. They'll assess your aptitudes, which are clearly exceptional. You'll catch up in no time at all. You'll qualify, and be an educated person." Educated? That was the torch that ignited the oil-well of her anti-intellectualism. Those exceptional qualities of mind became instantly apparent when she gave vent to her hatred of the written word. She was an orator of real stature, a natural.

Emerence could barely read. Her writing was crabbed. Addition and subtraction she managed with painful difficulty, and they were the only arithmetical skills she retained. Her memory, on the other hand, worked like a computer. On hearing the radio or television blaring out of people's windows, if the tone was positive she immediately contradicted it, if negative, she praised it. She had no idea where any particular place might be found in the world, but she related news to me about various governments with impeccable pronunciation, reeling off the names of statesmen, Hungarian and foreign, and always with a comment: "They want peace. Do you believe that? I don't, because who then will buy the guns, and what pretext will they have for hanging and looting? And anyway, if there's never been world peace before, why should it happen now?" She dismayed the representatives of a number of women's groups when they tried to get her to their meetings, or at least shake her hostile indifference. The street committee and the local council treated her as an Act of God, and the priest was entirely in agreement. Emerence was a born Mephisto, utterly perverse. I once told her that if she hadn't fought non-stop against the opportunities she'd been offered, she might have been our first woman ambassador or prime minister; she had more sense and intelligence than the entire Academy of Sciences. "Good," she said. "It's a pity I don't know what an ambassador does. The only thing I want is the crypt. Just leave me in peace, and don't try to educate me. I know quite enough already. I wish I knew less. Those who want something from the country are welcome to have it, since you tell me it's so full of opportunities. I don't need anyone or anything. Understand that once and for all."

And in truth she didn't need the country. She had no wish to join the people who oversaw the sweepers. But because she sought nothing for herself it never occurred to her that in her eternal negativity she was political. Had she behaved like that under Horthy, her employers of the time would have found it highly amusing. Józsi's boy told us she did once, during that period, spend a few days in prison for making inflammatory statements. Every phase of her life must have followed the same horrendous pattern. When she did get going, it was best to keep clear, and people fled when they heard her sounding off about Gagarin's space flight, or the dog Laika. When Laika's heartbeats were first broadcast she denounced it as cruelty to animals. Later, she consoled herself by claiming they'd used a ticking clock — no dog in its right mind would rush over and volunteer to sit inside a marble, or whatever it was, and race round the heavens for fun — who could believe that? As for Gagarin, she was a real prophet of doom. Projects like that should be left well alone. God usually ignored us when asked for something, but he invariably granted what we feared. If she levelled the score with a neighbour who trampled her flowerbed, why shouldn't God do the same to his intruders? The heavenly bodies weren't put up there for people to wander round. The day Gagarin died, when she was forced to see for herself the reaction of a shocked and horrified world, even the hopelessly dim Adélka stayed away. She stood on her porch, gesticulating vehemently, telling anyone who'd listen how she'd predicted that God wouldn't tolerate us exceeding our powers. She used other words, but that was her meaning. She was the only person on the entire planet who felt no more sorry for the young man who burned up like a star than she would have for Kennedy or Martin Luther King. She looked on East and West equally, without bias or sympathy, declaring that there were sweepers and their bosses in America too; that Kennedy was one of the bosses, and a negro who hadn't yet made it into the circus but still travelled around performing non-stop must be a king among sweepers. Everyone had to die one day. She'd shed a tear for all of them as soon as she could find the time.

Years later, when Józsi's boy and I met beside her grave and talked about how impossible it was to change her view of the world, the young man spread his hands in a gesture of help-lessness. He reckoned peace had arrived too late for his aunt. His father had taken a more rational view of things. He had never forgotten the hard times they had been through, but he was both contented and progressive. But Emerence had been prone to these bitter outbursts all her life. I must have noticed how peculiar they were, a hostility almost without an object. She was as much against Franz Josef as she was against anyone else in a position to influence the history of the nation, even for the good. I didn't tell him about the lawyer's son. I sensed that the cause of her rage somehow lay with him. In the end it was the Lieutenant Colonel who provided an explanation: Emerence probably hated power no matter whose hands it was in. If the man existed who could solve the problems of the five continents, she would have taken against him too, because he was successful. In her mind everyone came down to a common denomination – God, the town clerk, the party worker, the king, the executioner, the leader of the UN. But if she experienced a sense of fellow feeling with anyone, her compassion was all-embracing, and this didn't extend only to the deserving. It was for everyone. Absolutely everyone. Even the guilty.

I could have said more than anyone about that, because the old woman had confided in me. But I wasn't stupid. All it needed was for me to give them the full picture. On one occasion she was kneeling in front of me, using a damp cloth to pick dog hairs off the rug – Viola was shedding his winter coat. Sitting at my typewriter, I heard her talking away. "Dear God," she muttered into the damp cloth, "I hid the German because his leg – what little was left of it after the machine gun caught him – was falling off. I thought, if they found him they'd beat him to death. Then I stuck the Russian in with him, at the closed-off end of the cellar. They just stared at one another. Now you never heard that, and you never will, and if you once open your mouth about it you'll see what I do to you. When I moved in, there was no-one else living in the building, only that old cripple Mr Szloka, the one I later buried. The owners had gone to Switzerland, and the other tenants hadn't yet started to drift in. I went all over the villa, from the attic to the basement, and I saw it would be possible to make a perfect underground hiding place if I arranged the firewood in the right way. There was a tiny door behind it, opening on to a windowless space. So I dragged the wood in front of it, and I hid them all in there, anyone who was on the run. You can imagine the look on their faces when I moved the Russian in with the German. He must have been hit in the lung because his blood was all frothy. They babbled away at one another, neither understanding a word. I hid their weapons – I have them to this day – not that they'd be worth using, they make so much noise. But I knew how to. My boss was an officer and a big hunter.

"They died, both of them, before they had time to make friends. That night, I laid them out in front of the house. No-one has ever worked out how they came to be lying there, side by side, so peacefully. I also hid Mr Brodarics in the same place. Rákosi was after him. As if I'd just hand him over! He went off to the drilling site with his helmet on each day, and when I found him the oil wouldn't come off his hands. A spy – the hell he was a spy! Whoever said that about him was the real spy. So yes, I'd just let them take him away, and leave his poor wife, who scrubbed and cleaned all day, to fend for herself. And besides, Mr Brodarics showed a real respect for people. Often he would crouch down beside me when I had to light a fire for the cauldron. He showed me how to use less coal. I learned the secrets of fire from him – everything has its secrets, even embers. Rákosi's man arrives. I open the gate. Where is he? Well, he certainly isn't here, I say. The others took him away early this morning. But make sure you get him – he owes me money for bottling jam. So he survived it all, in my little nook. After that it was empty for a while, but then I hid a member of the secret police. He'd collapsed in the garden. He was a decent man, someone I knew. It would have been a real shame if anything happened to him. He helped me out when my arm was broken – he set up the drying rack – so why shouldn't I have hidden him? But as for the other one, the one I took in later, I wouldn't put my hand in the fire for him now. But I kept him for a few days because he was so miserable. He was sweating big clear drops like a dog when he sees them lifting the stick."

I listened in silence. St Emerence of Csabadul, the madwoman of mercy, who asks no questions but rescues all alike, since whoever is being pursued must be saved, the Grossmans and those hunting the Grossmans; on one side of her banner a drying rack, on the other Mr Brodarics' helmet. This old woman is not just oblivious to her country, she's oblivious to everything. Her spirit shines bright, but through a cloud of steam. Such a thirst for life, but so diffused over everything; such immense talent, achieving nothing. "Tell me," I once asked her. "You only rescued people? You never handed anyone in?" She glared at me, with hatred in her eyes. What did I take her for? She hadn't even informed on the barber, though he had cheated her, robbed her of everything. Even his dreams were lies. When he left her and made off with his loot, she said nothing. If he needed it, let him have it. But from that day on, if a man got close to her, he reminded her of the barber, and she wasn't going to lose everything she'd put together again, especially not the money. She made a plan for the future, and there were no barbers, or Kennedys, or flying dogs in it. There was no place for anyone but herself, and the dead she would gather in.

She threw down what was in her hand, and rushed out. She had remembered that she had to collect a prescription for someone who was sick. She asked if I wanted her to get anything. I stood there gazing after her, wondering why she still stuck with me when I was so very different from her. I had no idea what she liked about me. I said earlier that I was still rather young, and I hadn't thought it through, how irrational, how unpredictable is the attraction between people, how fatal its current. And yet I was well versed in Greek literature, which portrayed nothing but the passions: death and love and friendship, their hands joined together round a glittering axe.

NÁDORI-CSABADUL

Something else Emerence also almost never referred to was the part of the country where she was born, not far from my own birthplace. I was forever disparaging the city, its water, its air, and at the start of spring, when the sodden earth began to thaw and mists rose between the lingering mounds of snow, I would be seized with nostalgia and yearn to be back home. Emerence didn't join me in these little outbursts, though she too noticed the fragrances bearing the message of the season and the barely visible shoots of green, not yet a full canopy, or a bud, not even a baby leaf, appearing on the branches, reminding us that work was beginning in the fields; and in our villages the new-born light, diffracted in spring's prism, would bring back the girl who once jumped and danced without a thought or care – the girl I once was, the girl she had been.

On one such day, in late February, I received an invitation from the Csabadul library. I immediately dashed over to Emerence and asked if she would go with me if I accepted. She wouldn't have to listen to my talk, just travel with me, and while it was going on she could visit the cemetery or look up her relatives. She left me with no real reply, and I took this as a refusal, but I agreed to do the lecture anyway. Eight weeks stood between us and the appointed date, and a good month later she brought up the subject of the trip. She asked whether we would have to spend the night there, as that would be out of the question, but if we could set out early and be back by the evening, it was conceivable that she might come. Sutu had offered to sweep the pavement, and Adélka would do the bins, so if I still wanted to take her, she'd come. This surprising decision had breathed a hint of colour into her normally pale face. She went on to ask if, when we got there, I would refrain from telling anyone how we were connected. This really annoyed me. Did we treat her like a mere employee? I offered to introduce her as my husband's relative. I couldn't pass her off as one of mine because her family would know otherwise, but she might well be related to someone they didn't know in Budapest. The look she gave me, blending ridicule and forbearance, was unlike anything I'd seen from her before. "The master would be delighted," she said drily. "Don't trouble yourself. I was just curious to see whether you'd agree. But you did. And yes, you did because you're so stupid. You understand nothing. What do you imagine they think I became? A king? They put me into service when I was still a child. My family aren't dreamers. I shall tell them I am a caretaker: it's a perfectly respectable job."

By then I was so furious I lashed out at her in rage. As far as I cared, she could introduce herself however she liked, as a dog-catcher or someone who skinned dead animals. No-one could possibly respect her for keeping a multi-storey villa in order, plus all the other houses, and looking after us as well – and the best reason of all was the last, because, though she didn't believe it, I'd been invited to Csabadul for precisely the thing she set at nothing: my writing. There were people, even in the place where she was born, who didn't think writers were idlers; people, unlike her, who didn't dismiss out of hand names such as János Arany or Petőfi. She made no reply, nor did she mention the trip again. Right up to the last possible day I had no idea whether or not she would come. But I let things be. I was afraid that if I exerted any pressure, she'd stay at home.

In the days leading up to the lecture we carried on as before.

Emerence dusted the bookshelves, took delivery of the mail, listened whenever I spoke on the radio, but she passed no comment, she wasn't interested. She took note when we dashed off to a conference, meeting or presentation by some literary group, or occasional language lessons. She saw our names on the books. She returned them to the shelves duly dusted, as she would candleholders or matchboxes. They were all the same to her, misdemeanours that might be overlooked, like eating or drinking to excess. Some childish ambition made me want to win her over to what I saw as the irresistible enchantment of classical Hungarian literature. I once recited Petőfi's *My Mother's Hen* to her. I thought this poem might appeal to her because she loved animals. She stood there, staring at me with the duster still in her hand, then gave a dry, grating laugh. The stories I knew defied belief. *What is a stone?* What was all that about? *What is a stone?* And what was this word *thou?* Nobody spoke like that. I left the room, choking with rage.

In the end, she didn't go with me on the trip. It was no-one's fault in particular. Sutu was ordered to report to the city council offices that day about the licence for her stall, and the night before we were to leave she ran over to Emerence's to say there was nothing she could do about it, she was very sorry, but she couldn't stand in for her; she had no way of knowing when her turn would come, or how long it would take once she was called. The scene that passed between them was too brutal to imagine. The more clearly Emerence came to see Sutu's innocence, the more savage her insults became. More than anyone, she'd had the same experience herself, time after time: you planned something for a particular hour of the day, and then everything fell apart because someone somewhere else had made other arrangements. She knew that Sutu was as much a captive as the rest of us. If she was summoned, she couldn't tell them she had other things to do. So there was no point in arguing about it, or insulting Sutu left and right. But she did. Sutu withdrew, a veritable Coriolanus, and it was a long while before they were on the same good terms again.

On the day of my outing Emerence arrived at dawn (much earlier than usual) to take a sleepy Viola for his walk. While I was getting ready she never left my side. She found fault with my hair, my dress, everything. My nerves were in shreds. Why was she interfering and ordering me around, as if I were off to a royal ball? As she pulled and twisted my hair, she told me she hadn't been home since '45, and then she went there and came straight back again on the next available train, after trading a little food for various bits and bobs. In '44 she did spend a full week there, and didn't enjoy it, but in those days her people were in a miserable state. Her grandfather had always been a tyrant, and the rest of her family on her mother's side were unsettled because of the circus. "Circus", in Emerence's vocabulary meant national disasters – in this case the Second World War – all those situations where women become neurotic, grasping and stupid, and men go berserk and start knifing people, as happens in the wings of history's theatre. If it had been up to her, she would have locked the youth of 1848 away in a cellar and given them a lecture: no shouting, no literature; get yourselves involved in some useful activity. She didn't want to hear any revolutionary speeches, or she'd deal with them, every single one. Get out of the coffee houses, and back to work in the fields and factories.

Only when she saw the official car turning into the street, with Nádori-Csabadul, the name of her birthplace, painted on it, did she give me my instructions. If I could find the time, would I look to see what state the family graves were in, and if possible, the old house too, where she was born, on the outskirts of Nádori? Also, if there was time, she would like me to go to the station at Csabadul and walk all the way to the end of the goods platform. That was important — the goods platform. If I came across any members of the family — there must be some, because they wrote to Józsi's boy — they weren't Szeredáses; there were none of them left, only descendants on her mother's side, the Divéks — she had no message for them, but if they did ask I shouldn't say too much, just tell them the truth, that she was alive and well. I promised nothing. I had absolutely no idea what free time I would have. Any such meeting would depend not only on road conditions but also on whatever had been organised for me when I got there. These events almost never started when advertised, because they had to wait for an audience, or for the librarian to arrange lunch. I could hardly start inquiring about cemeteries, but I would do what I could. The car had in fact arrived rather earlier than arranged. Perhaps, if I really tried, I'd manage to make time for everything she'd asked.

At the very last moment Sutu appeared in the street and opened fire. She mocked Emerence for staying at home even when she'd changed the lock on her door. She knew why she'd done it. She didn't trust her, Sutu. She reckoned that she'd be burgled on the one day when everyone knew she was going with me, and who in all likelihood was best placed to do it but her, Sutu? And she could have taken Viola too. "Go and kill yourself," Emerence coolly replied. Sutu was dumbfounded, but she stood her ground. The curse was as unexpected, and as little justified, as her own accusations had been.

And that was my last view of them from the car. Sutu, with her head turned to stare at Emerence as if they were doing karate and the old woman had struck her such a blow that she was paralysed. I called out to Emerence that I'd do my best to be back early; I hoped before midnight, if possible, because by then I'd be so tired I wouldn't be able to speak. "Tired? What from? It's those poor people having to listen to you who'll be tired. By the time they've been herded into the cultural centre they'll have had to finish feeding the animals, milking them, bedding them down, and five million other things you know nothing about. All you'll do is sit and jabber a lot of nonsense."

I was not going to start explaining how much energy it takes to concentrate for hours, in the dog days of summer, in an airless hall, with the windows closed because of the noise outside. I asked the driver to start. Frankly, I felt rather cheated. I'd hoped that for once Emerence would refrain from needling me, and perhaps ask for something, perhaps a branch from the hedge round her old house, or some other memento. When I go home I always bring back a two-kilo loaf of bread. But she made no requests. As we pulled away, Viola gave a casual yap, as if he was quite sure the separation wouldn't last for ever, and we'd both be sure to manage until the evening.

Our trip went very smoothly. We didn't stop anywhere. I'd made a habit of not eating before my arrival because they almost always offered me something at the library, and it seemed rude not even to try it. Nádori was a lovely little village. I didn't have to ask for the cemetery; it began on the outskirts, by the sign announcing the name of the town, with a scent of sage and wild flowers wafting from the dilapidated headstones. We stopped the car and I went in. A woman was watering flowers near the fence. She was old enough to have heard the names Szeredás and Divék, but she told me she hadn't been born there, she'd only come to be married, and she knew nothing about the carpenter's family. The cemetery itself was quite clearly no longer in use. Those turning to dust lay under mounds of dirt, most of them unmarked, their gravestones and wooden crosses dragged away or stolen; or, if the dead person was of any importance, they'd been exhumed by the family. Perhaps twenty resting places at most were as well-tended as the one the old lady was watering. But I continued to search for a while among the rabbit holes and molehills, and I did it quite willingly. There is something very appealing, not in the least bit sad, about an abandoned cemetery in the summer, and I strolled among the graves, overrun with weeds. But there was nothing to see. Where I did manage to make out the faint engraving, it wasn't the name I was looking for.

However in Csabadul I was lucky straight away. As I stepped out of the car in the main square, I saw Emerence's mother's family name in red, on a sign right in front of me: *Mr Csaba Divék, Traditional and Quartz Watches. Mrs Ildikó Divék, née Kapros, Costume Jewellery.* A young married couple were working in the shop. If I had imagined I would cause a sensation by walking in with news of their relation Emerence Szeredás who lived in Pest – assuming this was the right place, and the late Rozália Divék, wife of József Szeredás did belong to their family – then I was mistaken. They hadn't kept in touch with Emerence, but they knew who she was. The watchmaker suggested I look up their godmother, another Divék girl. She was the cousin of their Budapest relative. They'd been little girls together and she'd be delighted to see me, mainly because after the oceans of time that had passed she might discover what had happened to Aunt Emerence's little girl, whom she hadn't seen since they took her back to the capital.

I now had to be very careful not to show that there were gaps in my knowledge, and that I was hearing for the first time that Emerence had a child. Pressed further, they could recall only what had been passed on to them by those who had gone before. During the last years of the war she had appeared with a little girl in her arms, who then lived with the great-grandfather for about a year. The young people knew nothing about the family graves, but the watchmaker's godmother would certainly remember everything.

Next I went to the library. As there was still a lot of time not just before the lecture, but before lunch, the librarian was happy to go along with my suggestion, and offered to accompany me.

The cousin lived in her own house. She had a distinct look of Emerence, the same tall, lean type, with the same dignified walk and bearing. You had only to look at her to see that even in old age she enjoyed life. The house was tastefully furnished, with light streaming in from the side windows, and one sensed the pride she took in her material independence. She offered pastries, lifting the platter from a fine old sideboard, and mentioned that the furniture had been made by Emerence's father, who had been a carpenter, which I obviously knew, and also a cabinetmaker. Her grandfather had the sideboard brought over when the Co-operative was formed in Nádori and the carpenter's workshop was altered to suit its needs. Now it was her turn to ask what had become of Emerence and the child after they disappeared. She thought there must either have been a very happy ending, or a very bad one, since Józsi's boy, for one, had never seen the little girl. Their grandfather, she went on, as we tucked into the thick golden pastries, and sipped the familiar wine of the Alföld sands, had been a difficult man. He had never understood the danger faced by young girls working in Budapest, and when Emerence appeared with the child they thought he was going to beat her to death. In fact, if he hadn't just had a stroke he might well have done so, but by then he was no longer his old self. Nowadays people took these things in their stride. Even if the family weren't very happy they didn't make a show of it. Both the authorities and society at large were protective towards the young, as I might have noticed. In those days the law sought to establish who the father was, but Emerence told them nothing and she produced no official documents for the child. If her grandfather hadn't been so highly regarded, and hadn't kept the town clerk supplied with a stream of gifts, she would have been in real trouble. But the clerk smoothed everything over. He conjured up some papers for the little girl to replace the documents "left behind" in Budapest. As the father was unknown, she became a Divék. In the end, the old man grew even fonder of her than of his legitimate granddaughters. Because the child had no-one else, not even her mother, she came to adore the old man. She climbed on to him and hugged him, and when Emerence took her away the old man burst into tears. Until his dying day he complained about having let her go when she was so dear to him. But all that aside, they would love to see Emerence at any time, either on her own or with the child, though by now she must be a young woman. Sadly, the grandfather had passed away, just as her poor husband had. They were the only Divéks living locally. The family was widely scattered.

The cousin then offered to take me to the graves, even in that sweltering heat. The old man and her own parents were there – Emerence's family were in the Nádori cemetery, which had since been closed. At this point she lowered her voice, clearly troubled. No-one could be proud of the fact that their grandfather had opposed his daughter marrying a Szeredás for no reason anyone could see; the carpenter made a good living until his death, and could hardly have been held responsible for the terrible tragedy. But he had never allowed the man, or the twins, or his daughter, near him. The funeral had taken place in Nádori, and the whole family were laid to rest beside Szeredás, as if they'd been his victims. It was possible that she had got it all wrong, because she'd been a child at the time, and indeed there were people who wouldn't go near a particular grave because they loved the dead person so very much they couldn't bear to see it. The second husband still had no resting place. Emerence must have told me that he ended up in a mass grave in Galicia. But in any case, if her Budapest cousin wanted to follow it up she shouldn't leave it too long, because the previous year Nádori and Csabadul had been merged into a single authority, and there were plans to plough up the old cemetery in the near future. She couldn't say exactly where the Szeredás family were buried, because she hadn't been there since a child, but we could take a look at the nearby Divék and Kopró graves. She had been born a Divék but married a Kopró.

Since I still had plenty of time I did have a look at the (very tasteful) obelisk. It was made of granite. Above the names it depicted, appropriately, the waters of Babylon, and weeping willows with violins hung from their branches. The cousin even made me a gift of two photographs. She took ages to find them, before they finally turned up in a drawer. Emerence's mother had indeed been a beautiful bride, but what upset me most was an ancient snapshot, its edges cut in wavy lines, of Emerence with a little girl in her arms. The lighting was poor and only the child was in focus. Emerence, even then, was wearing her headscarf, but her dress was rather more colourful, clearly a hand-me-down from one of her employers that didn't much suit her. Her face was essentially unchanged, but there was an attractive cheerfulness, rather than malice, in her eyes.

In the end, all the Divéks and Koprós came to my lecture. None had intended to do so, but it seemed appropriate since I had paid them a visit. The audience was unusually small. Those who did come listened without any sign of interest. Everyone was feeling the heat. As I delivered my text for the hundredth time, I kept wondering what had become of the child in Emerence's arms.

As we started back, I asked the librarian if we could make a little detour to the station. If he was at all surprised, he didn't show it. I walked all the way to the end of the goods platform, just as Emerence had asked. It was like any other, a series of raised concrete blocks, and completely deserted. On the way back to Nádori, the driver stopped at Emerence's old home. It was still apparently referred to as the Szeredás house. It stood out clearly in the gathering dusk of one of those improbable summer evenings when the sun doesn't linger but withdraws its rays suddenly, leaving variegated streaks of orange, blue and violet glowing behind the grey. We took a good look at this scene from the past. It was just as Emerence had described it — the painted façade, the trees round the side, the general line and height of the building. She had neither embellished nor understated. What was most surprising was her perfect recall of the proportions. She hadn't dreamed up a fairy-tale castle in place of her charming old home. It was quite beautiful enough the way József Szeredás had built it, a house designed not just with affection but with love. It had all the force of a timeless statement. There was still a workshop where the old one had stood, but this one had a power saw standing inside, and chained dogs that barked a warning. The little garden was still there. The roses had aged into trees, someone had planted a pair of maples near the sycamore and the walnut had filled out and shot up. A swing hung from one of its branches and there were children playing beneath it.

I didn't find the farmyard. A field of maize grew in its place, promising a fine crop. I stood gazing at the trees lined up in rows like soldiers, contemplating the memories the land must hold, with so much blood, so many dead, and all their dreams, all that failure and defeat. How could it bear to go on producing, with a burden like that? The works manager, a young man, had seen me stop the car and get out, and he imagined I'd come about one of his Komondor puppies, currently for sale. I told him I already had a dog and was looking over the building because someone in my street used to live there. As soon as he realised I didn't want a Komondor he lost interest. I thought about asking him for a rose from the ancient tree, but in the end I didn't. How could I know how far back her memories went, when to that day she had never mentioned that she had a child – or rather had had one? Standing in this place, in the unquestionable theatre of her early life, I tried to draw together the true co-ordinates of her being. But even here I couldn't do it. She was no more at home here than where she now lived, and even if that were where she belonged, it was in circumstances that had made her shut her home off from the world. In the fading light, with streaks of colour glowing between the blue of dusk, only one thing was clear: for her, the village had disappeared. She had arrived in the city and the city had taken her in. But she hadn't allowed it into her life either, so the only real elements of her existence that one might come to understand lay behind that locked door, and she had no intention of ever revealing them. I got back into the car, without plucking a single leaf for a memento, and we set off home.

I knew she wouldn't be waiting for me at our apartment – she was too proud for that. She would sooner not hear what fragments of her former life remained, than show interest. I greeted my husband, who told me that he and Viola had polished off a lavish holiday lunch. Then I went across to the old woman. The dog ran down from the porch to greet me at the garden gate. Emerence didn't even stand up, but remained airing herself on the laundry basket which served as a bench. I thought, just you wait. The atom bomb is about to fall. Still, you could have guessed that one or two details you had forgotten to tell me about your early life might have cropped up in conversation. First I gave an account of the watchmaker's, then I pushed a bit deeper. I described her cousin's agreeable circumstances; then added that her grandfather must have been a hard man, to punish the dead – who'd suffered enough. It was difficult to understand why a man would let graves to fall into ruin. Such behaviour wasn't very pleasant.

Emerence stared into the distance, as if she saw something in the darkness that had nothing whatever to do with me. A wave of shame engulfed me. Why was I thrusting myself into her private affairs? What did I expect from her – a confession? During all those years she hadn't allowed me to get one centimetre closer to her. Did I really want her to tell me about the child born out of wedlock, who had brought her only trouble and shame, and inescapable worry? Was I perverted? A sadist? Had I hoped she would boast about something she had until now felt she must conceal? She turned her back to the garden, and from then on looked only at me, holding Viola's head against her knee. It seems laughable to write this down, but I had the feeling that Viola had known all along about Emerence's daughter, because the old woman told him everything that I was curious to know.

"I've already told you," she began, in a conversational tone, "I've had the money for quite some time, but I decided to wait until my own death; then Józsi's boy can arrange for the crypt. I don't hate my grandfather. He was what he was, jealous and cold. He never forgave my father for taking my mother from him. He didn't like me either, but I don't hold that against him. But you have to honour the dead. I'll bring every one of them in. You'll see, it'll be a crypt like no-one ever built in Budapest. One of your painter or sculptor friends will draw up the plans, as I dictate them. The situation wouldn't have got as bad as it did, because my grandfather would have been afraid people in Csabadul would talk about him behind his back, but then I brought the child down on their heads. The old man was as clever as Satan, and he knew how deep the shame was, and that he could hit at me even harder by neglecting the graves; so he let the wooden crosses rot away. I was living in Pest, so I couldn't get to the cemetery."

Well thank God, she had brought the matter up, so I could

then hand her the pictures. She studied them both at length. There was no emotion visible in her face. I had imagined that she might be moved, or even blush, though I don't know why I thought that. So far as I was concerned, she might have had a whole album of pictures of the child. What did I know about the contents of Emerence's Forbidden City? But she wasn't looking at the picture as a mother might, even less like a distressed mother whose past was at that very moment coming to light; it was more like a soldier who always won his battles.

"This is little Éva," she explained. "The person I was expecting that day. She lives in America, and sends me money. She also sends me parcels, and I give most of it away. You get the useless things, like make-up and creams. This is how she was when I brought her back from Csabadul to Budapest. Now I don't even want to see her face, since she didn't come when I sent for her. If I invite her — as I did — then she should come, even if the whole world is blowing apart. If it hadn't been for me, they would have smashed her head against a wall or sent her to the gas chambers."

She pushed the photograph towards me, as if it was nothing to do with her.

"Did you think it was all so simple?" (She still clearly found it difficult to speak about.) "Up until then, everyone thought highly of me. I was everyone's ideal, Emerence Szeredás — a clean, respectable girl living a sober life, who had learned to her cost what men were like. When that man left her, and then the barber ran off with all the money and the few valuables she had saved up over the years, she didn't swallow caustic soda. She shook herself down as if nothing had happened and announced that never again would she be anyone's property, or let a man get near her — they could make fools of others and fleece them instead. No-one had ever laid a hand on me, so how pleasant do you think it was for me to pitch up at my grandfather's with a child in my arms and tell them, 'This is mine. You'd better feed it until the war is over, because I can't look after it in Pest and I haven't got time to sit around cuddling it. It can tear around here instead. I can't help it if some nasty little crook put one over me, so here she is.' I couldn't keep her in Pest, it was too dangerous. I couldn't just lock her up. A child needs to run around and breathe fresh air."

There was a deep sighing in the bushes. Viola was asleep, with his head on Emerence's shoes.

"You remember the Jewish laws, don't you? The old people drank cyanide, and the young paid to get out. But they couldn't make their way through the mountains on foot, practically on all fours, with a tiny baby, so they gave it to me. Mrs Grossman knew what my little Évike was to me, and what I was to Évike. The child cried if anyone else came near her. Even when she was in her mother's arms, she wanted to be back in mine. But not all the Germans were gangsters. This villa belonged to a German factory owner. He paid for the Grossmans to be smuggled out. He installed me as caretaker here and entrusted everything to me before he went back home. There was a plan. I settled in here, the young Grossmans set off for the border, and then I took the child to the village. It was better for people to think she had disappeared with her parents. Don't ask what sort of treatment I got when I arrived. It wasn't an ordinary beating – I thought I'd never walk again. You can punch me and kick me, I told my grandfather, and tell everybody what I've done, only leave the child alone. I gave him the money and jewellery I had from the Grossmans for the child's upkeep. There was so much he thought I'd looted it in the confusion of the war, that I'd stolen it from them. But don't worry, he took it. They used it well, looking after the little girl for a good year or so, until the Grossmans came back and I was able to go for her. The poor things wanted to start life here afresh, but in the end they went away again. Out of gratitude they gave me every-thing they had left, including the living-room furniture I'd brought here for safe keeping. And then they disappeared. They were afraid to stay because Rákosi was beginning to start the circus up all over again. Did you walk along the goods plat-form?"

"Yes," I said.

"I wanted you to see it, because I often see it in my dreams, just as it was when a pet of mine jumped off the train after me. We had a heifer. It was sandy-brown. I had raised it from a calf. After the two little ones it was for me the third child. Its coat was every bit as silky as the twins' hair, its nose was pink and soft, and it smelled of milk, just like them. People laughed because it followed me everywhere. But then we had to sell it. They locked me in the attic so I couldn't run after them. In those days hysterics weren't tolerated in the village. Children were given a good smack and told what to do, and if you still didn't understand, they hit you on the head. Maybe things are different now, and they are more tolerant down there, I don't know. Anyway they beat me round the head and shut the door on me, but I managed to get out. I knew that if they sold the heifer they'd take it to the station, so I ran to the platform, but by the time I got there they'd already bundled it into the wagon with all the animals the other farmers had sold. It was mooing away pitifully, up there in the van, and I screamed out its name. They hadn't yet closed the door, and when it heard me it jumped down from that great height. Children are stupid; I didn't know what I was doing when I called out to it. It landed on its front legs and broke them both.

"They sent for the gypsy to hit it over the head. My grand-father was cursing and swearing. It would have been better if I had died, rather than valuable livestock – I was such a useless good-for-nothing.

"They butchered it and weighed it. I had to stand there watching while they killed it and cut it up into pieces. Don't ask what I was feeling, but let this teach you not to love anyone to death because you'll suffer for it, if not sooner then later. It is better not to love anyone, because then no-one you care about will get butchered, and you won't end up jumping out of wagons. Now you must go. We've both said quite enough and the dog's exhausted. Take him home. Come on, Viola! Oh yes, the heifer was also called Viola. My mother called it that. Off you go, now. This dog's half asleep."

The dog, not I who'd been working all day; not Emerence, who'd been rushing around cleaning and sweeping. The pressing image of Viola. Viola on the goods platform, Viola running down our street, in the shape of a dog.

I went home, as she wished. I sensed that she wanted to be alone with the memories I had stirred. At that moment, I could see, it was all around her – the Grossmans and the factory owner who wasn't an evil man; the empty villa where at first she lived entirely alone, before witnessing an ever-changing series of tenants; first a flood of Germans; then Hungarian soldiers, who disappeared and were replaced by the Arrow Cross; and then when the Arrow Cross left the Russians moved in. Emerence had cooked for them, and washed for them, before the villa fell under state ownership and became an apartment block, as I knew it. And at the heart of all these events, beneath and behind them, lay the primal wounds – the baker torn apart by the mob, the barber who robbed her, little Éva Grossman who brought shame on her in Csabadul, the heifer, the cat strung up on the door handle, and the one great love of her life.

Was the cat, I wondered, also called Viola?

FILMING

In my student days, I detested Schopenhauer. Only later did I come to acknowledge the force of his idea that every relationship involving personal feeling laid one open to attack, and the more people I allowed to become close to me, the greater the number of ways in which I was vulnerable. It wasn't easy to accept that from now on I would always have to consider Emerence. Her life had become an integral part of my own. This led to the dreadful thought that one day I would lose her, that if I survived her there would be yet another addition to those ubiquitous, indefinable shadow-presences that wrack me and drive me to despair.

This realisation wasn't helped by her behaviour, which was so unpredictable. Sometimes she was so offhand, and so rude to me that any stranger would have wondered why I put up with her. But it didn't matter, because I had long ago learned to ignore the shifting tectonic plates under the surface of her being. She had probably made a similar discovery – like Captain Butler, she had no wish to put her heart on the line a second time, but she didn't know how to protect herself against the threat of dependence on me. If I was sick, she nursed me until my husband returned from work, but I could never reply in kind because Emerence was never sick. She didn't even think it worth bringing to my attention that she had suffered an injury in the kitchen or during the course of her work. If she burned her foot with sizzling fat, or sliced her hand on the carving knife, she didn't comment, but treated herself with household remedies. Emerence had a low opinion of people who complained.

With time, she felt able to drop in for no particular reason, and indeed no explanation was necessary. It was understood that she and I liked being together. When we were alone in the apartment, and we both had the time, we chatted. It remained impossible to persuade her to read any of my books, but it did now affect her when they were unfavourably reviewed. She understood the personal nature of the waves of politically motivated attacks on me, and she would fly into a rage of exasperation. She once asked me if she should report a critic to the Lieutenant Colonel. I tried in vain to calm her down. At such times she was possessed by anger and hatred. By now, without ever acknowledging its full worth, she no longer fought against the view that my work represented some sort of achievement, and she constructed an elaborate theory to avoid having to reject us. Writing was an occupation comparable with play. The child took it seriously, and carried it out with great care, and though it was only play, and nothing depended on it, it was tiring. She was forever putting questions to me that no writer, journalist or reader can answer: how did a novel come into existence out of nothing, from mere words? I couldn't explain to her the familiar, everyday magic of creation. There was no way of expressing how and from where the letters arrived on the empty page. I thought the process of film-making might be easier for her to understand, so when she began to take an interest in what was happening in the studio or on location, what it actually meant to make a film, I hoped I might draw her into my world, or at least its periphery.

An opportunity arose. We were making another film. Every morning the film crew's car would arrive for me and we raced off to the studio. When I got home she would pester me mercilessly about what had gone on – who had been there, how the day went, what we had done. So one day I announced I would take her the next morning.

In fact I didn't think she'd come. Other than to the cemetery, she never went that far from home. But early the next day she was waiting for the car at the gate, dressed in her best clothes, with a spotless headscarf and clutching a sprig of marjoram. With her there, I experienced real shame at every cynical remark that was made, and the way we all snapped at each other, or worse, let our rancour hibernate until the right moment came to put the knife in, because time was flying by and every second spent filming cost money. And there she was, dressed in her Sunday best, waiting to see something happen and taking it all in with deadly seriousness.

No-one bothered to ask who she was, or what she was doing there. The people on the gate assumed she was an extra. She strolled around with all the natural composure of a writer or actor, sat in the place assigned to her, kept perfectly quiet, remained fully alert without ever moving, and bothered no-one. The next scene was a difficult one, needing above all to seem spontaneous. The usual running around ensued; the familiar preparatory steps were gone through – make-up, checking the script, lighting, measuring distances, taking up positions, ready, clapper boards. Then we all set off to continue the work on Margit Island. Emerence gazed out of the car in awe. I think it must have been decades since she'd been past the Grand Hotel, if indeed she'd ever seen it. We were filming the outside scenes in front of it, with a second cameraman working from a helicopter. Emerence's eyes went back and forth between him and the operator on the crane. Here, the machines were as much a part of the show as the actors in their big love scene. With the trees, the earth, the whole world soaring around them, and the forest bending to embrace them, the man and woman were to seem dizzy with waves of passion. We played it back on the monitor. Every frame was brilliantly successful, much more so than usual.

We stopped to eat. Emerence refused to go inside the Grand Hotel. She had become hostile, unfriendly, no longer looking around her in wonder. I was familiar with her various faces and knew she'd seen enough, so I suggested we go home. I felt there must be something wrong, but as usual, I didn't know what it was. I thought she would tell me once we got back. Luckily my rôle was over, so I took my leave and we set off. In the car she immediately undid the top two buttons of her dress, as if they were choking her. I had rarely heard such bitterness in her voice as she revealed what had been upsetting her.

We were liars, cheats, she began – none of it was real. The trees had been made to move by a trick, it was only the branches. Someone was filming from a helicopter, circling around. The poplars hadn't moved at all, but the viewer would think they were leaping about dancing, that the whole forest was spinning round. This was sheer deception; it was disgusting.

I defended myself. "You're quite wrong," I said. "The tree really was dancing because that is how the viewer will experience it. What matters was the effect we achieved, not whether the tree moved or if a technician created the idea of movement. Did you think the forest could walk around, when the trees are held by their roots? Don't you think it's a function of art to create the illusion of reality?"

"Art," she repeated bitterly. "If that's what you were – artists – then everything would be real, even the dance, because you would know how to make the leaves move to your words, not to a wind machine or whatever it was. But you people can't do anything like that – not you, or the others. You're all clowns, and more contemptible than clowns. You're worse than con men."

I stared at her in astonishment. It was as if she were descending, before my very eyes, into the depths of an underworld I had never imagined; like someone fallen in a well, from which the only sounds to be heard were curses and a desperate gasping for breath. By the time she'd finished she was barely whispering. "Yes, there are such moments, moments when a technician wouldn't have had to lift a finger, when no helicopter was needed. The world of living, growing things could dance all by itself." Lord God, I thought. What had that one Faustian moment in her life been like, when she cried out for time to stop because the trees were swirling all around her? I shall never know, but it is there, somewhere in her past.

Once, after she'd been introduced to the tape recorder in our apartment and told that you could play back a text or a piece of music, she talked about what it would be like if someone's life were recorded and put on tape, to be rewound, stopped and replayed at will. She said she'd accept her own life the way it was; or rather, as it would be up to her death, but with the proviso that she might rewind it to any point she chose. I didn't dare ask where she would stop the machine, and still less, why there. I didn't think she'd tell me anyway.

THE MOMENT

However, she did tell me. Not when it might have seemed reasonable or logical to do so, but when she felt the moment had come. If Emerence believed in any sort of force, it was time. In her private mythology, Time was like a miller, grinding his corn in an eternal mill, funnelling the events of your life into your personal sack when your turn came. According to her, no-one was excluded. She believed, without being able to explain it, that the miller would grind the grain of the dead too, and pour it out into sacks, only it was different people who carried it off to make their bread. My own sack had its turn some three years later, when the white heat of her feelings had reached the point not only of love but of absolute trust.

Everyone trusted Emerence, but she trusted no-one; or, to be more precise, she doled out crumbs of trust to a chosen few — the Lieutenant Colonel, me, Polett while she was alive, Józsi's boy — and stray morsels to a few others. She would tell Adélka what she judged suitable and likely to be understood, but she would say quite different things to the Lieutenant Colonel, Sutu or the handyman. For example, she revealed to me quite early on how the twins had died, but only much later did it transpire that she hadn't told her nephew; he thought she'd had only one sibling, his father. It was as if she wanted to vex us all, even from beyond the grave. She gave none of us the full picture of herself. Once among the dead, she must have enjoyed a quiet smile at our expense as we struggled to work out the full story, as each of us tried to match his own allotted pieces of information with those granted to others. At least three vital facts went with her to the grave, and it must have been a source of satisfaction to her to look back and see that we still didn't have a full account of her actions, and never would.

The day her mythological miller finally filled my sack is fixed precisely in my mind, because it was Palm Sunday. I was not pleased at being stopped on my way to church. I was afraid I'd be late. I go a fair distance to talk to my God, in the much-loved chapel of my girlhood, further down the avenue. It still holds memories of my uncertainty and joyous hopes on my arrival in Budapest. Emerence was sweeping right outside our door. I knew this was intended as a statement. Once again, she had arranged her cleaning rota so that I'd find her here just before the service, and be reminded of her eternal message: how easy it was to be pious when your lunch would be ready and waiting when you arrived home from church. She remarked that when I was cleansed of my sins I should look in on her after lunch, she had some business with me. I was less than enchanted by the idea, not least because Palm Sunday is an especially precious festival to me, and also because ever since my mother was consigned to the dust in Farkasrét cemetery, my Sunday afternoons had their own fixed routine. I was to come over at four o'clock. At three, I answered. She shook her head. A friend of hers and her nephew were coming at three. Two o'clock, then. It couldn't be two, because she was giving lunch to Sutu and Adélka, and to fit in with them, I had to come at four. And that was that. I didn't take communion that Sunday, because I lacked the inner quiet needed for confession and absolution. Emerence had rattled me, and I went home strained and tense rather than calm. On arriving, I was told that Viola wasn't there. The old lady had taken him with her, having announced that she had invited him for lunch along with the others.

Emerence was capable of arousing the finest feelings in me, and also the most base. Because I loved her, I could become so furious with her that sometimes I was shocked by my own response. By now I should have been used to the fact that the dog was at my disposal only within certain limits. If it wasn't for this last absurdity, of his being invited for lunch, I might have kept my self control. But the thing so enraged me that, dressed as I was for church, I ran straight over to her. There was once an occasion when a writers' union meeting fell on the same evening as a dinner with a Western diplomat. We were nearly an hour late, and they never asked us again, snubbing us even on national holidays. But the diplomat's wife's behaviour after that meal was a warm, friendly hug compared to the icy superiority with which Emerence received me when I appeared uninvited before her as she sat, at a richly laid-out table on her porch, deep in conversation with Sutu and Adélka. When I rattled the garden gate Viola dashed towards me and leapt up on my dress. Emerence didn't even stand. She just glanced up and began to ladle out the chicken soup. Sutu moved over to make a place for me, but the old woman directed her with her eyes not to, as I wasn't staying. She asked me why I had come. I was so angry I couldn't formulate all the many reasons in my head. All I said was, "I'm taking the dog home."

"As you wish. But you'd better feed him. He hasn't had his dinner yet."

Viola jumped up beside the table, wagging his tail. An inviting aroma of chicken soup filled the air, overpowering the smell of chlorine and air freshener.

"Come on!" I said to him.

Emerence carried on serving. I thought all was well, because Viola obediently set off, without even looking back. But he came with me only as far as the gate, where he stopped and wagged his tail again, as if to say, "Don't waste any more of my time,

I want my dinner." I didn't humiliate myself by giving him any more commands. Emerence knew how to programme him with her mind, like a video recorder. He didn't even pause; he turned his behind on me and shot off back to Emerence's table. His behaviour upset me so much that when I got home I couldn't even swallow my soup. I lay out on the balcony with a book, unable to follow a single sentence. From my elevated position I could see Emerence's porch. I had no intention of looking that way, as I turned the pages, but even without wishing to I could see what was going on. Sutu and the others were eating and putting their heads together in earnest conversation; then the two women left, but only when Józsi's boy arrived, followed by the Lieutenant Colonel. They weren't served any of the meal, but Emerence placed wine on the table and something on a platter, obviously pastries. The nephew leant forward over a piece of paper and began to study it with the Lieutenant Colonel. What happened after that I don't know, because I came in from the balcony once and for all. I had decided that even though she had asked me to go over at four, I wouldn't. She wasn't going to amuse herself at my expense.

Four o'clock came and went. Then four-fifteen and four-thirty. I didn't look to see what she was doing. At a quarter to five the bell rang. My husband went to the door. Our neighbour from along the corridor told him that Viola was lying on the pavement outside, refusing to budge. His collar was missing and he had no muzzle on. As it was a Sunday, there were unlikely to be officials about, but it would still be wiser to bring him up.

Emerence Metternich of Csabadul, arch-manipulator! Now she was laughing, down in her little flat, because, oh yes, she knew I'd have to go back, for the simple reason that Viola wouldn't get up until he saw me or received different orders from her. She had sent him to fetch me. As I made my way it occurred to me yet again, with her unique combination of abilities, and her diamond-hard logic, what might she not have done if she hadn't been so hostile to her own opportunities? I imagined her alongside Golda Meir and Margaret Thatcher, and the picture did not seem at all strange. What I couldn't understand was why she hid behind a mask. If she were to turn around three times, whip off her headscarf, her smock and her face itself, and announce that it had all been a disguise, that divine command had fixed it on her at birth but thenceforth she would wear it no longer, I would have believed her. And why should I not?

Viola danced around her. He knew, better than anyone, that the crisis was over. As so often before, Emerence had won. And as a matter of fact I was no longer even angry.

Waiting for me on the table under a lace net was a freshly baked strudel, not yet sliced. She knew what I liked. Standing a good head and a half taller, she gazed down at me without saying a word. She had only to shake her head, and both Viola and I understood that I had behaved badly, thoughtlessly, improperly, though I was quite old enough to know that nothing happens without a reason. She sent the dog inside, and as the door opened the sweet aroma of the strudel was tinged with the even stronger smell of disinfectant that came spilling out. She pointed me to a place on the bench. Before her, under the makeshift paperweight of Viola's round pebble ball, was a folded sheet of paper. She pushed it towards me. There was no sound from within. I guessed that Viola must have lain down. I would have loved to see what he slept on, and where, but he alone had access to those secrets. I didn't. And I was about to be given a lecture.

"You have an appalling nature," she began. "You puff yourself up like a bullfrog, and one day you'll explode. The only thing you're good for is getting your friend in the helicopter to make trees dance by trickery. You never grasp what is simple.

You always go round the back when the entrance is at the front."

There could be no reply to this. I couldn't even be sure it wasn't true.

"I spoiled your Sunday, didn't I? But that's when these things are done, on a Sunday or public holiday. That's when you tell people what is to happen when you die."

Now I knew what was on the folded sheet of paper.

"I could have invited the master to come with you, but the two of us don't always see eye to eye, as you well know. Not because he isn't a good man – he is – it's just that he doesn't like sharing, and neither do I. We don't much like one another, because we would each prefer to have the other out of our lives. Now don't say a word, because I am speaking."

Once again her face changed. She was like someone standing in strong sunlight on a mountain top, looking back down the valley from which she had emerged and trembling with the memory still in her bones of the length and nature of the road she had travelled, the glaciers and forded rivers, the weariness and danger, and conscious of how far she still had to go. There was also compassion in that face, a feeling of pity for all the poor people below, who knew only that the peaks were rosy in the twilight, but not the real meaning of the road itself.

"I couldn't possibly have asked you to lunch because you are named in the will. I couldn't even ask my nephew, until I had talked everything over with Adélka and Sutu, and they'd signed the document. I've worked for a lawyer and I know how to make a will. It isn't very difficult. It'll stand, you can be quite sure."

A lawyer. She had never mentioned that.

"What are you staring at now? I told you that my grand-father put me into service when I was only thirteen, and the lawyer took me away. It was only later that I went to the

Grossmans, when he and his wife could no longer afford to keep me. But by then they didn't want to. Their son and I had grown up together. The reason I didn't invite the two of you wasn't that I begrudged you the food. I know we should be together at a time like this – it's something I did learn from my religious instruction, that Christ took his last meal with his friends. There's no need to jump up and down – I know it was a supper, and it wasn't on Palm Sunday but Holy Thursday – but Christ had all the time he needed and I don't. I couldn't invite you or my nephew because you are my heirs."

Christ took his last supper somewhere in Bethany, perhaps in the house of Lazarus. Bethany still counted as part of Jerusalem. I resisted the vision of her there, holding the will in her sacred hands, seated between Sutu and Adélka on her right and her nephew and the Lieutenant Colonel on her left, with Viola and myself at her feet. I resisted, but I saw it all the same.

"So, listen carefully. My nephew and I have agreed that any money I leave will be his. None of it will go to my relatives because, as you told me yourself, they neglected the graves of my family, and anyway they've got all they need. Józsi's boy has proved himself trustworthy in everything so far, and he'll gather together all my dead, and when the crypt is finished he'll have me put in there as well. The money for the building work and funerals is in the Post Office savings accounts; the rest is in the regular Savings Bank. The books are here. Everything inside the flat, you inherit. My nephew has signed before the Lieutenant Colonel that he accepts my instructions and won't contest a single clause. Anyway, he doesn't need what I'm giving you. He wouldn't know what to do with it. It's not his taste. And even if he could use it, he's getting enough. He'll inherit an awful lot of money. And don't try to thank me or I'll get angry."

I gazed into my lap, trying to work out how much it costs

to build a crypt, and exhume bodies, but I knew only the price of headstones. My family hadn't been buried in a crypt. But I didn't even attempt to think what I would inherit. The last few moments had been so utterly improbable, it was like a dream. Emerence stood up and lit the flame under her coffee pot. She always made much better coffee than I did. Where had she learned that? From yet another employer she hadn't mentioned?

"Why have you started to think about dying?" I said at last. "You're not sick?"

"No. It's just that there was an announcement on the radio that the lawyer's son has died, and it brought everything back to me."

Once, as a child, I watched a butterfly circling round and felt the same desire to influence it, desperately willing it to land. I didn't want to catch it, just to see it close up.

"For days the radio has been in mourning, and you'll be seeing all the films of the funeral on the news. I don't want to watch them, and I'm not going to the cemetery. Not me. It's a pity they didn't ask me a few questions, along with all those other people. I could have told them a few things. When I heard all those stories about him from people he knew, I thought, it's good there are so many coming forward, because I'm not going to. He rejected what I wanted to be to him, and I've been as good as dead to him for long enough now. It wasn't easy to raise myself from the dead – it's an expensive pastime. Well, that's why I've made my will, so what I have goes to you, the way I want it, without anyone else helping themselves to what I've put together. I've been robbed once already. I won't let it happen again. It's only my cat they managed to kill twice. No-one will ever again steal my belongings, or my peace of mind."

Her eyes were cold and bright as diamonds. Jesus, I thought, she was hiding this too. Not just Mr Brodarics, or the man from the secret police, but him as well. And yet how, and when? The press is filled with nothing else but him. The whole country's in mourning. When could it possibly have been? Only in the thirties.

"The programmes will show you what sort of person his wife was. When they were after him and he knocked on my door, he wasn't yet engaged. He must have got to know her later, when he was no longer in danger. 'I'll stay with you, I'll go underground in your cellar. You'll be my cover,' he said. 'You, Emerence, are as dependable and as pure as water.' Don't think we got up to anything. I hope you know me, and if you know me then you know him. I didn't even ask who was after him. I hid him in my room. By then the old couple had passed me on to the youngsters, and the young Grossmans had no idea what was happening. Do you think Éva's mother took an interest in what went on in her servant's room? Little Évike wasn't born then. They were always travelling, and going out to have a good time. There were separate servants' quarters in the house, and that's where the two of us lived. Drink your coffee and don't stare at me. Other people have been in love too.

"When he slipped out of the country I thought I'd lose my mind; and it would have been a pity if I had, because I did see him again – at the worst possible moment. He came at night; there was a moon, a bright evening. He was in disguise but I recognised him at once – perhaps at times like that you see with the heart. So you see, that was when the trees and the bushes did move, right here by the villa. I saw the moon shining on his face, and that fir tree dancing behind him. I thought, this time he's come for something else, perhaps he's understood something after all that time abroad, and now at last he's coming back to me, or perhaps, since he'd gone to the trouble of finding out from the Grossmans where I was, he'll take me away. I was sure it was the reason he'd come looking for me, even though he hadn't promised to. He'd never promised me anything, never lied to me. He made it clear straight away why he'd come. Could I give him refuge again? He had forged papers, identity documents, food rationing coupons – all he needed was somewhere to stay, just for a while. No-one would see to it better than I that he wouldn't be found. And then, as soon as he possibly could, he went off and left me here. And now he's dead."

I couldn't swallow the sip I had taken. I looked at her.

"So I took up with the barber, to get back at him. Haven't you heard the gossip? I would have gone with the devil himself if he could have persuaded me that I might be desirable to a man. But there must be something wrong with me, because he didn't just dump me, he also robbed me. I wasn't ugly. Not that it matters. It didn't kill me."

She was silent for a while; then she crushed a leaf of mint in her fingers, and sniffed it.

"You don't die that easily, but let me tell you, you come close to it. Afterwards, what you went through makes you so clever you wish you could become stupid again, utterly stupid. Well, I got clever, which shouldn't surprise you, because I was given training round the clock. He lived with me for two years in the Grossman's servant's quarters, and here also, for a while. When I could spare the time he talked and talked, about everything he knew. Do you think I'll ever in my life again hear a propagandist through to the end?"

Now that too fell into place: her anti-intellectualism, her contempt for culture.

"Soon after he'd gone the war finished and he came back – not to stay with me, or live with me, but to explain everything all over again. But that wasn't what I wanted. I wanted something else. Something that would have fitted in with the new world, with our freedom. So I laid into him. I said he'd lectured me quite enough, now it was time to move on. He wanted to enrol me in a school, but he would have had to wait for ever for me to go. He had recommended me for some sort of honour. I told him there'd be a scandal to surpass all others if I appeared in Parliament to collect it. Did he really think I was interested in the plans he was spinning in there, either alone or with his cronies, while I loved him and he had no love for me? I did love him. Do you hear? Not his head, his knowledge – that was what had taken him from me, his great big head with all its learning – but his body, the thing they're burying the day after tomorrow. But no matter. You wouldn't believe it, I know, but he told me he often talked to his wife about me. He even wanted to introduce me to her. I told him straight, don't bother about me, stay with her, like a good husband. You get on with rebuilding Budapest, and I'll rebuild my life. I took up with the barber; he found out and was furious. I was glad."

She didn't look like someone who was glad. Her face was a mask, her mouth a single straight line.

"Do you know how happy I was when they took him away in 1950, accused him of being a British spy, and almost beat him to death? I thought, go on, beat him, let him suffer as miserably as I did, like a dog. He couldn't even speak English. At the Piarists, where he grew up, they taught only French, German and Latin. I was with the family at the time, I know what he learned at grammar school. What a stupid accusation! But I was happy, because I'm an evil person, and stupid, and full of envy. Now, that's all in the past. Next comes the state funeral. There'll be his velvet pillow with all the decorations God sends, Hungarian and foreign. I believe he didn't mention me in his autobiography. But I was there, in his life."

"He did mention you, Emerence," I said, and felt such a terrible weariness it was as if I too had been beaten up. At that moment I understood our recent history as I never had before. "Not by name, only that he had been hidden for a long time, by many people, but longest of all by a truly admirable comrade. I heard it yesterday, on the third news broadcast."

"He was always very correct," she replied drily. "Now, I've chattered quite long enough. At least his death got me to make a will. You know, he was so brave, and full of life, so cheerful, he was like someone who could never die. And the great pile of books and all that boundless knowledge! Tell me, who would want to study all that? Not me, for sure. But you mustn't think him a cheat. I'll say it once again. He never promised me anything, so make a note of that. He did the right thing, hiding in my house. If he'd dared touch me I'd have thrown him out, I'm that stupid. Now clear off. I've had enough of you."

She produced a plate and piled it high with strudel.

"The master has a sweet tooth."

I stood up, but she held me back while she opened the door again, just a crack, and let the dog out. Again that peculiar smell filled my nostrils. Sensing her eyes on me I turned back to face her.

"One more thing – just a word," she said. "There'll be another inheritance, so it's better that you know about it. The flat is full of cats. I'm entrusting them to you. You won't know what to do with them, because apart from me they don't know anyone, just Viola, and if they got out into the street there'd be no hope for them, because they see dogs as friends. You're a good friend of the doctor who gives Viola injections. When I die, he must do away with the poor things. You can't give anyone a greater gift than to spare them suffering. That's why I don't open the door, because what would happen if it got out that there were nine cats living in here? But I won't give up a single one of them. And there won't be another hanging here. They're prisoners, but they are alive. This is my family. I never had any other. Now off you go, I've got things to do. It's been a long afternoon."

LENT

For several days I was unable to focus on anything other than what had taken place. Emerence had assembled her private parliament on the afternoon of Palm Sunday and, without any consultation or advance notice, had published her edict, like the Pope. The fact that Józsi's boy telephoned me suggested that he'd been hit by the same wave of feelings that I had. He asked if we could sit down and talk it over. He would come to me. We settled on the following Tuesday. I too thought it important that we meet.

What troubled him was the wisdom of Emerence keeping the two different sorts of passbook in her home when she possessed what to them was a substantial amount of money. He wondered whether the money shouldn't be held in some other form, because if the books were stolen, both the bank and the post office would pay out to whoever presented them. The passbooks bothered me too, but for a different reason. If somehow Emerence did lose them, I would be in an impossible position. I was the only person Viola would allow into the flat, and one thing I didn't need at that point in my life was the nephew's inevitable suspicion, however irrational it might be. We gave much thought to what might be done. The young man was anxious about the money, I was horrified by the unexpected responsibility I had been saddled with. And there was something dreadful in the fact that suddenly Viola had come to play a central rôle. In Emerence's republic he was the bodyguard, the source of security, the custodian of her wealth. As for the cats, I tried not to think about them. It wasn't only the fact of their number. What distressed me most was the duty I was charged with after her death. Who could do such a thing? I wasn't Herod. The nephew suggested that Emerence should open a deposit account, and we should put this idea to her. He would feel more comfortable if the Lieutenant Colonel and I dealt with it. He didn't want to look like someone who lived only for the money and wanted to tie it up in every possible way, and yet so many things could happen. What if she left the gas on, or Viola was killed, or the antiquated heating system gave up and a fire broke out one winter, while she was out? I promised to give it thought and we parted on the understanding that we would ask the Lieutenant Colonel. After that, nothing more was done. In most people there is a dull sort of shame.

My first idea was to bring the matter up with Emerence in a gentle, sensitive way. But after Palm Sunday she was clearly avoiding us. Small as our neighbourhood was, she managed to hide herself away like the Invisible Man. The ability to vanish ranked among her many accomplishments – she would have made an ideal member of any conspiracy. I finally caught up with her on Good Friday. I set out earlier than usual, so I could call in at the cemetery before the service. She was working away with her huge broom in front of our door. She advised me to give generously since on such occasions it would surely count double, and she hoped the charitable ladies would be pleased. I began to move away, not wanting to be upset by her and then unable to take communion as I had been on the last occasion. I told her that I'd be grateful if, on Good Friday at least, she would spare me her cynicism. The sufferings of Jesus were tragic – if she could see them performed, she wouldn't stand there dry-eyed. And anyway, if she asked me to do her a favour I didn't look for payment, I just did it; so perhaps she could stop annoying me and, when she'd finished, would she be so good as to make the plum soup? The fruit was already out on the kitchen sideboard.

She looked at me, then offered me the broom. It had a good solid handle; would I like to try my hand and help her with the sweeping? I went to church to remember, and to cry, so a little hard work wouldn't do any harm. I could do penance by sweeping. The broom was heavy, and the wooden handle was hard on the fingers. In her opinion, only those who knew what physical labour was actually like had the right to mourn for Jesus. I didn't even look at her. I scuttled off to the bus, the solemn serenity of my morning completely evaporated. Why did this woman needle me all the time? How could she dismiss the church, with all its claim to respect, its past history and its striving for good, on the basis of one, clumsily distributed aid package?

She's making these underhand remarks to settle the score, I told myself, but I quickly dropped the thought because I knew this wasn't true. Emerence wasn't getting even. The matter was more complicated than that, and rather more interesting. Emerence was a generous person, open-handed and essentially good. She refused to believe in God, but she honoured him with her actions. She was capable of sacrifice. Things I had to attend to consciously she did instinctively. It made no difference that she wasn't aware of it – her goodness was innate, mine was the result of upbringing. It was only later that I developed my own clear moral standards. One day Emerence would be able to show me, without uttering a word, that what I consider religion is a sort of Buddhism, a mere respect for tradition, and that even my morality is just discipline, the result of training at home, in school and in my family, or self-imposed. My Good Friday thoughts had taken quite a battering.

There was no question of plums for lunch. Waiting for us

were paprika chicken, cream of asparagus soup and *crème caramel*. The plums remained unwashed and unprepared, still in their blue skins on the sideboard where I had left them. Good Friday was the one day of Lent on which my father had expected us to fast, as he in turn had been taught in my grandfather's house. On that day the only nourishment taken at lunch was plum soup. We didn't even lay the table for dinner, as no-one had dinner. On Holy Saturday there was caraway soup for breakfast, without bread. In the afternoon the fast melted away, but only to the extent of a normal weekday meal, without meat. Within the microcosm of our family, we were served substantial nourishment only at dinner, and then custom required that no-one should eat too much. On Holy Thursday the piano lid was locked in case any member of our fanatically music-loving family forgot himself and started to play. Emerence had known for years that I held to what I had learned at home, and had never commented on it. She would bring over some delicacy of her own for "the master". At these times the two of them always joined forces against me, and amused themselves with little conspiratorial gestures passed between them at my expense.

So I didn't eat any lunch. That evening, I angrily cooked some caraway soup for the next day, and its taste defied imagination. But by that stage I could barely see from hunger. I gulped it down, and went across to Emerence.

Spring had come early that year, and she was sitting outside on her bench looking out, as if she was expecting me. She listened in silence to my assessment of her character, which was that she forced people to take on impossible tasks, and then insulted them whenever she could. She needn't look so smug, because I hadn't even tasted the paprika chicken, and I wasn't going to pay for it. If she made it, it was community service, because I hadn't ordered it. Even in the deepening gloom I could see her smiling. I felt like tipping the table over her.

"Now listen," she said cheerfully, without a hint of anger, like someone patiently instructing a slow-witted child. "I am going to hit you so hard you'll really feel it – though I first came to like you because you could take a few knocks. I've watched as your life has taken shape. I'm not interested in your fixed ideas. Believe me, it would have been a lot less work for me to do your plums than to cut up a chicken. I've always done them for you up until now, but you can eat what you like if you think it'll make any difference in heaven. You have a strange God who judges people on the basis of plums. My God, if I have one, is everywhere – at the bottom of the well, in Viola's soul, and over the bed of Mrs Samuel Böőr because she died so beautifully. She didn't deserve to – only the very good deserve that, but that's how she went, without suffering, and with dignity. What are you staring at? Didn't you see Mrs Böőr's granddaughter running along the other side of the street this morning, when I was sweeping – or were you paying attention only to yourself again? The child had come for me, and I went. Well, you can believe that if I'm holding someone's hand in the hour of their death, it's not difficult for them to die. I washed her, all very nicely, and prepared her for her journey. And I can tell you it wasn't easy finding the time. In between, I had done that lunch for you, for which you have thanked me so graciously. Pay attention, because this is going to hurt, but it's what you deserve. The master isn't going to live very long, as you well know. Do you think he's going to get stronger on plums? And what will he take to the other side as a memento? Because everyone going there takes something. Mrs Böőr took the honour that I, Emerence Szeredás, had seen to her, and that I'll be keeping an eye on the child. And you'll have to take care of her too, I promise you, because I'm not going to let you off that. I don't want her getting into the clutches of the charitable ladies. They don't even know that Mrs Böőr has a granddaughter with no-one to care for her, but you won't be able to forget it, because I'll remind you every day. So don't send the master on his way with plum soup, or that stupid diet food you keep him on; and it doesn't help that you're always running around some-where, and pounding your typewriter all day when you are home. You left him again today, and went off to church. Make him laugh for once, that's a real prayer. What must you really think of Christ, of God, when you make pronouncements about him as if he were a personal friend? How cheap you think salva-tion is! I wouldn't give a farthing for your week's religiosity. Your apartment is a mess, but you love order in your little life. I find that despicable. At three o'clock on Monday afternoon, heaven and earth can collapse into each other, but it's the dentist. You bare your teeth at each other, then come back in a taxi because there isn't time to walk. Every Thursday it's the hair-dresser. On Wednesday, the laundry – never at any other time. Thursday is ironing day, whether the clothes are dry or not. On Sundays and holidays, church. On Tuesday we speak only English and on Friday German, in case we forget them. The rest of the time we hit the keyboard non-stop. When he's dead the master will still hear the keys clattering."

I burst into tears. I cannot now tell whether I was crying because of what wasn't true or what was. Emerence, who was meticulous about her fine laundry and her starched, long-sleeved smocks, drew an immaculate white handkerchief from the pocket of her crisply ironed front and placed it before me. It was as though a child at nursery school was being repri-manded, and was so very ashamed of herself that she'd be a good girl from now on.

"Now, surely you didn't come about the chicken?" she asked. "So long as the master is alive there'll be no fasting in the house; at least, I shan't be cooking food for a fast. What are you doing here, on a holiday night? It's Friday. Go home and practise your languages. It's time to jabber away in German. Even the dog laughs at you. Tell me, what on earth are you practising for? God knows every possible language, and you're not likely to forget anything you've ever learned – your brain is like resin. Whatever gets stuck in it never gets out again. You pay back everybody who upsets you, even me. If only you'd shout and scream – but all you do is smile. You're the most vengeful person I ever met. You sleep with a knife under your pillow, and you wait till the time comes to stick it in. If it's something really bad you don't just scratch – you kill."

Pay her back? How? With what? They only thing I could possibly hurt her with had been hers from the start. Viola was her property, not ours. And – though he'd avoided the political errors of Imre Mező – they were burying the one person she had loved. I tidied up my face; her handkerchief was cool and lightly perfumed. I told her what Józsi's boy had asked and I could see from the set of her mouth that it made her very angry. That day I had seen her in all sorts of moods, but she became deadly serious when she heard the word "money".

"Now, listen here. You can tell that scoundrel not to keep pestering me with advice; and not to bother you either. The passbooks will stay where they are. Nothing will change, and there'll be no bank deposit book. Why that, in the name of thunder? Anyone who finds them in my house deserves to keep them. Not one of you has ever known me do anything stupid, so why should there be a fire here? I worry about my home too. The brat's obviously buried me already. Tell him from me: one more piece of advice and I cut him out of the will. You'll get everything. Let him come after you, if he dares. You're such a saint you'd deserve having to chase after my dead, and build the crypt. You'd really have a chance to pray there. The only reason I won't do it is because the ungrateful wretch would sue you. For money he'd even make his peace with the people in

Csabadul, and whatever I think of you I won't do that to you. But you deserve it, my Sugar Plum Fairy. Now, off you go. It's Friday. Go home and read your German Bible."

I was dismissed. Viola looked up at her for his orders. Emerence put her hand on the dog's forehead, and he closed his eyes dreamily, as if there was no other way to respond, receiving a benediction that flowed from those fingers, so gnarled and twisted by work. I walked away, slowly and with difficulty, like an old person. The events of the day, and everything leading up to it, weighed on me like lead. But it wasn't only the dog who followed me. Emerence came along too. I had become absorbed in the hedge of jasmine beyond the fence, and hadn't heard her footsteps — whenever she could, she wore cloth shoes with felt soles to ease her heavily-veined feet. I thought, with some bitterness, why is she coming after me? She's painted my portrait. She thinks I'm a hypocrite, that I'm stuffy, a snob. She doesn't understand how I've distracted my husband from thinking of death all the time; and if he was seriously ill, would I be likely to sit calmly at my work day after day? She finds fault with the one bit of me that is most utterly pure, the warrior who wrestles with the Lord.

"Now come back here, like a good girl. The master will have the radio on, he'll be listening to his music and enjoying the fact that Viola isn't home yet. Come on, I won't hurt you. In truth, I never want to hurt you. You're just slow, a bit of a thickhead. Why pay attention to my grumblings? Don't you see? You're all I've got left. You, and my animals."

We stood there. Soft sounds filtered out from behind the closed windows of the villa. The tenants who lived above Emerence were very quiet. They had turned the evening broadcast down low, but I could still make out the black and gold vision of the Mozart *Requiem*. There was no possible reply. After all, she had said nothing new. She didn't understand that it was because of our mutual love that she went on stabbing me till I fell to my knees, that she did it because I loved her, and she loved me. Only people truly close to me can cause me real pain. She might have grasped that long ago, but she understood only what she wanted to.

"Please come back in. There's no need to be stubborn. You've got the same cursed nature that I have, because we're both from the plains. Come on, don't stare at me. I've a reason for asking you."

Why? What more did she want? She'd finished the painting, she'd held the mirror up to my face, but for all her wisdom, she couldn't see the silver lining on the back, she'd simply used it to beat me over the head.

"Come on, I've got a present for you. A bunny rabbit laid it – the Easter Bunny."

Her tone was of one charming a child. When she spoke like that to anyone in the street I would turn round or stop where I stood. Children swarmed around and clung to her, just as Viola did. The Easter Bunny, on Good Friday. She hadn't cooked the plums, she mocked my mourning for Jesus, but of course she'd bought a present for me. She was allowed to give, I wasn't. For me, it was forbidden.

"I'm not coming, Emerence. We've said all we have to say to one another. I'll telephone your instructions to your nephew. You can keep Viola here for the night if you want to."

I could no longer make out her face. The sky had suddenly clouded over. All day I had been expecting rain and so far it had held off, but it is almost always windy on Good Friday, with driving rain. Now, towards the end of the day, the tears of lamentation for Christ were arriving once again, if rather late. I couldn't go back. They were falling in fat drops, and the legendary wind had sprung up afresh, signalling the outbreak of a storm, as if the universe were panting for air, or had begun to breathe in our ears. I knew the one thing Emerence dreaded was a storm, and that there was no point in resisting. If I didn't go with her she would drag me back in. Viola had drawn his tail in and was whimpering. He was already on the porch, scratching at the eternally closed door, wanting to hide. The lightning had begun to slash the sky and thunder rumbled between the howls of the dog. It was all pure electricity, a sudden sheet of pure blue flame, then nothing but pure water and perfect blackness.

"Quiet, Viola. It'll be over soon, my boy. Very soon."

The sky turned deep blue, then silver. The thunder raged. The lightning lasted long enough for me to see her fish the key out of her starched pocket. The dog whimpered.

"Shush, Viola, shush!"

The key turned. We looked at one another in the flashes of light. Emerence didn't take her eyes off me. I've got this wrong, I thought, I *must* have got this wrong. That door never opens. It can't be opening now. It's impossible.

"Now, pay attention. If you tell anyone, I'll put a curse on you. Anyone I curse comes to a sticky end. You're going to see something no-one has ever seen, and no-one ever will, until they bury me. But I've nothing else you would value, and today I hit you harder than you deserve, so I'm going to give you the only thing I have. You'll see it one day anyway – in fact it's yours. But you can have a look at it now, while I'm still alive. So come on in. Don't be afraid. Step inside."

She went ahead and I followed. Viola had slipped through the gap in the door. For the first few moments, while my feet picked their way step by step through the pitch black uncertainty, she left the light off. Viola was panting heavily and moaning. Along with his familiar voice I could hear tiny noises, as soft as that of a mouse scurrying across the floor in the deep of night. I stopped, afraid to take another step. I had never before trod in such total blackness. Then I remembered the shutters. In all the time we'd lived here, no-one had seen them open.

The light that flooded around us was harsh and raw; not yellow but a wintry white. Emerence didn't economise: the bulb must have been at least a hundred watts. The room we stood in was a large one, wide and white as snow, and looked freshly painted. It held a gas cooker, a sink, a table, two chairs, two large cupboards and the little sofa under an enormous violet-coloured cover which was frayed and had clearly seen better days. Its velvet upholstery had been shredded to a fringe. It was a "lovers' seat", of a type once in vogue. Emerence's home was as spotless as the row of glasses behind their translucent curtain in her old-fashioned sideboard. There was even an icebox, though it too was very old-fashioned. I stared at it, trying to think where she bought the ice for it, since the man hadn't been this way for years. Viola crawled under the lovers' seat, signalling that the storm was approaching its climax. The smell in the room — the familiar chlorine and air freshener — made me want to cough. Apart from that, it struck me as a lovingly and carefully furnished kitchen-dining area, one that held no secrets, even if it was hidden from curious eyes. There was nothing particularly odd about it, apart from the unusual arrangement by which the interior, which should have been the living room, was hermetically sealed off from the kitchen. An extraordinarily large, steel safe had been dragged in front of the door. Unless the thieves organised themselves into brigades, they were unlikely to move it. Former property of the Grossmans, I thought to myself. Beyond it must lie the furniture she had inherited. But who would ever manage to get past the safe, and how? Not even Emerence would manage it without help. Outside, the thunder roared and the rain poured down. She was deathly pale, but controlling herself. I discovered later that the safe was full of ceramic mugs.

Somewhat disconcerted, I gazed around. There were some flowers in a vase and several small pieces of carpet on the floor, as if someone had carefully cut up a tattered oriental rug and salvaged the pieces that could be used. Then my glance fell on what Emerence most wished to conceal from the eyes of the world: a line of bowls and trays of sand, essential requirements for cat hygiene. Under the sink, in the corner of the wall next to the sideboard, were nine small enamel plates, empty apart from a few leftovers, and nine little bowls. Between the two cupboards, like a statue, stood my mother's dressmaker's dummy, pinned all over with pictures, like a stark-naked female marshal clad in nothing but her medals. Among the pictures was a faded photograph, taken from a newspaper, of a rather intense, somehow old-fashioned, young face.

"Yes, that's him," she replied, to the question I had not asked. "When he left me I found the cat, the multicoloured one; the one that was hanged. There's no need for pity. I don't deserve it. You should never love anyone, or any animal, that much."

Viola whimpered in response to each clap of thunder.

"Anyway, I found another cat. There are always more than enough round here. People throw them out and chase them away. At first they're kept as playthings for the child, then when they start to grow up they're taken a little way off and chucked into someone else's garden. So, as I told you, I got another to replace the one that was hanged, and then that one was poisoned, obviously by the same person who strung up the first. This time I kept quiet. I'd realised that a pet doesn't have to go outside. It could stay indoors, the way Dobermann pinschers do, with the aristocracy. I could only keep them alive inside these four walls. I didn't have all these at the start – I'm not mad. I only wanted the first one, the old cat. I had him doctored straight away to calm him down. The second one was sick and moped around, and by the time I'd got him better I didn't have the heart to chase him away. They were dear little things, very gentle, and so happy when I came in. If there's no-one to show pleasure when you come home, then it's better not to live. I couldn't for the life of me tell you how there came to be nine. I found one screaming at the bottom of Devil's Ditch. He was trying to claw his way out, but he kept falling back in. The rubbish bin presented me with another two. As you know, the usual thing is to put the poor things in among the rubbish, inside nylon stockings. I didn't think they'd live, but they grew up to be the prettiest of all. The grey one was abandoned when the stove-fitter left. The three black-and-white ones were sired by the Devil's Ditch cat; they're like circus clowns, very odd. I destroy every new litter, what else can I do? But I couldn't bear to do it to these little clowns. They have stars on their chests. You couldn't push ones like that into the ground."

I stood there, stock still. The storm was receding, the thunder was much less and the lightning had almost stopped. The only blaze was from Emerence's huge light bulb.

"They know that they have to lie low, because they all remember that moment of danger. They can also sense death. Don't think that when you come with the injection they won't already know what's going to happen. But you needn't feel sorry for a single one. Being put down is more merciful than being cast out and going stray, with all its perils. Feed them full of meat before you finish them off. None of them are used to meat, and if you add a little sedative, you won't even have to chase them. Now, hold your tongue about all this, because nobody knows about them. You're the only one. They were all snatched from the jaws of death, and they are closer to me than my little brother Józsi's boy. If people in the building found out how many there were, they'd force me to get rid of seven, because we're only allowed two, and the Health Department would be let loose on me. I can't give you anything more than to entrust them to you, and let you see my home. Have a good look at them, but don't move. They're very timid. They don't know anyone but me, and Viola. Viola, where are you? Stop fooling around, the storm's over. To your place!"

Viola crawled out and jumped up on to the lovers' seat. I noticed the dip in the middle he'd made for himself over time.

"Supper time!" she called. At first nothing happened, so she spoke again, this time very quietly. The room filled with movement, and once again I heard those peculiar noises, and saw Emerence's family, all nine cats, emerging from their hiding places behind the armchair and under the cupboard. They didn't even glance at me. The only sound was the thumping of Viola's tail. They stood next to the empty bowls and turned their jewelled gaze on Emerence, who was at the stove, ladling out a sort of pepper and tomato stew from a large dish. She gave some to each in turn, the smile never leaving her face as she bent over them. The improbable vision didn't seem at all improbable, but rather like a circus act – this was real training. Viola, greedy as he was, didn't move a muscle, though he must have been ravenous. He just signalled with his tail that he was there too. The cats showed no fear of him. It was a long time since they had last thought of him as a dog. Last of all, he got his. He had a huge dish. It stood on the window sill, and – something he would never do at home – he wolfed down the stew, licked the bowl clean, and then looked at me defiantly, as if to say, see what a good boy I am here? "To your place," said Emerence. He jumped back up on to the lovers' seat, and the cats leapt up beside him and surrounded him. Those who didn't find a place either next to him, or on him, attached their graceful forms to the back of the sofa, clinging to the wood in charming, classical poses. Two even perched on the shoulders of the dressmaker's dummy, above the photographs, my own among them.

Suddenly she announced that she didn't have another minute.

The basement had apparently flooded and she had to go and sweep up some water. She kept Viola back, saying he should be allowed to talk with the others, but she packed me off home. We stepped outside and walked a little way together. The only perceptible fragrance was that of the rain. Once again, it was like *Book Six* of the *Aeneid*, as we made our way through the shadows, swathed in mist. Above us the moon hid itself only to deceive; soon it would pour down its rays. When I opened the door to our apartment, the tears began to flow. For the first time in my life I could not and would not explain to my husband why I was weeping. It was the only occasion in all our years of marriage that I refused to give him an answer.

CHRISTMAS SURPRISE

Viola is long dead, but I retain many images of him. Often, at dusk, I am tricked by the play of light and shadow in the street, and seem to discern a tiny, rhythmical pattering in the deep silence. I imagine I can hear him running along behind me, his claws clattering, and his quick, hot panting. But his image also comes to me on certain Sundays in summer, when the aroma of a meaty soup or pastry baking wafts out from behind the jars of pickled cucumber on the sill of the open window. No-one could gaze at the kitchen with such utter devotion, watching what was taking shape from the raw ingredients, as he. It was impossible to keep him away from the cooking area, though in fact no-one ever wanted to, because at such times he became a devotee, perfectly disciplined, but always waiting for some special morsel. His longing had its own peculiar sound, as if he were sighing, and always, in response to this doleful note, the person standing at the stove would throw him something. These sighs too are often brought back to me by the stream of memory.

More often than not, the face of Emerence that looks out at me from the past is the one she wore as she asked me, in a voice empty of all emotion, whether I wasn't bored with forever offering to help her and then gazing dreamily at her, as if she had asked for my hand in marriage. What did I want from her? Friendship, or to be fondled like a close relation? "Your ideas about everything are very different from mine. You were taught how to do a thousand things, but not to be aware of what really matters. Can't you see that there's no point in trying to dazzle me? I don't want anyone unless they are completely mine. You like to put everyone in a box, and then produce them whenever they're needed: this is my girlfriend, this my cousin, and this my elderly godmother. This is my love, this is my doctor, and this pressed flower is from the island of Rhodes. Just let me be. Once I'm no longer here, visit my grave now and then, that's quite enough. I rejected that man as a friend because I wanted him as a husband, but don't pretend you're the child I never had. I offered you something, and you accepted it. You've a right to a few of my things, because we got on well even if we had our little tiffs. You'll get something when I'm gone, and it won't be just anything. That should be enough. And don't you forget that I let you in where I never allowed anyone else. Beyond that, I've nothing else to offer you, because I've nothing else in me. What more do you want? I cook, I wash, I clean and tidy. I brought Viola up for you. I'm not your dead mother, or your nursemaid, or your little chum. Leave me in peace."

She was right of course, but that was little comfort. The one favour she had asked, that after her death I dispose of her little zoo, I would have done for anyone, though in my heart of hearts I hoped that when the time came the whole menagerie would have dwindled away, or been got rid of, and that she wouldn't be mad enough to take in any more. The existing nine were terrifying enough. It certainly wasn't an easy task, but there was nothing else for it. I had to accept that she had set the terms of our relationship, and the thermostat she had installed was an economical, rational one. We kept in touch with various diplomatic couples in the same polite way. Before each encounter, we would repeat the unwritten paragraph of the foreign service code: feelings are to be kept under control; every three years diplomats are sent elsewhere; they cannot allow themselves to form lifelong relationships with the natives; we too must ration out our fellow feeling in this measured way, but we should enjoy their presence while they are here as it's so good to be in their company, and enjoy the mutual exchange of sympathies.

To this diplomatic convention only the three of us subscribed. The fourth member of the family, Viola, did not. Once, in a rage, he bit the old woman, and received such a beating with the shovel that it broke a rib. Despite his howling he submitted to the attentions of the vet. The old woman held him while he was being treated, explaining all the while, "You asked for that, you village bull. Don't tell me it's the mating season. And don't you sulk. You're a disgrace, you got exactly what you deserved. Now, open your ugly mug." His reward, a piece of pastry, instantly disappeared between his brave, gleaming teeth. Emerence made it a condition that if you loved her, she should be the leading figure in your life. Of all those around her whom she considered really important, only the dog took that as natural and accepted it – even as he bit her.

As a rule, relations with her were at their most harmonious when one of us was in some sort of difficulty. There was no shortage of such times. Both my husband and I were in generally poor health during those years and were often ill. Either our bodies failed to fight off an attack, or our nervous systems told us the game wasn't being played fairly against us. In times of crisis, Emerence stood by us in ways that could really be felt. Her gnarled fingers brought relief and healing. There was nothing more blissfully restorative after a serious illness than when she washed us all over, gave us a thorough massage, and dusted us down with some fragrant talcum powder sent by little Éva Grossman. My husband once suggested that we should live with one foot permanently in the grave, or sink into some bottomless pool from which she could pull us out – then she would be thoroughly content and satisfied. If we ever achieved lasting success or relative security in our lives, she would lose interest. The moment she could no longer help, she would see no justification for her existence.

One thing we never got used to was that, although she never read anything, all the bad news on the literary front that was turning our lives upside down seemed nonetheless to reach her. She always made us aware that she knew about it, and assured us that she was making it her business to inform everyone in the street who mattered – if they hadn't discovered it for themselves – that the conspirators were on the move again. From the members of her private circle she required declarations of solidarity and denunciations of our enemies.

Thus, as the years flew by, our relationship continued to strengthen. Emerence was one of us, as far as she would allow. She continued to receive me outside on her porch, like any other visitor, and she never again allowed me into her flat. Otherwise there was no change in her habits. She continued to carry out all the various jobs she had undertaken, though it was clear she no longer did so with the same fresh energy. She didn't even stop clearing the snow. I tried occasionally to establish just how much her fortune was worth. I had my suspicions that, as well as the crypt, Józsi's boy might well be able to build an owner-occupied building for his entire family. Emerence made precise distinctions in the way she rewarded each of us. The Lieutenant Colonel was given high respect, Viola had her heart, my husband her impeccable work (and he also greatly appreciated her keeping my rustic amiability within acceptable bounds through her own restrained behaviour); to me she entrusted her instructions on the approaching, and critical, final moments of her life. She also demanded of me that, in my art, it should be real passion and not machinery that moved the branches. That was a major gift, the greatest of her bequests.

But I still felt it wasn't enough, that I wanted something more. For example I would have loved to give her the sort of hug I had shared with my mother, and to tell her things I would tell no-one else, things my mother understood not with her intellect or as the result of her education, but through the subtler antennae of love. But Emerence didn't want me in that complete way. At least that was what I thought; that I wasn't essential to her. Long after all trace of Emerence and her home had disappeared, the handyman's wife, seeing the cut flowers from the garden in my arms and realising I was on my way to the cemetery, threw her arms around my neck. "You were the light of her life," she said, "her daughter. Ask anyone who lives round here how she described you. 'My little girl.' What do you think? Who did she talk about non-stop – when the poor thing actually sat down for a rest? She talked about you. But all you ever saw was how she lured the dog away and kept him from you. What you never noticed was that she'd become to you what Viola was to her."

Emerence accompanied our lives for something like twenty years. During that time we spent countless weeks, even months, abroad, while she looked after the apartment, dealt with the mail and the phone, and took delivery of what money came in. Though he squealed loudly, she never took Viola to her flat, not even for an hour, so that our home would never be empty in our absence. Once, on our return from a Book Week in Frankfurt, we brought her a portable TV. We knew of old that she didn't accept gifts, but we thought it might bring the wider world into the Forbidden City. At the time, such things weren't available in Hungary – it was almost the only one in the whole country – and, since she seemed to aim for exclusivity in her emotional life, we thought this time she might react differently. She would be the only one in the street to have one of these small-screen sets.

We got back in time for the holiday. It was Christmas again, just as when we had found Viola. In those years, there were far fewer religious programmes on TV. Instead they showed folk dramas, with children in fur coats and boots, singing and chanting. But after dinner there was to be a sweetly sentimental film, set during the Second World War. We imagined that Emerence, who was serving our meal, would be delighted. But she gave no sign of pleasure; she looked at me with her mysterious, solemn eyes, as if she could tell us something if she chose, but wasn't going to. I was in a state of total euphoria, since she had actually accepted the present. She thanked us, wished us a merry Christmas and left. That year Christmas was particularly good, like those in the lacquered cards of my childhood. Outside, huge, soft, feathery snowflakes circled down. All my life winter has been my favourite season. I stood at the window, looking out. I was enchanted, full of the spirit of Christmas and home, and my seasonal thoughts mingled with thoughts of Emerence, the proud owner of a television, sitting in her room celebrating.

I think that everything that happened later followed from what took place that evening. It was as if Heaven itself had thrown the present back in our faces, or as if Emerence's God – whom she had always scorned and denied, but who was there watching every step she took – stirred, and gave me one last chance to see, rather than look. We were standing at the window, above the streetlight, whose rays flooded in even in the wildest snowstorms, gazing in wonder at the winter and the feathery flakes dancing, when suddenly the image of Emerence swam into our picture of the street. She was sweeping. Her headscarf, her shoulders and her back were turning white under a thick veil of snow. She was sweeping, on Christmas Eve, because the pavement couldn't be left uncleared.

The blood rushed into my face. From above, she looked like the straw man in *The Wizard of Oz*. Sweet, kind Jesus, newly born, what sort of gift had I brought this old woman? How often would she be able to sit at home in peace, with her chores tugging at her from one breakfast time to the next? That was why she had given us that special, wounded look. If the fabric of her emotional life hadn't been woven with a finer thread, and more sensitive strands, than mine, she might have refused the set; or asked us if we'd sweep the snow off the streets for her, or do her duty in the laundry, since by the time she'd be able to sit herself down on the lovers' seat, Budapest would have stopped transmitting.

We didn't dare say a word to each other. My husband had come to the same realisation. We were too ashamed to continue looking, and turned our backs on Emerence and her broom. Viola scratched at the door to the balcony, wanting to go out, but I didn't let him. Neither of us spoke, and why should we? The need was for action, not words. But we went back to our own television. Even now I cannot forgive myself when I am reminded of what I ought to have done, but went no further than the thought.

I've always been good at philosophising, and I wasn't ashamed to admit that I had done wrong. But what didn't occur to me was that, compared to her, I was still young and strong. And yet I didn't go out and sweep the snow. I didn't send her home to watch the film, though I could have handled the broom perfectly well. As a girl in the country I had danced with one often enough. I was the one who kept the front of the house clear in those days. But I didn't go down. I stayed right where I was. It was Christmas, and I too exchanged my usual taste for savoury and bitter things for something sweet — for that sweet, sad, lovely film, after all those grotesque, existentialist productions.

ACTION

Yes, I'm sure that's when it all started to unravel. At some point towards the end of February Emerence caught the flu virus that had been on the rampage since the autumn. Of course she took it in her stride and ignored it. That year the winter brought exceptional snow, and she turned all her attention to keeping the street in order, though her cough was almost choking her, as everyone could hear. Sutu and Adélka rushed around, bringing her hot tea laced with spiced wine. Emerence would throw the sugary alcohol down her throat, and stop from time to time to lean on her broom for protracted fits of coughing. Adélka fussed over her until she too collapsed and was so ill she was hospitalised. Emerence was visibly relieved when she no longer saw her constantly popping up. Sutu was more discreet in her support, but Adélka's big mouth didn't stop working for a moment. Emerence found it highly distasteful to have the whole street echoing with: that old woman doesn't go to bed for days on end; the godforsaken snow keeps coming; sick as she is, she skates around from one house to the next – there are so many – and then has to start all over again. The former class- mate who first told me about Emerence suggested one day that I should speak to the old woman and tell her to go to a doctor, and above all, to take a break from clearing the snow and lie down or she'd be in real trouble. She had heard her coughing, and in her opinion it was no longer flu that was plaguing her, it was pneumonia. When I took Emerence's arm to make her stand still and pay attention, she was gasping for breath. She shouted at me to leave her alone. If I was so eager to help I should see to myself and my husband, and do the cleaning and cooking. As long as the cursed snow kept falling she couldn't move from the street, and she certainly didn't want a rest – what a stupid idea, that she should go to bed when I knew perfectly well she didn't even have one, and anyway how could she possibly lie down when absolutely anyone could ring for her at any time? – the tenants had their own keys but the authorities might pitch up, some official she didn't know and wasn't expecting – and it was better for her to sit up at night, it was less painful for her back; so would I please stop worrying about her, she'd had quite enough, it wasn't anyone else's business whether she lay down or not; she'd never asked me why an old woman like me had so many cosmetics in her bathroom; my classmate and the doctor could take to their beds, and any other troublemaker who wanted to order her about should stay in theirs.

Fury – and fever – blazed rose-red in her face, and she resumed her sweeping with even greater violence, as if she had a personal vendetta with the snow, which she alone could settle. Sutu and the handyman's wife, she shouted after me, were bringing her food, enough for the whole street, so there was nothing for me to worry about. She hated being spied on; she'd never in her life gone in for hysterics, but if we nagged her enough she might experiment to see it was like. Her words were drowned by choking, followed by a fit of coughing, then she turned away. Those days she never had Viola with her. She said she didn't have time to run around with him, and it wasn't good for a dog to stay still; so I should take him home, into the warmth. There was no need for him to catch a cold as well.

In every way, it was a most unusual year, and this applied to us too. In the period after the Christmas when we gave Emerence the television, my life began to open out. From the very first day of the new year, it was as if an invisible hand were turning the mysterious tap from which good and bad flowed into people's lives, sometimes off, and sometimes on. Just then, the tap was in full flow. It wasn't spectacular, but it was distinctly perceptible. I had never before had so many things to organise and to do, and I didn't understand the reason until almost the very end. For so many years I'd been held down by outside forces, inside an invisible but almost palpable circle. It took some time for me to grasp that somewhere a decision had been taken, that the barrier which had always been down was being raised, the door on which we hadn't knocked for years had opened of itself, and I could enter if I chose. At first I didn't even attempt to interpret the signs. Emerence swept, and coughed; I did the shopping, and cooked. I kept the rooms in order, fed and walked the dog, and wracked my brains as to why this organisation or that was pressing me with such insistent demands; and all the while Emerence's condition cried out for her to speak, even once, to a doctor, but whenever I raised the subject she shouted at me to get out of her way — everyone had the right to cough; as long as the snow fell she had work to do on the street; it was enough if I looked after our home until she came back to work; but I needn't pester her about medicines and doctors, I was wasting my time.

I was scuttling about between tasks like a beetle on the run, without the steadying hand of Emerence at my side, and suddenly every editor in the business popped out of nowhere, and photographers called me up to take pictures. By then I had realised that something really exciting was about to happen — if they'd wanted to harass me they'd have made a different sort of fuss. Never before had I been given such glowing reviews; never before had the outside world been so interested in me. I was forever having to go somewhere, journalists were phoning non-stop, radio and TV people kept appearing; the world had turned upside down. Even when my colleagues started dropping repeated hints, I failed to understand. Then one morning, after a phone call from somewhere rather important, my husband, his face shining as I had never seen it before, not since those hours that followed our wedding, finally spoke the words. The prize.

Of course it must be the prize. It was already the middle of March and all these signs, especially the latest, a friendly phone call on a totally different subject, could mean only one thing – that the award was coming my way. I should have been so happy, so very happy. After all, my ten years of struggle were finally over. How happy I should have been.

But all I felt was tired to death. Without any period of transition, my life had become public, and the constant exposure was exhausting me. And our domestic order had collapsed – there was no Emerence. This see-saw existence, which put me ever more strongly in the spotlight and should have produced real happiness, made it very difficult to co-ordinate attending to Viola, to the heating and the cooking, to the laundry, to the cleaning and tidying, and running back and forth to the dry cleaners. At long last Adélka emerged from the hospital, and we hoped that she and Sutu would take over Emerence's street-sweeping. At first she was rudely rebuffed. Emerence screamed at her, as loudly as her sore throat allowed, to get out of her way, but then she suddenly fell silent and left the street. Sutu shut up her stall, which was now selling fried potato and roast chestnuts, and put up a notice, "closed due to illness", and took charge of the birch broom with Adélka. Within a single afternoon it became clear that the two of them weren't able to finish half of what Emerence would do on her own, when in good health. By now the old woman was in hiding. When Mr Brodarics called to ask if she needed anything, she shouted at him through the door to leave her in peace. No-one was to visit her; she wouldn't let a soul in anyway; no-one was to bring her any medicine because she wouldn't take it – or a doctor. All she needed was a bit of rest; as soon as she'd had a good sleep she'd be back on her feet. She didn't want Viola, because he would just bother her by jumping up. I shouldn't even think of coming over, because she didn't want to see or have to listen to me. No-one, let's be quite clear. Not even me.

So Emerence vanished. Without her, the street seemed unreal, a wasteland, a desert. It's typical of me that when I finally took it in that the old woman had withdrawn and shut herself away, even from me, I felt neither pity nor panic, but simple, futile rage. So she didn't want anyone to see her; even I wasn't to bother her? How very thoughtful of her! Just when every single minute of my life was being claimed by someone, I got stuck in this mess. Instead of things getting better, the place was falling apart, and it was all up to me. My husband wasn't allowed out in the cold; the dog howled all day long; the apartment had to be kept spick and span for the constant visitors. When I was supposed to do it all was a mystery. And added to everything, the phone never stopped ringing, and I was surrounded by journalists. Whenever I went out, I found a street humming with activity, Sutu and Adélka chatting away as they swept, and the neighbours, who had learned from the old woman how decent people behaved when others were ill, tramping through the snow on their way to Emerence's porch with mugs and bowls and food containers. From me she got nothing. At mealtimes I would open two tins and the three of us, including the dog, lived on that. I couldn't have offered that to a sick person. The others, to be sure, quite outdid themselves. No-one else failed the test, only I, though I went over several times a day to her door and called out to ask what I could do for her. But that was the full extent of my nursing activity, on which the old woman made not one second's demand. As I stood there asking if she needed anything, I shook with anxiety, praying she would refuse. I couldn't cope with what I already had to do, let alone take on more, and besides, the snowfall had so disrupted transport that I had to run down to the shops four or five times a day, dragging Viola with me, because nothing was being delivered on time, and I couldn't get the simplest things. Almost everything in the kitchen had been used up and needed replacing. I slithered all the way home with bulging carrier bags, but never quite caught up with myself. Meanwhile the photographers were beavering away in our apartment. I had never looked quite so haggard, unattractive and worn out as in the photographs taken just before the announcement of the prize.

Emerence never opened her door, never once showed herself. Enraged by the constant knocking, she demanded that no-one bother her. Her voice had lost all its strength; it was somehow altered, not muffled but strange-sounding and raw. She continued to refuse entry to the doctor, and only I knew why this was. The gifts of food stayed outside on the little bench. At first, she had collected them and taken them in, and the empty dishes were washed and returned. But when she stopped going out to get them, and the christening bowls from the neighbours sat there side by side, untouched, I really began to worry. When we challenged her about it she replied through the gap around the door that she had no appetite and anyway her fridge was full. By now her speech was slurred and broken; I thought she was treating herself with too much alcohol. I knew what she was saying wasn't true. I had seen the "fridge". It wasn't electric, and it was years since ice was last sold on the street. As in that moment when I'd watched her sweep the Christmas snow, I registered only part of what I saw. I knew she was lying, but I didn't think through what she and the cats might be living on. Perhaps, I tried to persuade myself, she had rationed out the food she'd had earlier. After all, she took so much in at the beginning that the bowls might still be full; the sills between the windows and shutters were very cold, so perhaps the rest was piled up in there? But I didn't think about it too long. I was always rushing off somewhere, always being phoned or receiving visitors. And yet every day I made my way to her door and repeated my offer to call someone, such as my neighbour who was a professor of medicine. I knew in advance that she would refuse, and when she did I was secretly glad, because there was no room in my life for anything more.

Luckily my brain was still working sufficiently for me to try to contact the Lieutenant Colonel and let him know that Emerence was ill. He wasn't at the police station. He was on holiday somewhere – they weren't free to name the resort. I informed Józsi's boy, and he came over, but he didn't get in either. He left some oranges and lemons and a large saucepan of stuffed cabbage on her doorstep. Finally, Mr Brodarics walked over to our flat one evening and asked if I had worked out how long it had been since the old woman had appeared on her porch, because it was now the very end of March, and if his calculations were correct, it was two weeks since she had last opened the door. The tenants were worried that they'd be in trouble as a community if they didn't call in a doctor or other assistance, even if she didn't want it. He also pointed out what I already knew, that her bathroom opened directly on to her porch, and she kept that private area padlocked, but she hadn't been using it lately. The snow was blowing on to the porch, but for days there had been no footprints in it going from the front door, only those leading to it, made by people bringing food. What was Emerence doing when she needed to answer Nature's call? There was a strong smell coming from behind the kitchen door that gave him cause for concern. We couldn't allow this ridiculous business of locking herself away to go on for ever.

We had to do something, or the old woman would suffer. If she carried on refusing to let either the neighbours or a doctor in, they were going to break down the door. A district official had already tried to get in to her – Adélka had taken him there early that morning – but Emerence had chased him away. According to Adélka, she had almost no voice left, and had mumbled her complaint about being disturbed. This wasn't darkest Africa, so would I be kind enough to contact the rescue service, and quickly, or the poor thing would soon be dead?

I was plunged into despair. No-one else was allowed in there without her permission, and she had let me in only once. It was impossible to know what might happen if she thought we were planning to force our way in. I was so worried that I finally came up with a possible solution. I told Mr Brodarics that we should wait till the next day. I would have to talk to Emerence face to face, with no-one else present. Then I would let them know whether my idea had been successful, and if not, we would speak further.

That afternoon I ran over and called out to her through the door. I promised to respect her wishes and keep in mind her reasons for not wanting to open up No-one would set foot inside, I would go in and do everything that had to be done, but she had to come out. She wouldn't have to go to hospital if she didn't want to. She could stay with us, in my mother's room, with Viola. The doctor was already waiting. He would examine her, and with his medicine she would soon be well.

The suggestion enraged her, and her voice grew stronger. It was no longer a slurred mumble – she positively shouted at me. If we didn't leave her in peace, the moment she was back on her feet she'd indict us for neighbourly nuisance. We were all pushy, base, thoroughly nosy types. She had a right to convalesce for as long as it took to get better, and to lie down or sit up or stand as she pleased. If I set foot – I or anyone else –

people should know she had a hatchet and she'd kill them. Repulsed, I made my way home, horrified. Mr Brodarics came over again that evening with the handyman, and Józsi's boy also presented himself. They decided to break down the door, with the doctor waiting outside. However Józsi's boy wouldn't be taking her home – he was afraid his little girl might catch something – but he'd help drag her up the stairs to our flat. If I could get her to open the door a tiny crack, or even turn the key, the rest would take care of itself.

My husband uttered not a word of protest, even though we'd planned and decided everything behind his back. What did puzzle him was why the thought of breaking down the door upset me so much, when it could be fixed back on again. It wasn't exactly news that the old woman wouldn't open her door. Emerence had never been quite right in the head, so why was it so terrible that she'd gone all stubborn and withdrawn, like Achilles? We'd get her better in spite of herself. I should bring her home, if she was willing. He didn't like having strangers in the house, but that wasn't the point. The old woman had to be looked after, and kept in a properly heated place. Anyone who could leave her to her fate would have it on their conscience for the rest of their life – *that* would be indefensible – but my panic was irrational. After all, I liked the old woman, so why did the thought of bringing her here so upset me that I was crying my eyes out? I didn't reply. I couldn't reply. I alone knew about Emerence's Forbidden City.

The doctor, Mr Brodarics and I had decided that Emerence should spend this last night in her home. The next day, once the surgery had closed, we would take action. It was a difficult night. The hours dragged slowly by, as I continued to deliberate. But finally I made up my mind. There was nothing else I could do. If she didn't get medical attention it would be the end of her. The only way to save her was to betray her. She was made of iron — perhaps it wasn't too late. If I played it right I might still be able to preserve her secret. It would mean an appalling amount of extra work, a string of well planned lies, and a huge expenditure of energy.

At dawn I went over to her flat and knocked. I asked her to do this much for me: to step outside her door for a moment that afternoon, to reassure the neighbours. It wasn't wise to let no-one see her. They would only think the situation worse than it was. No-one wanted people to think they didn't care — she knew how much they all loved her. My plan was to get her to open her door a crack, the doctor would move in behind me, seize her by the arm and pull her out, then the handyman, Mr Brodarics and Józsi's boy, with my help, would take her over and settle her in our apartment.

She replied that she'd been about to give me a message. She certainly wouldn't step outside her door. But if I would stand close to it, with a large box, a long one, her old cat, the neutered one, had died, and I should bury it. She didn't need a doctor, and no-one should come anywhere near the flat. If they didn't believe she was still alive they could all go and hang themselves. They'd know she was alive if she gave me something. I could say I was taking her rubbish away. That should be more than enough for all the nosy neighbours and their fears. I could barely decipher her mumbled whispers, but when I did I thought I'd go mad. I had never hoarded boxes. Where would I get hold of one suitable for a cat's coffin? And what was I supposed to do with a corpse when I was up to my ears with everything else? But I promised.

Back home, I fished out a discarded box from our cellar, and my mood began to lift. The dead cat had actually made my task easier. She would have to open the door to pass the corpse out, and the doctor could then seize her. It was just that everything would be happening at the same precise moment. The doctor couldn't get there until just before I had to leave for the TV studio, to do a personal profile. They had asked me for four o'clock; the car was coming for me at a quarter to, just as the doctor would be arriving (he couldn't do it a moment earlier). I'd call to her, the old woman would open the door, I'd give her the box and be given the cat in return, and at that moment the doctor, Józsi's boy, Mr Brodarics and the handyman would haul her out, the men would bring her to our apartment, and I'd be able to go off to the TV studio. My face was green with anxiety and I was gobbling tranquillisers like sweets, even though earlier it had all seemed so simple, and I'd been ashamed that such a practical solution hadn't occurred to me sooner.

I changed the bedding in my mother's room and lit the fire. Journalists kept popping in, to be mildly surprised by the first great clean-up, that afternoon, of a room that hadn't been heated all winter, while Viola barked non-stop. I now realise why it never occurred to me that things might go wrong. For the first time in my life I was in the limelight, caught and held in its blaze. Everything else barely sank in. To be fair, no sensible person would have doubted the feasibility of my plan. Everyone knew that Emerence was fond of us, that we didn't use my mother's room, that it would make Viola happy, and that even in her moments of darkest suspicion the old woman felt sure that if I had promised I wouldn't allow anyone into her locked apartment, and had accepted responsibility for the creatures living with her, I would keep my word. In fact there was only one detail that worried me – the moment when she realised that it was not just me standing there, the one person on earth to whom she might open her door, but also someone else, her arch-enemy, the doctor. Though I suffer so badly from stage fright that I break into a cold sweat at the very thought of being before a camera, I was more afraid of that moment than of my planned television appearance.

We had arranged to meet the doctor on Emerence's porch. At home, I even managed to serve lunch. Viola was not at all his usual self that day. At first he barked continuously, then later he fell silent. When I took him downstairs for his walk, he immediately insisted on going back inside. When the doorbell rang, he didn't even lift his head. But he wasn't asleep; he was watching. I ought to have understood this total dejection, but I wasn't Emerence. I didn't realise why he went berserk with rage when he saw me leaving the flat without him. I took the cat-coffin, giving the others a rather confused account of how it fitted into the plan to bring Emerence's belongings to our flat. Józsi's boy arrived at the same moment as the car from the studio. The driver brought the message that they were very sorry but the make-up people were already waiting, and before that we had to talk things through with the director. Unfortunately they had miscalculated when I needed to be there, and we had to leave immediately, so would I please get in?

I told him I couldn't come immediately. I had something to do which couldn't be postponed – it wouldn't take a moment, they would have to wait. The driver gave me five minutes. In theory it should have been enough – all I had to do was run over to Emerence's, take the cat in its coffin through the opened door, and let the others pull her out and bring her home. While they were reasoning with her I'd lock her door, come back to the apartment, give her the key, reassure her that everything was in order and that no-one would be able to break in, and then – after the broadcast – I would sit with her and persuade her that we'd get along perfectly together, and I'd take good care of her menagerie for as long as she remained ill.

Persuade Emerence! How could I have imagined that? I had obviously taken leave of my senses, believing what I wanted to believe. And in the midst of all this turmoil, I was trying to think what sort of questions I would have to answer in the studio. When the moment arrived, it was exactly a quarter to four. The driver ostentatiously pointed to the watch on his left wrist and spread out the five fingers on his right hand. Fine. I had given my word. Five minutes and no more.

It was the very end of March, cold but fragrant with the violets that teemed in Emerence's garden. Even the grass beneath her window was lilac. The doctor, Mr Brodarics, the handyman and the nephew were waiting in ambush. I had warned them not to make a move until I had taken the package from her. Meanwhile the whole street was aware of what we were up to. It was like a canvas by Breughel, with people gathered in brightly-coloured groups. They all knew each other, and fully approved of the solution we had finally reached. The handyman pointed out the stench around the door. It had been disturbing the day before, now it was even thicker and more oppressive. Had he not known it was impossible he would have thought there was a corpse in there. He knew that smell from the siege of Buda.

I asked everyone to retire to one side, as I would have to be completely alone at the door, and even the onlookers in the street moved back, though they would have paid serious money to watch us rescue Emerence in the teeth of her protests. When the porch was completely deserted, I knocked on the door. Emerence asked me not to enter, but to give her the box, then stay there and wait. The man from the TV honked his horn in front of our house. I couldn't respond, I was watching the door moving and Emerence's hand starting to appear. I could see nothing of her face. She had either been sitting there in the dark all along, or had turned the lights off, because behind the door it was pitch black. The stench that came pouring out made me desperate to put my hand in front of my nose, but I stood there, straining like a dog at a shoot. It really was like the aftermath of the siege, with the stench of decay wafting out from the flat, mixed with that of human and animal excrement, though it was impossible to take in every detail in the heat of the moment. I handed over the box. The TV man honked a second time. Emerence closed the door, and I heard the light switch click inside. The doctor peered around the corner and I signalled him to wait. As the TV man honked yet again the door opened a crack and Emerence produced, not the box, but the corpse itself, wrapped in a shabby little coat. The box had proved too short; at full stretch the animal wouldn't fit inside. I held it in my arms like a murdered infant.

She would have slammed the door, but the doctor had already forced his foot into the narrow gap and Józsi's boy was rushing forward. Whether they actually went in, or hauled her out with the help of the handyman as we had agreed, I couldn't be certain. I ran off towards our apartment carrying the dead cat. Outside the gate, passing through the lines of Breughel figures, I was seized with nausea and threw the corpse in a rubbish bin. The horn was now unremitting, but I rushed up to the apartment, filled with the insane feeling that if I didn't run hot water over my fingers that minute I wouldn't be able to utter a sound, no matter what questions they asked. Why was everything happening in such a topsy-turvy way, in such confusion? Emerence would now be on her way to us, resisting all the way. They would be dragging and pushing her along. I should have been there with her, but it was impossible. I wasn't there, and there was nothing I could do about it. "Would you do something for me?" I asked my husband – he told me later my voice was unrecognisable, as was my face. "Don't wait for them to get here. Run over and lock the place up, before the whole street looks inside. And don't you look in either, and when they bring her up, you must give her the key and tell her I'll take care of everything myself. The TV man won't take his hand off the horn, I really can't stay to explain any of this to her myself."

He promised. I ran to the car, he towards Emerence's flat. The old woman was nowhere to be seen, nor was the rescue squad. All I registered was some sort of noise, a deep rumbling. I acted as if deaf. I fell into the TV car and we raced away from the street.

WITHOUT HER HEADSCARF

When you do something truly unforgivable, you don't always realise it, but there is a certain inward suspicion of what you have done. I told myself the bad feeling clamped up inside me was stage fright. But it was simple guilt. When we got there it became clear that even after all the rush, we were still running late, and I found myself in front of the camera without make-up, with my nerves in a jangle, looking a wreck. I could sense that the interviewer wanted more from me, some more original ideas, but even as I responded to his questions my mind was elsewhere, on the problem at home. We had agreed with the doctor that if her illness appeared not to be serious, and disaster not imminent, she would stay with us. If it proved more grievous, or indeed life-threatening, the ambulance would take her. But all this would have already been decided by the time I got home.

There were a large number of people involved in the programme, and it dragged on. Even then the meeting didn't end with the interview, because they wouldn't let me go. I couldn't wait to get away, and yet it was also my hour of glory. For the first time in my life I was in the world of television. Had I strongly insisted, they would obviously have let me go, but this was no ordinary experience, meeting the people I watched on the screen every day. I knew I ought to rush off, but I didn't. Finally it occurred to me to glance at my watch, and I was shocked to see the time. Then nothing was fast enough. I asked for a taxi and we raced away.

When I stepped out of the car the day was almost over; the street was silent and strangely empty. The only noise was coming from our flat, where Viola was complaining bitterly. So, I realised, Emerence wasn't with us. If she were, he wouldn't be grieving. I knew, without being told, that the situation was more serious than I had imagined – something I should have understood a lot earlier, on the day Emerence suddenly gave up working for us and told us to fend for ourselves. But lately I had paid attention to nothing but myself. I got out of the taxi outside our apartment. The rubbish bin was a step away; I peered inside to see if that appalling bundle was still there, as of course it was. With a shudder I slammed the lid back down. But I didn't go on up the stairs. Instead I set off to check that my husband had actually locked Emerence's door.

Standing at the window in the villa, the handyman was closing his shutters, gently, the way he treated everything. What followed was not what I expected – that he would wave to indicate that he had something to tell me, and reveal what he had witnessed while I had been mouthing platitudes at the TV studio. He pulled the blind shut, and the thick wooden slats separated his face from mine. This man does not wish to speak to me, I thought. Terrified, I started to run through the garden. I'd been in such situations before. Lit from behind, his face had worn the same expression you sometimes saw on the faces of nursing staff – you approached the patient in a hospital ward, but someone else was in their bed, and the sister calmly, with no trace of emotion in her voice, sent you off to the chief doctor who had something to say to you. Merciful God, how had things turned out so very differently from what we had planned? Surely the door hadn't been left open? Surely her cats hadn't scattered in every direction? That was the very first moment – there were countless more to follow – when I shuddered at the realisation that, whatever kind of award I'd received, even if I'd been not just a contributor in a group discussion but had the entire TV network for a day, with every member of the government wishing me peace and comfort while I broadcast all the humiliations I had suffered to the four corners of the world — even then I should never have left Emerence alone, to face whatever it was that had happened. My much-lauded imagination had run only so far as to reckon that that evening I would have to clean her place up and get rid of the stench, whatever its cause, so that no-one in the building would complain. But now I knew I should have been with her at the precise moment when she lost her independence, when they forced her door open, even if it was only wide enough to let a doctor in, and took her protesting from her home — that idea had never entered my head. The prize, I reflected bitterly, had already begun to work its influence. I had rushed off in a TV car towards its radiance, away from illness, old age, loneliness and incapacity.

Once on the porch, I lost the ability to walk. I remained frozen on the spot in my smart shoes. I expected bad news, but not on the scale that now met me. No imagination could have conjured up what appeared before my eyes. Emerence's door was neither open nor closed: she no longer had a door. It was propped up against the wooden slats of the washroom, with the lock still in place. It had been torn off its hinges. Its middle section was missing — someone had hit it with a hard object and only the top half was intact. It was of the sort you see in Flemish paintings, the door split across the middle with the upper part folded down, and a smiling woman leaning out with her elbows on the half-door, as if posing for her portrait. I imagined Emerence gazing out from under her headscarf, taking stock of the situation; that I wasn't there; that the doctor was standing in my place, ready to grab her. The reconstruction went no further. I was so weak I had to sit on the bench and try to pull myself together. I knew I couldn't avoid it. I would have to walk into that stench. I rested for a few minutes, then steeled myself to go. I remembered where the click of the light switch had come from, that particular night. I felt around for it and then turned the lights on. This time there were no mysterious sounds of scurrying and rustling. The silence was total. If the cats were still hiding in there, they must have flattened themselves out somewhere in their terror.

The light, which on the previous occasion had seemed so oppressively stark, once again spared nothing. In a room that had once been as clean and sparkling as polished glass, I stood among human and animal excrement. Stinking piles of rotten food were strewn around the bare floor or on sheets of newspaper. The christening bowl had been overturned and armies of maggots swarmed around the contents. A half-rotten raw fish and a carved duck were in a similar state. The food brought by callers had been dumped on the floor, and God knows how long it had been since Emerence had washed or tidied up. Even the cockroaches were dying. The horror spread out before me was covered by a thick white powder. It was as if some obscene, verminous, medieval Death's head had been sprinkled with fine sugar, while just below the surface, the teeth in the faceless skull maintained their sardonic grin. Emerence was nowhere to be seen, nor were the cats. None of the windows were closed — the casements and the shutters had been taken off — but the suffocating smell of disinfectant still lay heavy in the room, not the usual chlorine and air freshener, but something altogether more brutal. Quantities of this kind of powder weren't to be found in kitchen cupboards or even in shops. It wasn't only the doctor and the ambulance who had called. The decontamination unit had been as well.

When I arrived home my hands were so rigid with terror and guilt I was incapable of turning the key in the lock. I had to ring. My husband opened the door. He had never scolded me for anything, and he didn't then. He shook his head like a man who had no words for what had taken place, and went off to make tea, while Viola crawled towards me, cowering. As I sipped my drink, my teeth chattered against the cup. I asked no questions – the key to Emerence's flat lay on the table. Nothing was said about my television appearance. My husband waited for me to force the tea down my throat, then he called a taxi and we set off, still without speaking, for the hospital. The first time we spoke to one another was when we learned that although the doctor had assigned her to a ward, where she was known about and expected, she hadn't yet appeared. How was that possible? Hadn't they taken her there? "They are bringing her," the sister said, "she just hasn't arrived. First they took her to be decontaminated. In the state she was in when they found her, it wasn't possible to put her in a bed."

I didn't at first understand what she was saying; I stared at her stupidly, and slowly sank to the ground. We were surrounded by helpful members of the nursing staff. Could they get me anything? – I was looking terrible – some medicine, or would I like a cup of coffee? I wanted nothing. We sat and waited. By that stage it had become impossible not to ask my husband for details. He told me what he had witnessed.

By the time he reached Emerence's flat, the doctor had managed to seize her arm. She was fighting him off but was unable to offer much resistance because, as the doctor and the ambulance man discovered, she had suffered a mild stroke. The brain haemorrhage had been largely reabsorbed, but she was barely able to use her left arm, and the left leg not at all. She must have been totally paralysed for days, but her amazing constitution had already begun to fight back. She had managed to snatch her arm free, yank the door shut and bolt it. She refused to answer any questions. By then everyone in the neighbourhood who had any time to spare was out on the porch. For a while she remained mute, ignoring their pleadings, but when the doctor threatened to call in the authorities she shouted out that if they didn't leave her in peace she would kill the first person who touched her door. Respect for her was so great that no-one was prepared to resort to violence. A total stranger passing along the street, drawn by all the shouting and discovering what was going on, did make an attempt to force the door open. But just as the lock began to move a plank was smashed open, not from the outside as might have been expected but from within, and through the gap, as in a horror film, an axe shot out and flailed about in all directions. After that, no-one dared go anywhere near the door – not least because of the stench that came billowing out.

For about a week following the stroke she had been totally unable to walk. She had lain there, propping herself up on her elbows. Somehow she had to resolve her desperate situation without moving out of the flat, and she must have reasoned with herself that if she didn't let anyone know how helpless she was, no-one would discover the truth, no doctor or ambulance would come, and there would be no hospital. Faced with the two horrors, she preferred the one she had previously decided on. If the cats could see to their own needs then she wouldn't have to drag herself on all fours on to the porch, and her secret would be kept. If she recovered from the illness she would make everything right again as soon as she could move. And if she died, none of it would matter. She would no longer know about anything. She had proclaimed often enough that, among many other things, she did not believe in the afterlife. Meanwhile the animal and human excrement lay rotting. Between and around it the piles of food, raw and cooked, had also disintegrated, and were either fermenting or covered in mildew.

They finally managed to bring her under control when the stranger squatted down at the bottom of the door and used the handyman's axe to hit the lock so hard that it burst apart. Trying to defend herself, Emerence fell out on to the porch at their feet. The catastrophe could no longer be concealed. Even the dress she'd worn for God knows how long bore witness to what had been happening – with bits of dried filth swirling down around legs that had always known immaculately clean underwear. Mr Brodarics telephoned for an ambulance, which came immediately. By then Emerence was unconscious. She had passed out the moment she got out into the fresh air. The two doctors – the neighbour and the one from the ambulance – conferred and she was given an injection, but the ambulance did not take her away, as her condition wasn't considered life-threatening. She would have to go to hospital, but first he would send for the decontamination squad. It wasn't just the patient, the flat too needed immediate attention.

The squad arrived. First they scattered some sort of powder around, then they sprayed everything with a liquid. They bundled Emerence up and took her off to the decontamination unit, saying that once they'd dealt with her she could go on to the hospital, but first they would have to clean her from top to toe or they wouldn't be able to put her in the ambulance. As the men were spraying and spreading insecticide around the scraps of stinking food, all sorts of creatures had leapt out and fled through the door, including some huge cats. The Health Department would have to decide what to do about the flat; it couldn't remain as it was, if only out of consideration for the other tenants. It wasn't possible to close it up, and anyway there would be no point. No-one would break in with the rotten food stinking the place out; the door would be boarded up as soon as the team had completed their work.

Now this was what was missing from my life, this image of the old woman lying in her own filth, surrounded by rotten meat and fermenting soup, recovering slowly from paralysis but not yet capable of walking. Józsi's boy, sitting with us on the bench and looking anxious, aroused a very real concern in me that there might be thieves whose stomachs were quite equal to Emerence's Empire. The passbooks had become easy pickings and would have to be recovered. I said I'd wait for Emerence up at the hospital if he'd go in and have a good look for the wretched things. In fact the young man found them immediately. The moment he began to search, there they were, both of them, pushed deep into a gap in the upholstery at the side of the filthy lovers' seat. He'd remembered it had been his father's usual hiding place – the gap you could feel with your fingers between the padding.

My husband was buried in his book – he always had one with him. I sat there, massaging my fingers – it felt as if my left arm was dead. When the old woman finally arrived, we barely recognised her without her usual clothes. She remained mute, letting them do whatever they wanted to her. Her eyes were closed and the muscles around her mouth twitched spasmodically. She was barely conscious. They connected her up to a drip and covered her up. I felt so weakened by shame and grief I would gladly have got in beside her, but the doctor told us to go home. There was nothing we could do, we were only using up her air and anyway, because she was in shock, she wouldn't recognise us. More generally, he didn't know what reassurance he could give us at this stage. The paralysing clot was continuing to be reabsorbed, an X-ray had established that she was largely over her pneumonia, but her heart was so worn out it was impossible to say how much more it could endure, or – he hesitated a moment – how much longer she wanted it to. It was by no means clear that getting better would solve her problems, because her illness, and the circumstances in which she had been brought here, might well have humiliated her in the extreme. Medical science had performed many miracles, but in this case it would have its work cut out. He'd very rarely examined a heart that had been so desperately overworked.

Now for the first time, the very first since we'd stepped into one another's lives, I saw Emerence without her headscarf. In her lightly-fragranced, freshly-washed hair, aged to a snowy white, I glimpsed her mother's glorious, radiant mane, and from the contours of her head I was able to reconstruct the perfect proportions of that other one that had crumbled away so long ago. Emerence, closer to death than to life, had without knowing it been transformed into her own mother. If at our first encounter, our very first, among the roses, when I wondered what sort of flower she might be, someone had told me she was a white camellia, a white oleander or an Easter hyacinth, I would have laughed. But now her secret was out, exposed as she lay before us, with nothing to cover her rounded, intelligent forehead, her beauty radiant even in careworn old age. The body lying in the bed wasn't so much undressed or half-dressed, it was above and beyond every form of costume. The simple, rational garb of terminal illness had translated her into an aristocrat. A truly great lady lay there before us, pure as the stars.

It was then that I realised what I had done in deserting her. Had I been there, I might have been able to use the new-found fame I had already misused to persuade the doctor to leave well alone and to let her stay with us, and that I would look after her – there'd be no need for decontamination, Sutu and Adélka would help, I would bathe her and get her straight. The TV could make their programmes without me. It was more important that I ward off the shame of strangers ravaging her home, whose real nature I alone had seen. When I stood there in Parliament and received my medal, everyone would think I was a success. Only I would know that I had failed at the first hurdle. Now, in the final phase at least, down the last straight, I would have to try to make things right or I would lose her for ever. I would have to work genuine magic, to rise above myself and persuade her that what had happened that afternoon was nothing more than a dream, it had all been simply a dream.

THE CEREMONY

I telephoned twice that night. Emerence's condition hadn't changed, for better or worse. Arriving home, I sliced a few mouthfuls of meat on to a plate and made my way back to the dreaded flat. The doctor had said the animals had scattered, but they might make their way back, since they knew no other home. It was now night, and all was quiet; even if they'd been scared to death, they might have returned by now. I looked behind and beneath everything, the stench almost choking me, but the flat was empty, there wasn't the tiniest sound to be heard. At dawn, when I ran over again, the plate of meat hadn't been touched. For all my hoping, not a single cat had come during the night. And yet I knew it was better for them that they had vanished, that they were no longer there. I was beyond thinking practically or realistically, or even of my own interests. I breathed a silent prayer that one or two at least would turn up, so that when I'd cleaned and restored everything to order, and Emerence was allowed back, some of her loved ones might be with her. But like the decontamination people, I failed to find a single one, alive or dead. When the door came flying in they must have felt as if the whole world was exploding around them. They had fled back into the unpredictability, danger and death from which Emerence had saved them. Never again did a cat prowl around the flat – it was as if some secret signal had scared them off. Viola, who knew the way better than anyone, refused to go anywhere near the wreck of her home. After her death, the flat was refurbished and soon found a new owner, but the dog wasn't interested. The light on the porch shone as before, without the slightest attraction for him, and every summer her lilacs bloomed in vain. He looked for her in all the places they had walked together, but never at her home. He recognised the field where the battle had been fought and lost, even though he hadn't witnessed it himself. On that first morning the street was eerily silent, as when a head of state is grievously ill and the distressed populace mourn in anticipation; a silence not directed from above but genuinely heartfelt. The dog lay on his mat as if his throat had been cut. He uttered not a whimper. When I took him out for his walk, he didn't once raise his head, even to glance at other dogs.

*

In my youth I took a lot of photographs, with a rudimentary camera and no talent whatsoever. Now, when I think back to the day they gave me the prize, it seems to live in my memory like a replica of an old snap I took in which, by some optical illusion, the subject appears to be moving in opposite directions at the same moment. I had taken a picture of my mother, and when I brought the developed roll of film back from the shop, I couldn't believe what I saw. The person I had sought to immortalise was both coming and going, her image progressively increasing and diminishing in size in a double and contrary series of movements. My family would show visitors this ghostly apparition of someone behaving in self-contradictory ways at the same point in space and time. This was how I too must have been on the day they awarded me the prize. During those hours, every thought and every action had its reverse image, within, behind and around me, as in a mirror.

It was a busy day. It began at dawn, when I checked the plate of meat and looked for the strayed cats. From Emerence's flat I dashed off to the hospital. I wasn't alone. Sutu had got there before me, as had Adélka. The three of us together faced an Emerence who was fully conscious, but making it plain by her silence that she was not to be appeased, not prepared even to consider forgiveness. Sutu kept jumping up with a thermos flask, but Emerence didn't want any coffee; or a cool drink. Nothing. In addition to her own christening bowl, Adélka's carrier bag held two other gifts, sent as tokens of friendship. The handyman's wife had prepared some chicken soup, and Mrs Brodarics a bowl of *îles flottantes*. Emerence didn't even glance at them. She wasn't interested, either in the gifts or the message they conveyed. The nurse told us later that visitors had been pestering her the whole day, morning and afternoon. It was the start of a national holiday weekend, and people wanted to get the visit over. But no matter who called, their journey proved fruitless. The neighbours went away rather offended that the old woman hadn't even looked at them.

I hadn't brought anything. I kept looking at my watch to see how much longer I had to sit with her. I didn't trouble her with talk, but now and then I touched her under the sheet. Each time she pulled herself away, but otherwise gave no sign that she was aware of me. After a while an exasperated doctor almost shouted at Sutu and Adélka that it might be too early to say whether she would pull back from the grave, but if she did, one thing was clear: she didn't want anyone to witness the process. Feeding her, bombarding her with plates of food, was a waste of time. She was ignoring them and she wasn't going to eat. Everything she needed to sustain her was being given intravenously. If they really wanted to help, they should leave her in peace. He was right. No matter who was addressing her in hushed tones, they were treated in the way she treated me, shutting her eyes to avoid having to see anyone. What I took away, as I rushed home from the hospital to put on my black dress in preparation for the festivities, and get some sort of order into the careworn features that stared back at me from the mirror, was the image of her eyeless face, resembling nothing so much as a death mask.

The large envelope in which the award notification arrived had also contained several other useful bits and pieces, including a sticker for the taxi's windscreen to allow us all the way through to the carpeted main entrance. This was fortunate, because I was barely capable of walking. I said not a word as we drove there, and very little at the ceremony. It wasn't the first time that I'd been given something in a way or in circumstances that almost crippled me, and now it was happening again, as the pictures taken clearly show. Before the prize-giving had even begun they ushered us into a vast room for photographs to celebrate the great day. Even in that extraordinarily anxious time, all I could think was how tragic, and how comic. The photo of me that would be filed away in an official album would immortalise a quite surreal image – the lingering horror on the face of some ancient heroine who had looked on the Medusa. I had gone to the ceremony from a deathbed. I didn't need a doctor to explain that Emerence would not recover, and that I was in some way responsible. She will never again be completely well, I kept thinking, as I mouthed "thank you" and "yes, but of course" and "very much" and "absolutely"; not because her amazing constitution wasn't capable of surmounting even this hurdle, with the doctor's care and if she would take her medicine. This was about something else, something medical science wasn't equipped to deal with, for which it had no cure. Emerence no longer wished to live, because we'd destroyed the framework of her life and the legend attached to her name. She had been everyone's model, everyone's helper, the supreme exemplar. Out of her starched apron pockets came sugar cubes wrapped in paper and linen handkerchiefs rustling like doves. She was the Snow Queen. She stood for certainty – in summer the first ripening cherry, in autumn the thud of falling chestnuts, the golden roast pumpkin of winter, and, in spring, the first bud on the hedgerow. Emerence was pure and incorruptible, the better self that each and every one of us aspired to be. With her permanently veiled forehead and her face that was tranquil as a lake, she asked nothing from anyone and depended on no-one. She shouldered everyone's burden without ever speaking of her own, and when she did finally need my help, I went off to play my part in a TV show and left her, in the squalor of advanced illness, for others to witness the single moment of degradation in her life.

How can I truly describe her, or trace the real anatomy of her compassion – this woman who peopled her home with animals? Emerence was spontaneously good, unthinkingly generous, able to reveal her orphaned condition only to another orphan, but never giving voice to her utter loneliness. Like the Dutchman, she steered her mysterious ship entirely alone, always into unknown waters, driven by the wind of everchanging relationships. I had long known that the more simple a thing was, the less likely it was to be understood; and now Emerence would never have the chance to make anyone understand either herself or her cats. No matter what she might say, her credibility had been destroyed by the stench that had poured out of her home and the dirt that remained there to be cleaned. The chicken and duck carcasses that surrounded her, the rotting fish and boiled vegetables, testified to what had never been true, that she was mad, not that her body had left her iron will stranded. After the stroke, how could she possibly have cleaned and tidied up, or taken the leftovers out to the bin? It was a medical miracle that she had been able to drag herself out to bring in the gifts of food at the start of her illness. A well-behaved and very mild embolism, which had begun to heal almost immediately, had made her life impossible in the eyes of an entire community, and, by taking the huge birch broom out of her hands, had annulled a lifetime of unstinting work.

As it happened, so many people – family members, distant relations and others – flooded into the presentation room that I didn't even get a seat, and I was glad, because it meant I wasn't trapped in one place. I waited for them to call out my name when I would step up to the table, receive the box and then be free to go to the buffet and pretend to be eating. But I would have much preferred to dash away. I had the feeling that if Sutu, Adélka or anyone else realised what needed to be done and finished the job before me, Emerence wouldn't be the only one to break down, I would too. If I didn't do it myself, I would never again be able to look her in the face. But the ceremony dragged on interminably. It was the greatest formal occasion of my entire life, outshone only by the reception ceremony later that evening. But that too ended on a surreal note, which echoed one of my childhood dreams. I had always wanted to make my way up an immense stairway in a long dress, with everyone watching me and noticing my beautiful figure, how attractive I was. If one can walk badly, just as one can sing out of tune, then that evening I did it. Bent over, I shuffled miserably up the steps, shook whatever hand had to be shaken, and slipped out of the building by a side stairway, certain in the knowledge that if they did let me into the hospital they wouldn't even remark on my dress. If I approached her stark naked or in a borrowed royal gown, Emerence wouldn't even glance at me.

When I think back to that day – the day I was awarded the prize – the one thing I remember, apart from the continuing sense of helpless bitterness, is how very tired I was the whole time. My part finished towards one o'clock. The moment I arrived home I changed into my working clothes and set off for Emerence's flat armed with cleaning implements. I was not going to leave her to her shame. There would be no need for the decontamination men. By the time they arrived I would have removed everything that shouldn't have been there. It was the Saturday of a public holiday weekend and I was sure I'd be able to complete the job, because the sanitation workers would have already begun their break. By the time they pitched up they would find nothing but order and cleanliness. Then the bucket fell from my hands. There on the porch, taking a cigarette break, were the decontamination men. The doctor had forgotten to tell me one thing: the department had ordered immediate action, including the total destruction of all the furniture (with full compensation) in the interests of public health. I stood before them, stunned. I must have looked like a melancholy circus clown in full paint – I had changed only my dress. I still had the make-up on my face and my hair was done up in curls. But who could accept, or even consider accepting what they were about to do? Did they think they could just demolish someone's home, like vandals?

Nothing of the kind, replied the man in charge. First they would clean everything thoroughly, in a neat, orderly way, get rid of the dirt, scrub the floor, the furniture and the walls, then they would burn anything that was still filthy or infected. "So kindly put that bucket down, and don't attempt to help, if you please. There's no place here for private initiatives; this is a job for professionals, for the authorities. But you could, as a repre-sentative of the family, attest that the work is carried out in accordance with regulations. Strictly speaking, it should be the sick person herself, but I'm told she's not all there, so would madam be so good as to act as temporary legal representative and check the inventory to make sure it is accurate, because the owner is to be reimbursed by the city council for any property destroyed? There's no point in complaining. Please don't argue with us. This is official."

I spun on my heel and dashed back home to the phone. I'd been told it was once again possible to contact the Lieutenant Colonel, back on duty for the public holiday after his break. I couldn't speak to him because he was already on his way to the flat – we arrived at almost the same moment. The officials had already begun, and all six were hard at work, wearing rubber gloves, aprons and masks. They shovelled up the putrid slush and dumped it in a decontamination tanker reeking of chlorine, washed everything down very thoroughly with a spray of chemical solution, scrubbed all the furniture and then took it out into the garden, on to Emerence's beloved lawn, where the slime-covered chairs, fouled lovers' seat and wardrobe were left to sprawl. Items that were relatively unscathed or had already been treated were moved a short distance away. And there, against Emerence's lilac bushes, I saw my mother's mannequin, stuck all over with faces, like something in a vision. Pieces of paper, stinking books and scraps of fouled clothing that had fallen into the dirt were piled on to the lovers' seat, along with old calendars, newspapers, boxes and copies of my own works, inscribed to Emerence, which she had insisted on having but had never even opened. When everything was finally outside, and some pieces of furniture and other objects had been separated out from those selected and officially recorded as being for destruction, they sprayed the lovers' seat and chairs with petrol, and set them on fire. As I stood watching the flames I thought of Viola. This was where he had grown up, on this sofa; this was where the old woman had always rested; it had been her bed. And here too the cats – the sometime, never again, eternal cats – had sat, like birds on a telephone wire. Into the conflagration went Emerence's shoes, stockings and headscarves.

Now, for the first time, the Lieutenant Colonel assumed the

rôle of policeman and investigator. Before consenting to the destruction of each item, he examined it carefully, and if it was to escape the bonfire, put it to one side. He even emptied out the drawers. There was now only one thing left in the kitchen. They had disinfected it and scrubbed down all the walls. Out on the lawn, the old furniture looked thoroughly ashamed of itself; everything else was in flames. Passers-by would spot the blaze, stare into the garden and have to be chased away.

By now the only thing left in the kitchen was the safe that blocked the entrance to the inner room. A metal plate announced that it had been made in the older Imre Grossman's steelworks. Its door had been forced open once before, during the Arrow Cross period. This time it contained nothing but the ceramic mugs that had already been removed: if Emerence had had any jewellery or cash, it had vanished in the blaze. We found nothing in the drawers; neither of us bothered to poke around in the corners of the upholstered chairs, which Józsi's boy had already gone through anyway. Towards lunchtime, the men decided they had dealt with everything that had been contaminated; next after the kitchen they would make a start on the inner room. But here the Lieutenant Colonel took charge. The men accepted his argument that its contents weren't a hazard either to the occupant or the neighbours because the safe would have denied Emerence access, and neither animals nor parasites would have been able to squeeze through behind the huge object that had kept the room sealed off. The fact that it was the start of a long weekend focused the brigade's minds on the good and useful work they had accomplished, and the superfluity of attempting anything more. After all, the Lieutenant Colonel served in the local police, he knew the owner, and it was his view that the inner room should be left untouched. They had incinerated most of her kitchen and personal effects – it was quite enough for the old lady to take in. He would personally take charge of whatever else remained to do, and if further sanitation measures were necessary, he would contact the department. If they didn't hear from him, it would mean that he'd found everything in order. Meanwhile he would put his signature (alongside mine) to indicate that he took responsibility in the name of the local police. Everyone was pleased. The squad leader decided that he saw no further source of risk, and that the Lieutenant Colonel's suggestions had merit. But they carried out one final task. With enormous effort, they moved the safe back from the door, so they could say in all conscience that they hadn't neglected anything. There was no key in the door, and they were reluctant to break it down. The condition of the wood, the snow-white, undamaged paintwork showed that Emerence hadn't pulled the safe away, and couldn't have gone into the inner room since the time of the Lieutenant Colonel's visit as a junior officer. They were free to go. There couldn't possibly be any food or insects in there. No-one had been in there for decades. They took their leave and made off.

Meanwhile Józsi's boy had arrived from the hospital, and was staring in horror at the bonfire. He reported that Emerence's condition hadn't changed. The greatest cause for concern was now not her heart but her total passivity. She was giving no help to the doctors, and making it clear that she didn't care what happened to her. My message from Parliament had reached her, and the doctor on the case was concerned, because though she had evidently understood what she was told, she had made not a single comment. She wasn't interested.

My message from Parliament? I had to think what it might be. It was difficult to concentrate, standing on the porch of a wrecked home that stank of disinfectant, while a short distance away Emerence's past life went up in smoke. On to the fire they had thrown pillows, wooden spoons and simple, old-fashioned housekeeping implements, objects that must have held countless memories. I realised with a start that I didn't even know whether I had brought home the box containing the prize, so dazed had I been during the ceremony. Now I remembered that after the photographs were taken, an even more surreal moment had followed. I'd been seated in a separate room with a colleague, and a TV person was grilling me about what I thought and who I had to thank for helping me get where I was. I had named Emerence, as an example of someone who had taken care of everything around me that might have kept me from writing – behind every public achievement there was some unseen person without whom there would be no life's work. The sisters in the hospital had heard the report, the nephew said, and one of them had dashed over to the old woman to tell her they were talking about her, and put a little radio against her ear so she could catch the end. Emerence showed total indifference and said nothing. She was on all sorts of medication, and that might have been the reason for her silence. I knew better. Emerence had understood perfectly well, but she didn't give a damn. She had loathed publicity and polished phrases all her life. I should have been with her in the lion's jaws, at her Golgotha, and I wasn't, and she had had to stand alone and bear what was done to her. So now she had no interest in my chatter, my cheap phrases – I'd spend my time lying on the bier at my funeral service, looking around to see how many people had come. She knew me like the back of her hand. She knew that no shock to my nervous system could ever be so great as to stop me finding the right words.

Józsi's boy took his leave and rushed off home to his family. Before he left he commiserated with me, with a kind of gauche sympathy, over the damage to the kitchen and what I stood to inherit. What they had burned, he said, was a real loss. The thought hadn't even occured to me, and despite my depression I burst out laughing. There goes half my inheritance – hard luck! The Lieutenant Colonel and I sat for a while on the bench, with the handyman's pretty young wife, who was always so kind and attentive to everyone and had brought us coffee. But neither of us drank. We just stirred it and stared into the distance.

"So how did it come to this?" the Lieutenant Colonel finally asked.

My God, because of me, I told him. I failed her. It was a relief to pour out all the details of what had happened while he had been walking in the woods near Visegrad. If I had got through to him, so many things might never have happened, or at least not this way. Even if I had left Emerence in the lurch, he would surely have shared the fateful hour with her, the one hour in her life when she really did need help. He made no comment. He was sufficiently sensitive neither to blame me nor to offer consolation. He asked me what I planned to do. Nothing. If she survived, I would bring the old woman to live with us and abandon our trip abroad. We were due to leave in three days for Athens, as members of the Hungarian delegation to an international peace conference organised by the Greek writers' union, and we'd planned to stay on for a few days by the sea. It was to have been a real rest, but events had swept it all away. Never again would I fail her the way I had – not even if I never saw Athens again. Not even then.

He became angry, and raised his voice. I'd made quite enough mistakes already, did I want to cause even more trouble? Those foreign officials wouldn't be pleased if a delegate failed to arrive. They'd think of every possible reason, including that we'd been banned from travelling. I had no right to involve the country in my private business, so would I please go? There was no point in my staying. If the old woman died the next day there'd be nothing for me to save her from. If she lived – and the doctor was quite certain she would – she could wait for my return.

One short week was nothing. During that time he would take care of everything. The door would have to be replaced, and he'd get the money from the council for what had been destroyed. There was no question of Emerence being prosecuted. If a paralysed body couldn't move, and a paralysed hand couldn't put things in order, that was unfortunate, but it wasn't a crime. The old woman hadn't endangered the public health for fun. He'd get her some furniture, better-looking and more comfortable than her old things. He'd go to the state warehouse, where they stored things from the liquidated homes of people who died intestate. There was no point in arguing with him. International relations were important. He would remain on duty beside Emerence, and my husband and I should go ahead with what was both a professional obligation and what the nation expected of us. By the time we got back Emerence's constitution would have come to its own decision. If she was capable of getting better she'd be on her feet by then; if not, they'd delay the burial. There'd be time for us to open up the other room once I got back. He'd have her empty doorway boarded up that day. When the public holiday was over he'd send someone round from the station to unpick the lock on the inner door and board that up as well. Once we were in, we'd be able to see if any more serious degree of cleaning was necessary. But he didn't think it would. Emerence had never used that room.

Back at home at last, I tore the dress off my back as if it were on fire. I hadn't even had lunch. I wanted to feed the dog, but my husband had already tried and failed. Viola had begun his hunger strike. When we took him out, he dragged himself along beside us; as soon as he had finished marking the trees, he wanted to go home; he didn't bark, he wouldn't drink. The crisis was at its height and there was nothing we could do – he was responding in his own way to what had happened. I couldn't eat either. At the Parliament they had piled my plate high, but there too I had been unable to swallow a morsel, and kept giving meaningless answers to questions I hadn't understood. I lay down for a few moments on the balcony, then leapt up, convinced that if I weren't there to care for Emerence, she would die. I alone could protect her from the horror that had engulfed us both. I rushed over to the hospital ward. Emerence was fully conscious and the doctor was smiling. He told me she was quite a lot stronger and had started to talk. She'd told the nurse to cover her up and make her decent, she couldn't bear nakedness. Later, she demanded a headscarf, and they'd given her a surgeon's cap. She painted a singular picture in it, but it had calmed her down. He thought she was beginning to haul herself out of the pit. In any case we ought to bring her some night clothes and other necessities, as she had arrived with nothing.

While he was talking to me I hardly dared look at her — not just because of what had happened, but because of what she was. She was an incredible sight in her surgeon's cap, not because it didn't sit well on her head but because it did. I saw her as a great professor finally revealing his true, perversely unused, talents. I listened to him in silence. What could I have said? It was of no concern to the doctor that she no longer possessed any towels, night dresses, or any of the things she had once kept in her wardrobe, or that what remained lay sodden with disinfectant, giving off fumes on her lawn. If I brought in my own underwear, which she would have branded indecent, she would become suspicious; she'd recognise my towels. My things weren't linen, like hers. Well, I'd have to think of something.

The moment she saw me enter the room she pulled a hand towel over her face, just as ancient kings, following royal tradition, veiled the spectacle of their death agonies from the eyes of the court. But this wasn't a question of dying — she seemed livelier than she had that morning. It was rather that she no longer wished to see me. Oh well, so be it, I thought. I trudged off homewards, first looking in on Sutu's stall. I asked her, if she intended a visit, to take Emerence whatever she thought appropriate in the way of supplies – towels and toiletries – and to make up some story about why she hadn't brought Emerence's own. Sutu had company. The neighbours were trying to plan who should visit when, and what they should cook for the sick woman. I went off home again, to watch out for the Lieutenant Colonel's men coming to board up the kitchen door. I knew that I would have to wait until he came himself, whenever that was, to see at least that task through with honour. I was close to the limit of what I could bear. Circles and waving lines were dancing before my eyes. I would have given my soul's salvation for someone to shake me and say, "there's no need to weep and wail. You've had a bad dream." I felt more and more that what was happening to us couldn't be real. It seemed impossible that so many terrible things could rain down on one person.

The plain-clothes policemen arrived quite promptly with the boards. These days, coffins are no longer nailed shut but sealed with clamps; but as they reinforced the two half-doors with four upright and four horizontal planks it felt, for me, like the nailing down of a coffin. The hammering proclaimed a multiple burial: the death of a human life, the end of a home, the final chapter in the saga of Emerence.

It was time to set off for the festivities in Parliament, but I didn't feel at all like dressing. It was as if I had been ground in a mortar. First I called in at the hospital. Her condition had again slightly improved. They told me they'd given her a powerful tranquilliser and she was sleeping. She was also taking antibiotics, so there was cause for hope. But when she was awake she was saying very little, and when visitors approached her bed she would cover her face with the hand towel. There were a lot of them, rather too many in fact. They kept shaking her drip.

Emerence was alive and getting better; so I could prepare myself for the most wonderful and glittering night of my life! Well, the dress would pass muster, but no make-up expert could have done anything for my face that day. When I told the first acquaintance I met in the Parliament building that I was sorry but I wasn't feeling up to the occasion, I didn't need to explain. She understood immediately. No-one was at all surprised when I disappeared from the great hall, which that evening was more like a starry summer sky. The glitter of medals and jewellery was all around me, and from all sides the flashing lights of the chandelier danced back off the mirror-polished floor. This was how it must have been in the ballrooms of old. But all I wanted to do was go, get home as quickly as I could and, once there, to crawl into bed. Next morning, I would know with more certainty to what I was sentenced. If she died, there would be no escape. If she lived, then the power that had so far never let me down would, yet again, pluck me back, perhaps for the very last time, from the abyss over which I trembled.

AMNESIA

I had a troubled night, mercifully free from dreams, but I kept waking with a start, thinking I could hear the telephone ringing. I had asked the nursing staff to keep me aware at all times of any change. But the receiver stayed silent. In the morning I took the apathetic Viola for his walk – he was still refusing to eat – then dashed off to the hospital.

Emerence was now visibly improved. They had just finished washing her and a sister was bringing her breakfast in on a little trolley. The moment she caught sight of me through the open door she started to fumble around and clapped the hand towel over her face. With bitterness in my heart, I knocked on the door of the duty nurse who had been with her during the night. There was only good news. If she continued to recover at this rate we could go abroad without any real concern. The old woman was going to pull through, and even be well again. But I wouldn't be able to take her home, not for some weeks, and then only under certain conditions: for instance, there was no possibility of her working. Did she have a home, where she could be cared for? "Of course she does," I thought. "If only she could see it." I replied that we had agreed she could live with us until she was fully herself again, physically and mentally.

Now it really did look as if we were going, and my husband was rushing around sorting out travel documents; but I felt little enthusiasm for the journey. I packed in a sort of reluctant dither, clinging to the ridiculous hope that at the last minute the hosts would withdraw the invitation and the conference would be cancelled. During my last hospital visit I had spoken to the doctor. As far as Emerence's physical condition was concerned, he could let us go with a full guarantee, but what was going on in her mind, he added, was the domain of the neurologist. The embolism, which was now almost fully reabsorbed, hadn't affected the speech centres. It was still hampering her movement, and one leg remained paralysed, but the cause of her silence was psychological. I thought back to the moment when I arrived at the ward and she again covered her face with the wretched bit of towel so that she wouldn't have to see me. Well, I wasn't going to irritate her any further. Anyway, Viola was the only one she wouldn't hide her face from, or look on with hatred. I turned to go, without even wishing her goodbye. As I slowly made my way home I noticed two of the neighbours walking up the hill, carrying casserole dishes. Back home, the dog was maintaining his hunger strike, but by now that didn't interest me either – I was so bitter, so wracked with guilt, and so very tired that nothing mattered. I gathered his things together, his pillow, bowls and cans of dog food, took them over to Sutu and asked her to look after him for a few days while we carried out our mission abroad. He flopped down in her little home with complete passivity, and didn't even look up when I left. It was as if he wasn't our dog. I continued packing. By now I was like a machine, without feelings. I think the only thing I did grasp was that nothing mattered, not even myself. After dinner I phoned the hospital once again, but didn't go. Why should I? Emerence was well, and eating normally. I wished her a speedy recovery, I said politely, and sent her all our greetings. By now my message was as formal as an official communiqué. There was no need for her to worry about her work, I told her via the nurse. Everything was in perfect order. Her friend the Lieutenant Colonel had taken over, and her flat was for her, in exactly the state she would wish, and spotlessly clean. Everything necessary was being done. I was thinking that there would be time for her to find out what had really happened after she had been discharged. I added that she shouldn't expect me (expect? she hadn't even looked at me!) for a few days. I didn't tell her we were going abroad, but I phoned Józsi's boy so he would know why he couldn't contact me if he happened to try, and we left on the night flight for Athens.

We were woken the next morning, in the hotel, by a phone call from the Greek writers' union. I was still so exhausted I couldn't understand what they were saying. It wasn't the language, or even the sound quality. I must have been suffering from a certain amount of shock, because suddenly I couldn't understand anything, in any language. I wouldn't have been able to ask for a glass of water, let alone discuss the prospects for peaceful international coexistence. At the conference we were seated in the front row, and I fell asleep almost as soon as it began. My husband took me back to the hotel, apologising on my behalf to everyone he could, and letting the chairman know what had happened to me earlier, or as much of it as could be explained. I was supposed to lead one of the sessions but by then I was stammering incomprehensibly. They took pity on me, put me in a car, sent me off to a hotel in Glifada and left me there – what else could they have done with a delegate who was so clearly ill?

Through clouds of myrtle, hibiscus, jasmine and thyme, the Aegean lay glittering before me, but I was on the verge of a nervous breakdown and barely conscious of it – it was my husband who pointed these things out to me. When we arrived the water was sapphire blue; as dusk fell it turned amber; when the sun dipped into it it became a burning red. I know this from him; I saw none of it myself. I slept for almost an entire day. When I finally roused myself from this state of near unconsciousness, we wandered slowly around Glifada, though I don't remember a single building, or even the name of the hotel. The only thing I registered was that different fragrances were wafting around me, and that the waves were carrying the corpse of a dog out to sea. I thought of Viola, but distantly, as if I had merely dreamed him, and myself as well, and everything that had happened to me. The prize, Emerence, the decontamination squad, the door split open by the hatchet.

Easter fell early that year, at the beginning of April, and our last day there was Good Friday. I have an enduring memory of going to church, and of the dead Christ laid out on a bier. A gilded basket stood in the doorway, filled with rose petals, and as you entered you scattered them over the body of the Son of God, until He was completely covered. Later, they rang the bell in a little campanile, and all the old people of the village came and stood around it. When they noticed us in the entrance to the church throwing handfuls of petals over the sacred corpse, they came up to my husband and gestured to him that he should join them in mourning the Saviour. I can still see him ringing the bell, his thick blond hair, already shot with grey, tugged by the sea breeze. Next they put the bell rope into my hands. I think I must have pleased them, because I wept copiously all the time I was pulling it, but the tears had nothing to do with the ceremony, they were only for myself. The next day we went back to Athens and left for home from Helicon airport. The journey was as unreal as they always are. The Greek writers were kinder to me than seemed possible, pressing farewell baskets laden with gifts into my hands as to someone who had been knocked over by a goods train. They even accompanied us to the airport. If they never again invite another Hungarian writer, I am the cause.

On the plane we decided that my husband would take the luggage back to the apartment while I went straight to the hospital. By the time I stepped into the lift I was almost whimpering, as my mind went over every possible change that could have occurred. During my time away anything could have happened. What if everything had gone wrong, and Emerence was down in the basement preserved in ice and waiting for burial? Or still living but better off dead because incurable after all? Or perhaps someone had taken her off, without consulting me, to another part of the hospital? After all, legally, these things were in the hands of her nephew.

The only variation I hadn't considered was the one that awaited me. Peals of laughter met me some way down the corridor – her laughter, so rarely heard, which I would have recognised among everyone else's. The nurses smiled at me as I started to run, someone shouted something out to me, but I had no time to listen. I dashed towards the open door where the sound was coming from. The room was dark with visitors. It was clear that here too Emerence had cast her spell over everyone – such large numbers weren't allowed. Half a dozen people were in attendance around her bed, and Sutu was clearing away the remains of a meal, not standard hospital fare, but from the neighbours. Dishes and bowls I didn't recognise, together with jugs and plates, filled the window sills. Emerence was sitting with her back to the door, propped up on pillows, and she must have realised from the faces of the others that some new and interesting guest had arrived. Still laughing, she turned round, no doubt thinking it was the doctor. The instant she saw me the blood rushed into her face, flattening its features, and flooding out every sign of pleasure. As I came in she was already making use of both hands; a few days earlier she'd only been able to grab the hand towel with the fumbling right one. She had been sitting in front of the other guests bareheaded, but the moment she saw me she covered her face. The visitors fell silent. It was a coarse gesture, and it had the same force as if she had struck me. Suddenly everyone had urgent things to do. The women gathered up the dishes and bowls, washed her cutlery and bid each other a chastened farewell. Sutu uttered not a word to me, not even about the dog; all she did was wag her fingers at me from the doorway, and I understood I was to call on her at six o'clock, or she would come to me, and then we could talk. I would never have thought that those people could have so much tact, and would sense with such precise mental antennae that in my absence Emerence had taken my measure and found me wanting, no-one understood exactly why, but there was no point in getting their knickers in a twist about it. Whatever had happened, it was wiser to keep their distance, and more decorous not to get involved.

For the first time, the very first time since the whole avalanche of events had been set in motion, I was filled with resentment and my self-reproach began to fray at the edges. For Heaven's sake, of what crime was she accusing me? That I hadn't left her to die? Without the injection, and the medicine, she would have long since been dead. I hadn't stayed with her because I couldn't. I hadn't wanted to leave her. I didn't go off to enjoy myself but to work. She of all people knew that for me television was work. So, if she didn't want to see me, then that was her choice. Józsi's boy could come and visit, and the Lieutenant Colonel, Sutu, Adélka and the others. I certainly wasn't needed there. I made no attempt to speak to her, or to begin to explain myself. I knew Emerence better than that. She could stay under her headscarf till Judgement Day. There was no point in running back and forth to the hospital, dead tired, for another experience like this, when I could be sitting in a bathtub at home. I went out, and was on my way to the lift when the nurse stopped me.

"Please, Lady Writer . . ." she began, obviously choosing her words. "The old woman isn't well. They just think she is. She's only frisky like that with visitors. The rest of the time she's completely silent."

Then let her stay silent. The nurse could see from my face that she would have to say more.

"The improvement seems impressive, but it's very superficial," she went on, trying another approach. "When you were last here, we weren't in a position to make a full assessment, but now we have. She can move her limbs, but she can't walk. The Lieutenant Colonel comes every day, and we're trying to decide the way forward with him."

Well, if the Lieutenant Colonel was coming every day, I was clearly free to go home. The police choir could come as well, and why not the scouts? I was fussing to no purpose. The whole neighbourhood was plying her with things she needed, and gossip, and the Lieutenant Colonel providing the all-important security. If I wasn't needed, so be it. I'd made my last offer.

"That would be fine, if . . ."

The nurse stopped. I understood well enough what she was unable to express. Words were my *métier*: I shouldn't let any of it hurt me; I should swallow it all, every unjust gesture, every caprice – because not only was she going to stay paralysed, perhaps she wouldn't even live very long. Nonsense. She was going to live for ever; she wasn't my concern.

Now, as I type these words, I have the sense that that was the moment when, for the second, and last, time I decided her fate. That was when I let go of her hand.

"At all events, I'll phone you if she needs you."

"No, don't bother to phone. She won't need me. She won't accept anything from me, either practically or emotionally."

I made my way slowly home, and told my husband what I had found. He listened in silence, and for some time made no reply. I then heard something I had not expected from him, something quite new. It took me completely by surprise. He gave a deep sigh and said, "Poor Emerence."

Poor Emerence! For years I had argued with the local priest about what sort of person she was. Just then I felt closer to his view than I had ever been.

"Sometimes you can be astonishingly unjust," my husband went on. "How can you not have understood what is so clear to everyone else? Everybody else can see it – the whole street, the Lieutenant Colonel. It's so obvious from what you've told me."

What was "so obvious"? I looked at him the way Viola did when my instructions weren't clear and he was trying to decode my imprecise signals and commands. What crime had I committed over and above what had happened on that wretched day? Ever since then my life had been one of constant self-reproach. It hadn't left me for one minute. The night of the prize ceremony was filled with unconscious terror, Athens had been pure hell, and when I wasn't asleep my cares circled round me like wolves.

"Emerence is ashamed, before you and before the entire street. She pretends she's lost her memory because that way it's easier to bear the thought of lying there in full view, in all her filth, with her human dignity smashed to pieces. Do I have to teach you, of all people, what shame is? You, who effectively brought this upon her? Wasn't the 'day of action' your doing? You handed her over chained and bound, the cleanest of the clean, with all her secrets, when you should have protected her, whatever the cost. You were the only person on earth whose words would have induced her to open her door. You are her Judas. You betrayed her."

So now I was Judas? Wasn't it enough that I was half-dead and desperate for rest? I'd had quite enough of everything, and I didn't think this was the time for a lecture. All I wanted was to lie down. Sutu had promised to come at six o'clock. I asked my husband to wake me if I was still asleep and I crawled into bed, away from myself and from Emerence. I thought I would be overwhelmed by exhaustion, but even then I couldn't relax, and I was the one who opened the door when barking and scratching signalled Viola's return. He was very thin, but happy. For the first time in his life he was truly glad to see us. It was as if he wanted us to feel he was back at home again, and since he'd found us, perhaps his nightmare was finally at end and Emerence would appear as well. I thanked Sutu for taking care of him and asked her what I owed her. She named a reasonable sum, and I paid her. But she had no intention of leaving.

"Please Lady Writer," she began, "there's something you should know, if the doctor and sisters haven't told you already. Emerence is getting better, but in a very strange way. She remembers only bits of what happened; there are gaps. She has no idea what happened earlier – not the hatchet, or the ambulance or the way she struggled. She asked us how she was brought there, and I told her that you had arranged it. The thing she was most concerned about was whether her flat is properly locked up, and we told her that it was, straight away, and that the writer lady has the key. She knows the story the Lieutenant Colonel instructed us to tell her. One day she didn't answer when we knocked on her door, so we were worried and ran over to you, but she didn't answer for you either. By then we were sure something was seriously wrong. The doctor gentleman forced the door open (the whole street referred to him as the doctor gentleman – I tried to visualise him, without much success, with a crowbar in his hand), and we found her unconscious in the entrance. The handyman bundled her up and we brought her in Mr Brodarics' car to the hospital, where she'd been looked after ever since. Not a word has been said about the decontamination people, or the cats, or anything. And no-one has tipped her off that you went to Athens. So please tell her everything's all right, that you locked the flat up straight away but you go over every day and see to everything. There's plenty of time for her to find out that her room has gone, and all the horrible things that were in there. Everyone is treating her very gently. The Lieutenant Colonel lies like a leaking tap and so does the Szeredás boy. After everything she's been told, she even believes she'll recover. I just don't know how she will take it when she finds out the truth."

She was expecting praise, and had probably earned it, but I said nothing. The whole neighbourhood had passed the test of honour, and of tact, but I stuck to my silence. I knew the real Emerence. A flash of insight had finally penetrated the massive darkness, and I began to find my bearings again. Emerence's amnesia? What a joke! How could you reconcile that with the towel over her face? All her life she'd been like royalty, adjusting her memory to suit political reality. What I had finally realised didn't surprise me. It terrified me. When we said goodbye and shook hands, Sutu remarked on how cold my fingers were. She hoped I wasn't sickening for something.

My husband had reached exactly the same conclusion, so there was no need to argue about it. I threw myself down in the chair and ran my fingers through Viola's coat. I had to decide what to do. I called the Lieutenant Colonel; he didn't answer, but they promised to tell him I'd tried to contact him. I phoned the nephew and actually got through. He was living in the same optimistic fairyland as Sutu. What a Heaven-sent mercy that his aunt didn't remember anything! Later on, once the flat had been refurbished and painted, with a nice clean kitchen and a new door waiting for her, we'd be able to console her for what had happened. My medical knowledge was no greater than his, but I knew Emerence better. I had watched her destroy the celebratory meal she had prepared in vain. I had wandered with her through the labyrinth of her memories. Forget her cats? Impossible. If she had, she would never have asked about the flat. No, she remembered everything. She just didn't dare to ask openly. In the early days the medication would have caused mental blankness, washing certain images from her mind, but as the days went by the procession of figures that had been reduced to mere shadowy outlines would have become ever more brightly coloured. If she could recognise Sutu, and everyone else from the street, then everything about her home must be firmly in place in her consciousness, including the animals living in it, the half-prepared duck, the putrid fish — everything that surrounded her during that final period when she was temporarily paralysed. She was keeping it a secret because she hoped she could battle her way through this too, just as she had from the depths of so many chasms throughout her life. Poor, unhappy Emerence, to whom no-one would tell the truth, and who didn't even dare ask, but was left reaching out after shadows! So what was I being so sensitive about? This wasn't the time to consider who she might have offended or how, if indeed a sick person can give offence. Off you go, back to the hospital. In this drama there's only one protagonist, and it's not you, it's Emerence. It's a one-woman show.

She wasn't alone. The medical professor's wife had come to see her and Emerence was responding to her in a lively, cheerful manner. Apparently this lady had also spoken in support of her. The hospital must have been amazed that this old woman mattered to so many people. The beautiful young woman had been an unexpected and flattering visitor, and Emerence didn't dare carry out the face-covering ritual in front of her. But the moment she left us together, Emerence reached for the hand towel. I hadn't been mistaken, not in the least mistaken. Her brain was functioning perfectly. The professor's wife had been innocent — she obviously knew nothing — so the veil wasn't appropriate for her; but for me it was. As I approached the bed she donned it as a priest dons his surplice, and with it she distanced herself both from me, and her shame. I looked around. On the table, beside various medical accessories, was the placard proclaiming *NO VISITORS*, which had been tacked up outside while the battle to save her life continued. I hung it from the door handle out into the corridor, then plucked the towel from Emerence's head and threw it on to the other, unoccupied bed. She couldn't reach it; she would have to look me in the face. Anger and hatred blazed in her eyes.

"Let's stop this," I told her. "If you've come to hate me so much because I didn't leave you to die, I can accept that. But don't keep on covering your head. Tell me straight, because this can't go on any longer. I wanted to help. It didn't work out the way I'd planned, but I meant well, even if you don't believe me."

She never once took her eyes off me. It was like facing an interrogator and a judge in one person. And then, unexpectedly, tears sprang to her eyes. I knew what she was weeping for – her secret which was no longer a secret, her animals whose fate she dared not even ask about, the hideous parody of her former impeccable conduct, the hatchet, the death of her legend, and my betrayal. She said nothing, but I understood all the same that if I could have accepted that in her impotence she had chosen death, and had I not made her degradation public, while she was still alive, before the street which had held her in such high esteem, then she would have felt I loved her. Emerence didn't believe in Heaven but in the present moment. When I made her open her door her whole world was overturned, and she had been buried under it. Why had I done it? How could I have been capable of doing it? Not a word of any of this was said, but the unspoken sentences hovered between us.

"Emerence," I began again, "if it had been the other way round, would you have let me die?"

"Of course," she replied, drily. Her tears had ceased.

"And you'd have no regrets?"

"None."

"But even if I hadn't managed to save you, it would still have all come out: the fish, the cats, the filth."

"And so? You could have left me to die, and then it wouldn't have mattered what came out. What does a dead person know, or see, or feel? It's only you who imagine that they'll be waiting for you up there, and that when Viola dies he'll go there too, and your home and everything else will be just as it is now, an angel will bring you your typewriter and your grandfather's desk, and things will continue. What a fool you are! To the dead, it's all one. The dead person is a zero. Why on earth haven't you worked it out? You're old enough."

So it wasn't just shame, but anger and hatred too. So be it. But don't expect penance from me. I'm not Adélka.

"Then what's the point of the tomb, Emerence? Why gather up your mother and father and the twins in that fairy-tale crypt? Wouldn't the wild mallow beside the ditch be enough? And the weeds."

"For you, but not for me, and not for my dead. Your family can lie among the mallows. The dead may not feel, but they do expect to be honoured, you owe it to them. But what do you know about honour? You think if you toss me a nice juicy bone from Parliament I'll put my hand on my heart and be your slave, like Viola? Well, don't bank on it. You know how to make grand statements, but to stay when you're needed, when you're saving my life, to cover my misery from the eyes of the world, no, you didn't have time for that. Get out of here, go and make another pronouncement. You actually had the nerve to say you had me to thank for the prize?"

She knew what she was doing, saying all this to my face. We knew each other. I stood up. I hadn't gone through the door when she called after me.

"Did you at least pick up the rubbish? Are you taking proper care of my pets? Did you patch up some sort of door?"

For a single, tantalising moment I thought I would tell her that only half her flat remained, the door had vanished and the animals were lost. Had I yielded to the temptation I should perhaps have never got over that night, but luckily it was one mistake I didn't make. I replied that no-one, apart from me, had set foot in her home. The instant the doctor hauled her out my husband and Mr Brodarics had put the door back together and nailed her pastry board over the gash, so no animal could get through. By the time they'd settled her in here I had seen to everything – that same night. All I'd had to do the next day was deal with a few finishing touches. Cleaning up hadn't been easy, but I managed it. I took the rubbish away in a bucket, but not to her bins. Instead I divided it among the ones out in the road, on the opposite side of the street, so no-one would realise it was my doing. The words flowed like water from a spring; it was like the public reading of a novella. The cats were well, except of course for the one who'd died. I had buried him under a wild rose. They were being fed on meat because I didn't have time to cook. And now I had to dash off home, because we hadn't eaten yet – only the cats had – and I was afraid I'd get caught in the rain.

I was on my way. It had been more than enough for one day. But she stopped me with a single word: "Magdushka!"

Only my parents had ever called me that. No-one else. I stood rock-still, waiting for what came next. My heart was thumping; conflicting emotions clashed inside me – the shame of having lied, hope, guilt, and a flooding sense of relief. She raised her hand slightly, summoning me to her bed. Once again, she pronounced my name. The word seemed to hold something else, something more, something hidden, a secret tremor, like an electric current. The tone was low, almost rasping, but not unpleasant – like the drawing back of a curtain, or a soft husk splitting open. I sat down again beside the bed, and she took my hand, examining my fingers minutely as she spoke.

"All that horrible stinking mess? All that rotten filth? With these useless little hands? And all on your own, so no-one else would see? At night?"

I turned my head away. I couldn't bear her look. Suddenly she opened her mouth and caught my hand in her toothless gums. It was the most astonishing, most truly shocking, moment of my life. Anyone seeing us would have thought us perverted or insane. But I knew what it meant, just as when Viola was unable to express himself through sounds – I was so familiar with his nibblings, the ecstatic dog-language of boundless happiness. Again and again she thanked me. She had been wrong, I hadn't betrayed her, in fact I had saved her. She hadn't become an object of ridicule. The neighbourhood knew absolutely nothing, had not seen the filth. She hadn't lost face. And now she could go home.

There aren't too many moments of my life that make me shiver with horror when I think back on them. But this is one. Never before or since have I so palpably felt this blending of horror and ecstasy. All was well at last – Emerence's cats running around us playing chase, the shutters guarding the re-assuring gloom, the lovers' seat – the whole empire of Emerence that had long gone up in smoke. I pulled my fingers away. It was too much to bear. I became aware that my tears were flowing. She caressed me around the eyes and kept asking what could be wrong, because now she could go home without shame, and she promised she'd get well quickly.

I tidied up my face before leaving. She gathered up the cakes and bars of chocolate and instructed me to take them to Viola.

SUTU

Her recovery proceeded smoothly. The thick tresses around her finely-formed, unlined face had grown back strongly after their cropping at the time of the decontamination. Everyone noticed that some sort of weight had been lifted from her mind – the doctors, visitors from the street, the Lieutenant Colonel; but the more relaxed and cheerful Emerence became, the more my anxiety grew. I had become inextricably tangled up in lies from which there was no escaping. So I had another conversation with the doctor who was treating her. He was less than delighted by the way things had turned out, but he too was unable to offer an alternative. We would have to delay telling her the truth till the last possible moment; meanwhile the Lieutenant Colonel would have the kitchen painted and new fittings installed, and a new door delivered. I didn't waste my breath explaining to him that even if the flat was fitted out with a suite from Windsor Castle it wouldn't satisfy her, because what she loved was irreplaceable. Had she wanted to replace her furniture she would have done so long before, but God knew what sort of memories were linked to her kitchen. There were no two items in it that matched. And there was another problem. It wasn't just that she'd disapprove of everything, but that her health would be put at risk. If there was new furniture then something must have happened to the old, and if that was the case, she'd know exactly what I had lied to her about. "You must understand," I said to the doctor, "this old woman is being kept alive by the belief that I kept her secret, that I put everything in order, and she wasn't shamed before the entire street – so she can go home with confidence, and she won't even be alone because the cats will be waiting for her." "She'll survive," he comforted me. I looked at him without hope. He hadn't understood. Nor did he understand Emerence.

Meanwhile the entire neighbourhood was on the lookout for the cats, in the hope that she might get them back at least. But I couldn't even provide a description of them, having seen them only once. I remembered that there had been black-and-white ones among them, and some with stripes, and we actually found the corpse of a grey, run over in the main road, which no-one had claimed and which might have been one of hers. There was no trace of the others. By now we were all dreading what, sooner or later, was bound to happen. Emerence's porch was once again crammed with people, the circle growing steadily as one after another they came, with footstools and kitchen stools, to talk over her problems. And their business was serious. Sutu had apparently become their leader. Even the stray cats were brought before her for inspection. Adélka was her zealous assistant, though she had never set eyes on the animals. The only one who refused to step on to the porch was Viola. He could sense an unfamiliar odour, some hostile emanation, and he hated it.

Around this time he embarked on a course of behaviour that went on for months. Luckily it didn't end in tragedy, thanks to the Lieutenant Colonel, who sent a circular with his details round all the police stations, local councils and dog wardens stating that a stray dog who answered to the name of Viola had taken to wandering and was looking for his owner, so please take him home to me. Shortly after our return from Athens, Viola began to absent himself regularly for days on end, scouting round the neighbourhood, sometimes as far as the woods, looking for Emerence. On one occasion he came for me, summoning me with his bark. He was in a fever of excitement, frantic and obviously wanting to show me something. He ran across two streets, leading me to a fence, then looked at me guiltily as if asking me not to be angry – the thing he'd dragged me out for was no longer there, but he had seen it. I knew why he had called me. He must have found one of Emerence's cats in that garden. It hadn't run away from him because it knew him, but while he was fetching me it had hidden further off. Later, we had our suspicions about another corpse, found by the women near the market. It was a black-and-white cat with a star on its breast, which had been savaged by a dog. Such an end was comprehensible, given that Emerence had brought all her cats up not to fear their ancient enemy or think dogs would harm them. The rest had vanished, as if they had never existed.

By now I was no longer going to the hospital every day. I didn't have time, and I didn't see the point. At first I tried to hide from my cares and concerns, but it was no use. I would have loved to write, but as I've said, creativity requires a state of grace. So many things are required for it to succeed – stimulus and composure, inner peace and a kind of bitter-sweet excitement – and these elements were missing. When I did think of Emerence, I had no sense of relief that she was still living. Instead I was confused and helpless, with a persistent feeling of shame.

One day Adélka ran across to call me over to the porch. The neighbours were there and we needed to start talking again.

Sutu came straight to the point: what did I think would happen? What would become of Emerence when she was strong enough to come home? I said that, as far as I knew, it was as we had agreed. She wouldn't be allowed to work at first, and while she was recuperating she would be our guest. Her mind and her hands were functioning normally, but she couldn't walk unsupported. But the doctors were very reassuring, it was only a matter of time. I was holding forth like a bad actor, acting worse than usual, in a bad play. Sutu stopped me with a wave of the hand.

"But you see, she'll never be able to work, and there's no question of a full recovery," she stated, almost cheerfully, as if she were trying to persuade me of the exact opposite. "Emerence is finished, dear writer lady, if not now, then within a year, and this is a service flat. The building has to be seen to. The entrance and the stairway have to be cleaned. This place needs a new caretaker. You can't go on sharing out the chores among the tenants till Judgement Day. It wouldn't be possible even if Emerence hadn't taken on a workload that's more than enough for five people."

The handyman's wife snapped back at her, as if her own reputation had been attacked. "That's not the way to talk," she shouted. In the name of everyone in the villa, she declared, they would never abandon the old woman. And yes, they would carry on sharing out the chores, and wait for her to get better, however long it took. Everyone was doing something. It was what they had done up till now, and what they would do in the future. What was Sutu thinking? They weren't going to put Emerence out on the street.

"Who said anything about the street?" Sutu gave her a look. She was like Fate herself, the classical Moira. But she was only being realistic. As I now know, Sutu was the only one amongst us who had thought every possibility through, in a responsible way, and she alone had the courage to face up to them. "She needn't end up on the street; if the Lieutenant Colonel helps her they'll get her into a nursing home, or one of the better old people's homes, or her nephew might take her in; or, if she really means it, the writer lady will. But the building must be attended to, the snow swept, and not just from here but from the other houses as well, according to the contract she signed. The writer lady has no help of her own. If she can't manage for herself, how does she think she can take on anything more?"

Silence. Then everyone started to talk at once. It was like the Pentecostal outpouring of tongues, but in reverse — suddenly no-one understood anyone else. I was the first to speak up: of course Emerence could live with us. Someone would step in to take over the houses. She'd be happy with us, she liked us. Sutu burst into laughter, and there was nothing good-natured about it.

"Come off it," she said. "You don't actually imagine she'd stay with you? Emerence will live only while she believes she has her own home. Shouldn't we be thinking about what's going to happen when she finds out the truth? She hasn't heard it yet. It's very good of you all to share the work out amongst yourselves, but have you actually asked her if she wants to be supported in this way? The writer lady will take her in. Good. And she'll provide for her. But is that the solution she wants? Does Emerence want someone else to keep her? Has she agreed to that?"

Adélka was sniffling away and dabbing at her eyes, but otherwise everyone was silent. I was the most silent of all. From the outset I had been alarmed by what Sutu was saying.

"What are you playing at here?" Sutu continued. "You know her. She's not going to stay with anyone, anywhere. Once they send her home and she finds out about her flat, you'd better watch out. She's already quite strong, so you'd better hide that axe. She went after the ambulance men, and once she's home, we're next, whether it's the doctor, or the writer lady, or the Lieutenant Colonel — whoever let them set fire to her furniture. Emerence doesn't want any kind of life. She needs her own life, and she doesn't have that any more."

The meeting broke up, leaving everyone depressed. Adélka

was so shaken she was incapable of protest. Sutu packed her things up and left. I left too. We had got nowhere. Mrs Brodarics kept the tenants back and, with the help of the handyman's wife, drew up a plan for Emerence's replacement on a sheet of lined paper. I was touchy and irritable for the rest of the day and I didn't sleep well either, like someone terrified of some unforeseen change for the worse. I really did expect trouble – either something new or a twist of the old – and not without cause. A week later Mr Brodarics, who had been chosen at the tenants' meeting to act as caretaker in Emerence's absence, phoned in some distress to tell me that Sutu had called on him and announced that if her turn ever came, and the tenants wished it, she would be happy to give up the stall, hand back the permit and take full responsibility for Emerence's round of jobs – everything that went with the position. So what was my verdict? What did I say to that?

I had always analysed the night at Gethsemane from Jesus' point of view, but now for the first time it occurred to me how it must have felt for John say, or Philip, when they realised that the man who'd accompanied them on their journey, whose powers they understood better than anyone – they had after all seen Lazarus and Jairus' daughter raised to life – and from whom they had, until the very last moment, drawn both strength beyond understanding and the certainty of life eternal, had been betrayed. Mr Brodarics asked me again, what did I say to that? Nothing. It was shameful, a disgrace. I put the receiver down. Sutu had the nerve to apply! Sutu, who was a hopeless case until Emerence, with the help of the Lieutenant Colonel, got her the stall. Sutu, whom she had fed and given clothes when she found her wardrobe bare. Well then, now anything was possible! But I wasn't just angry, I was beginning to panic. Mr Brodarics had resisted her offer for the time being, but if Emerence returned home unable to work the residents would sooner or later have to act. They couldn't stand in for her for the rest of her life. They were either very old, or running around performing countless tasks themselves. They almost all had second jobs; there was no-one who could be reached at any hour to deal with snow, or a burst pipe, the postman or the chimney sweep; and the authorities weren't going to accommodate themselves to the personal schedule of whichever tenant happened to be on duty. Either Emerence would make a full recovery and do everything she had done before, or she would have to vacate the villa and stay, perhaps, with us, since she would have to give up the flat with the job. My God, what would I do with her, if she couldn't walk, or take charge of things, wash, cook, go shopping or dash about with the christening bowl? What on earth was I going to do?

The next day, at the hospital, I was told the chief doctor wanted to see me. I already knew what he wanted to say. He resembled a certain kind of critic. Those who play by the unwritten rules of the craft toss in something inconsequential, some faint praise, for the writer to chew over like an old dog, then shoot him while he gnaws on his bone. With a shining face he extolled Emerence's amazing ability to heal, the strength with which, after the initial wave of depression, she had begun to fight for her life, the positive results, the kilograms of pure muscle she had gained. Was I aware that cataracts were forming in both her eyes? No? No matter, it was just a sign of age. It hadn't bothered her so far because she never read, and she would still be able to watch television. I was waiting for the gunshot, and it came.

"I must ask you to start getting her used to the idea that she must leave and go home. In any case, it's what she now most wants. She talks about it, and longs to be in her garden. She says she's missed the early part of summer; and it's her favourite time of the year. I know that the truth has been kept from her.

That was wise. She would never had got better if she'd known everything from the start. But now she has her strength back, and in my judgement she'd be able to face the facts. So would you be kind enough to ask the Lieutenant Colonel to get things ready in the flat, because we're sending the old woman home?"

"Not yet," I replied. "It isn't possible yet. We haven't made any decision about her future. The flat is just as it was after the decontamination. Nothing's been done; we have to give it further thought. We can't do what you are asking. It's unthinkable."

"Not at all," the doctor replied. "It's not even worth arguing about. I'm keeping her here for one more week, and you can sort things out during that time. Do bear in mind that she will need help with everything. But as for walking, she won't be up to that for the foreseeable future, if ever. However, we won't leave her without state help. We've spoken to the local council about it. You'll have to organise someone to do the shopping and cooking for her, because she can't get out of bed. And she'll need a bedpan. But the district nurse will be there for the injections, and to bathe her and change the bed. If you can't sort things out among her family and friends, then obviously the Lieutenant Colonel will find a suitable place for her. But from all the sympathy and affection we've seen, we feel sure someone will take her in."

It was like listening to Sutu. The same conviction.

"But, doctor, what will happen if she doesn't want to live with anyone?" The moment the words were out I realised what nonsense I was talking: *doesn't want, doesn't wish, won't, might object*. How could she? Everyone knew that from now on things would only ever happen to Emerence. Nothing would depend on Emerence, except death.

The doctor gazed at me benevolently, as if he hadn't heard my last foolish remark. He stood up and grasped me by the hand.

"Let us understand one another. I don't let her go with a light heart. Everyone here likes her, and so do I. Her constitution is a gerontological miracle, and so is her mind. She's an unusual case. But I can't keep the bed from someone whom we can put back on their feet, and the old woman, I am sorry to say, will most probably remain paralysed. We can't keep her here until she dies. Believe me, as it is we've done more for her than for anyone else. And there's something else. This is perhaps the most important thing of all."

I waited for the second shot. The nice juicy bone had fallen from its mouth, but the animal was still alive. And what I heard next was indeed the most important item of all.

"Don't put her in the situation where the ambulance men take her to a room she's never seen before, freshly painted and filled with brand-new furniture, and then move her somewhere else because she can't stay on her own. At this moment she's strong enough to take it, so tell her the truth: the hatchet, the decontamination, everything. You must tell her. And tell her here, where I can treat her. Don't let her get back home and hunt for her old furniture and her cats. I've already discussed this with the neighbours, and they tell me she's closest to you, and that you are the one to tell her. After all, it was you who set everything in motion. And you're the one she has to thank for her life. If you hadn't got her to open her door, she would have been dead within forty-eight hours."

Yes, I thought, she can truly thank me for this life we've rescued her into; for the lost or dead cats who eased her loneliness; for the cherished belongings that went up in smoke; and for the generous offer by the residents to share the tasks – which they so obviously can't keep up in the long term. Emerence would never go into a home, not if they killed her. Only her own will do. But after all that's happened, where is that? She won't be happy with us. She needs her own things, her private belongings, about her. And how would I fit a paralysed patient, needing constant attention, into our lives? And since it's the only option, when would I have time to bring her the bedpan, wash her, cook for her, keep her from getting bedsores? The district nurse won't come every day, and what shall I do when I have to be away from home? And what will my husband do? Will she even come if I ask her? She'll reject the idea straight away, but then where will she go? There's no room with anyone else. József's boy won't have her. The Lieutenant Colonel is now married for the second time. There's no other way. She can only come to us.

I set off home, wondering all the while what I should do if she raised objections when I invited her. I didn't even look in on her but hurried off to talk things over with my husband. It was clear that something was afoot at Emerence's villa. People were swarming round a parked goods truck in the street outside. I went along to see what was happening. They were painting the walls of her kitchen and renovating the porch. The boarding had been removed and someone was fitting a door in place of the damaged one. Women were busy scrubbing – the Lieutenant Colonel's brigade of convicts. So the work was under way. I carried on to our apartment to use the phone. The Lieutenant Colonel couldn't understand what was bothering me now. The door was in place; the painting done and the floor freshly scrubbed, the furniture would be arriving in a few days and the whitewash was drying fast in the summer heat. So what was the problem? Why all this desperation?

What was the problem? Couldn't anyone see? I told him about Sutu's betrayal. This did shake him, but he immediately insisted that the law would protect Emerence. They couldn't drive her out of her flat. They couldn't even pressure her to move out, because it was only an assumption that she wouldn't ever again be fit to work. And anyway, the committee would have to wait two years, since that was the rule governing sick leave. And a great deal could happen in two years. She might recover, or the poor thing might die. Until then, the neighbours would have to cope with things the way they were, and he'd make sure there was a district nurse. So what was I worrying about? Everything was under control. We'd got over the critical period. Everyone had the right to get ill. What he was asking was, would I see through what I had begun? Emerence was still alive because I had added the weight of her trust in me to the neighbours' touchingly beautiful lies, but there was no longer any need for them. I should now crown my achievement, soften the bad news with the good, and explain that what had been lost had taken a new form, that the old home and the new one were one and the same, and were waiting to receive her.

So he didn't grasp my meaning either; or perhaps he couldn't. We were dealing in such different currencies. Emerence's dictionary featured *filth, scene, scandal, laughing stock of the street* and *shame*. His contained *law, order, solutions, solidarity, effective measures*. Both phrasebooks were accurate, it was just that they were in different languages. So, could he at least do this: would he explain to Emerence what really happened? I hadn't been there, I'd gone off to the TV studio; she knew who'd stayed, and who hadn't.

"I'm not afraid of doing that," he replied. "Emerence is a wise woman. You underestimate her if you are scared to tell her that you saved her, not for a hopeless defeat, but for this strangely happy ending — because that's what it is. I'll tell her everything, this afternoon. Don't say a word to Sutu, there's no need even to greet her. I'll tell Emerence about her betrayal, don't you worry. That'll get her going better than any medicine. Her anger might even get her back on her feet. What Sutu's in for, if she dares show her face, will be something special.

Anyway, I'll see to all that, but I have to say I am disappointed in you. It's just lucky you kept your nerve until this last and final phase."

I had of course endured hours similar to what I went through that afternoon. I was filled with the same tension I'd experienced when my husband underwent lung surgery, or the night before my parents were buried. I lay where my mother had slept, with a Viola who never once stirred. Somewhere around six o'clock Adélka called in to tell me, with a worried look on her face, that I wouldn't believe it, but they wouldn't let her in to see Emerence. She had no idea what had happened. There was a sign outside her door banning visitors, and when she spoke to the nurse about taking her soup in she was asked to take it away. Emerence didn't want anything, and for the time being she was not to be visited. The handyman's wife hadn't been let in either, and she'd also come away with a bag full of things. So the axe has struck, I thought, now I can go. I dragged myself to my feet. On the street outside our door Sutu, obviously driven by some innate work ethic, was sweeping like someone in a dream. There was no suggestion of guilt in her face when she noticed me, rather a look of deep thought. Perhaps she had heard from Adélka about the new visiting restrictions and was wondering whether what had happened would help or hinder her cause, much as she'd done when she put her cards on the table on Emerence's porch.

Along the road leading to the hospital I met two of the neighbours making their way back with their christening bowls. The women were worried that Emerence must have taken a turn for the worse. The sky was a dark steel-grey, a cold front had blown in and the wind was tearing at the branches in the avenue; perhaps she was sensitive to it and that was why the nurses had shut her away from everyone. They hadn't guarded her so strictly even when the poor thing seemed to be dying. So I should go on up – perhaps they would tell me the truth.

I made my way up and removed the sign forbidding entry. The nurse saw me, and nodded. Clearly she had had instructions. As I went through the door I was thinking that the Lieutenant Colonel had been right. I had thrust myself into her life, and now that I had dared strike the fatal scissors from the hand of Atropos I ought to have the courage to look around the Fates' workshop. Emerence was lying with her back to the door. She didn't turn round, but she recognised my footsteps, just as the dog did. The one striking difference from the day before was that once again her face was veiled. But I knew she was aware of my presence.

We both stayed silent. Never had there been a more mysterious, more mute or inscrutable figure than hers that afternoon, with the dark descending and the branches beating on the windows. I sat down next to her, with the *NO VISITORS* sign in my hands.

"How many cats are left?" she finally asked, from behind her veil. Her voice was every bit as unreal as her invisible face.

At this stage it would make no difference.

"Not one, Emerence. Three of them we think we saw dead. The others are lost."

"Keep looking. The ones that are still alive will be hiding in a garden."

"Certainly. We'll do that."

Silence. Twigs rustled against the window panes.

"You told me a lie. You said you cleaned everything up."

240

"There was nothing left to do, Emerence. The decontamination people had done it."

"And you let them?"

"I can't go against an order. Nor can the Lieutenant Colonel. A tragedy occurred, a disaster."

"A tragedy! You could have gone to the Parliament later that day, or the next."

"Even if I'd been at home, I would have got nowhere trying to pester people. I'm telling you, there's a regulation covering such cases, a public health measure. I can't overrule something like that."

"You weren't at home? Where did you go?"

"Athens, Emerence. There was a conference. You'd forgotten about it, but we did speak about it some time ago, at home. We were delegates. We had to go."

"You went, when you didn't even know if I would live?"

I had no answer to this. I watched the raindrops slide slowly down the window. That's how it was. I had gone away.

Suddenly she pulled the scarf from her face and glared at me. She was pale as wax.

"So what sort of people are you? You and the Lieutenant Colonel? The master is the most honourable of you all. At least he never lied."

Again no answer was possible. It was true that my husband had never lied. But then again, the Lieutenant Colonel was one of the most admirable men I had ever met. As for me, I am what I am. And this is what I am: I went off to Athens. I would have gone though my own father were in a life-threatening condition – because the Foreign Ministry of Greece would have put a certain construction on things if the official Hungarian delegate stayed away; because, after the prize, my being named a delegate was a gesture from the state which I couldn't ignore; because I am a writer and have no personal life; and because things happen to me as they do to actors. I have to play a part, even if there are problems at home.

"Get out of here," she said softly. "You never bought a house, though I asked you to – and I had planned so many treasures for you to have in it. You never had children, though I promised I would bring them up. Put the sign back on the door. I don't want to see anyone who witnessed my shame. If you'd allowed me to die, as I made up my mind to when I realised I would never be capable of real work again, I would have watched over you from beyond the grave. But now I can't stand having you near me. Just go."

So she did believe in the next world, after all. She had simply been provoking the priest, and us as well.

"From now on you can do what you like. You don't know what it is to love. And yet, I believed you might, one day. You would rescue me for this, for what's left? And you'd even take me into your home and look after me? Idiot!"

"Emerence!"

"Get out. Go and make a speech on television. Write a novel, or run off back to Athens. If they send me home from here, don't any of you try to come anywhere near me, Adélka has left her scissors here and I'll use them on anyone who comes near me. Why are you so concerned about my fate? There are plenty of care homes. This is the most wonderful country in the world, and I've the legal right to be sick for two whole years. That's what your friend said. Now go. I've things to do."

"Emerence, with us . . ."

"With you! You as a housewife, you looking after me! And the master! Go to hell! There's only one sane person in your flat – Viola."

Her supper was beside her, untouched. In her exasperation she moved slightly and almost knocked the dish over, but I didn't dare go near. I really believed she would stab me with the scissors. She was now lying on her back, staring at the ceiling. I could see very little of her as I went out. I didn't say goodbye. I ran home in the rain, wondering all the time what else I should have said. But I could think of nothing.

An hour later I felt calmer. I believe I had been unconsciously prepared for even worse. But the illusion of peace didn't last long before my husband brought my fears flooding back. He was pacing back and forth in the flat and saying he didn't like this restraint, this calm. It wasn't like Emerence. A major explosion would have been more in character. But my analysis of her mental state was cut short. Suddenly the dog went mad, quite literally. He howled, scratched, kicked the rugs into a tangled heap, and hurled himself on the floor, foaming at the mouth. He was in such a state I thought his last hour had come. I phoned the vet and asked him to come straight away, which he did, just as he had on that first memorable Christmas Eve. Viola worshipped him; he would even show off his tricks to him after an injection. Now he lay there, not even standing up when called. The vet knelt down beside him, talking to him while his lean, sensitive fingers played piano sonatas all over his body. Then he dusted his knees and shrugged his shoulders. There was nothing physical. He must have had some sort of shock; something dreadful had upset the balance of his nervous system. He tried giving him various orders, but Viola made no effort to obey. He wouldn't sit, he wouldn't walk. If the vet stood him up he fell on his side, as if paralysed. We parted on the understanding that he'd have another look at him the next day. That night I was to give him some glucose and a child's dose of tranquilliser. He had no idea what had happened to the dog, and if I nailed him on a cross he still wouldn't know. With that, he left.

I was setting the table for supper. Viola hadn't moved. I asked him to show me that he loved me, but he didn't even glance up,

243

he lay there like an old rag. Then suddenly he howled, in a voice so far beyond imagining it left me frozen with terror. The fully laden tray fell from my hands. I dared not go near him. I was convinced he'd gone mad and might savage me. I didn't want to believe what that sound was telling me, even with my calm, rational husband at my side in the kitchen next to the burnt remains of the dinner. He glanced at his watch and said, very quietly, "quarter past eight." "Quarter past eight," I repeated after him, as if some mad person were speaking through me, announcing the hour. "Quarter past eight; quarter past eight." When I'd declaimed it for the third time, my husband produced my raincoat and I fell silent. I suddenly felt that nothing that was happening around me was real. I'd been calling out the time like a parrot. What was wrong with me? Was I going insane? But I was lying to myself, as if my life depended on it, to avoid somehow putting into words what Viola had announced. But he knew, and my husband knew. The dog had been the first to understand and he had told us both. He was sobbing like a child.

The hospital corridor was teeming with doctors, and the matron could be heard on the phone from outside her office. "No questions, please," the doctor said when he saw us, clearly impatient to give us the news. After I'd gone, Emerence had at first lain in silence, tugging at her headscarf and refusing to answer when spoken to. This wasn't unusual behaviour. There'd been other times when she'd indicated she wanted to be left in peace. Some time after eight, when the nurse looked in to switch off the light, Emerence demanded to be sent home immediately, that very night. She had to search around the neighbouring houses, in the gardens, where her loved ones were waiting for her – no-one was looking after them or feeding them. They explained that this was impossible, for so many reasons. First of all, it was evening, so they couldn't give her a discharge note; in any case, there still wasn't anything to sleep on in the flat. Her manner became harsh and domineering, and she loudly informed them that they needn't bother to take her, she was quite strong enough now to overcome her cursed weakness. She had to go that minute, she couldn't stay, she really needed to. Then she actually tried to leave, throwing herself out of the bed. Of course she couldn't walk, or even stand. As she hit the floor, or perhaps even while she was falling, a new embolism, triggered by the Lieutenant Colonel's revelations and her subsequent meeting with me, paralysed not her brain this time, but her heart. I would never have believed it possible, but even in that surreal moment, as they were giving me the same facts that Viola had communicated without words, I found something else to take away from Emerence. I robbed her of the last thing she had of which she might have been properly proud, the well-deserved applause for a dignified finale in death. Though she continued to lie there, having been put back on the bed, from then on no-one paid her the slightest attention. The moment I saw her I had collapsed in the doorway as if struck down, and the entire medical team turned their attention on me. It was some time before they managed to bring me round. They wouldn't let me leave, but kept me in for a week. So now the visitors with the christening bowls came for me, Emerence having gallantly vacated the stage of public attention. They put me in a room with a telephone and a TV, attended to all my needs, watched over me and comforted me. I bathed in the warm glow of sympathy, rather like the newly honoured Toldi, leaning on an invisible spade, having just received the glorious message of pardon from King Lajos, with the dead body of my servant Bence at my feet, and above my head romantically shredded clouds bearing a legend of legends. My husband came every night, but only after nine, when he could be certain of not meeting strangers. Everyone else approached my bed with smiles of encouragement; his face alone never lost its expression of pity and overwhelming grief.

I often think back to how simply it all went in the end. Emerence placed no further burden, no more insoluble problems on her few blood relatives and loose circle of friends. Like a truly great commander she settled everything around her in person, with a single impressive gesture. If there was nothing to be done about herself, nothing she could do, then better to put an end to it. Humankind has come a long way since its beginnings and people of the future won't be able to imagine the barbaric early days in which we fought with one another, in groups or individually, over little more than a cup of cocoa. But not even then will it be possible to soften the fate of a woman for whom no-one has made a place in their life. If we all lacked the courage to admit this to ourselves, she at least had done so, and politely taken her leave. Now it seemed as though even government departments with no personal knowledge of her, and officials overburdened with work, were behaving as if ordered by her not to drag things out. The tenants' book had ended up in the lovers' seat along with other soiled documents, but the Lieutenant Colonel managed to arrange her burial without a scrap of paper changing hands, and the hospital found it quite natural that an excitable patient of some eighty years should be carried off by a heart attack. Dates were quickly named for the probate hearings and the cremation service. This was deemed to be only a preliminary burial, since Emerence's last resting place, according to the will, was to be the Taj Mahal, still waiting to be built. Józsi's boy showed me the relevant invoices and asked me to speak to the reverend minister about the church burial. I didn't agree to do this immediately because, in truth, I didn't want to. In this one particular at least I hoped to act in accordance with Emerence's wishes – she had never wanted a religious funeral. But the nephew thought the street would be scandalised and criticise him for not doing the right thing. We decided we wouldn't prepare a death notice but rather announce the time of burial in the paper. He informed the Csabadul relatives by letter, and they sent their condolences. Regrettably, other engagements prevented them saying their farewells in person; but they thought it proper all the same for Emerence to have left what she had to her younger brother Józsi's son, since they had never really provided for her (not that she would have asked) and in any case they had long been out of touch. And if the nephew intended to gather together the dead relatives from Nádori, they certainly would have no objection, but would in fact be grateful.

We were drawing up the list of what remained to be done, on the site of Emerence's former court, the entrance to the Forbidden City. Viola lay at our feet, supremely indifferent. I could now bring him here, to the old woman's former home, without a qualm. He behaved as if he'd never been there. For three consecutive days my husband had listened to his sobbing, then the whimpering died down and finally he fell silent. Then suddenly he gave up posing as a rag rug, stood up, shook himself, stretched his body, and looked at my husband as if he'd woken from a dream. From that day on he had no voice at all, quite literally: he never again drew our attention to anything. He never again expressed either pleasure or protest. At most, if he was ill he might snarl at the vet. But till the end of his life, he never barked again.

The Lieutenant Colonel had arranged for the probate

hearing to be on the same day as the funeral. We arrived at the council building at nine in the morning: myself, the nephew and the Lieutenant Colonel. There was no on-site inspection. The Lieutenant Colonel presented the Health Department's records and explained that there was still one room containing personal effects which he had inspected some years before – beautiful old furniture – but nothing else. The deceased had owned all the usual things found in a well-equipped household, but a good part of the kitchen contents had been destroyed. If they wished they could go and verify this. But there was no wish to verify anything. Józsi's son stated that while she was alive Emerence had supplemented his income, and the personal effects were for me. It was over in ten minutes. The young woman who conducted the meeting smiled and asked me to let her know if the deceased had been hoarding any treasure, in which case there would be tax to pay, and I promised to comply. The proceedings had been swift and courteous. They even offered us coffee. We were all in black, including the Lieutenant Colonel, in the uniform he wore when detailed to receive heads of state. We went in his car to Farkasrét Cemetery. Józsi's boy advised us that Emerence's real home would be up by St Stephen's Day, 20 August. By then the exhumations at Nádori would have taken place, and he would receive us again on 25 August, at the newly built crypt, for the final deposition of Emerence's urn.

A crowd of mourners in black darkened the square where the bier stood. I didn't see it for myself, but I was told afterwards that every self-employed person in the neighbourhood had shut up shop for the funeral – the shoemaker, the woman who decorated scarves, the soda-water vendor, the tailor, the invisible mender, the waffle maker, the podiatrist, the furrier and of course Sutu. On the door of every one of their shops was a sign with variations on the same text: *Closed until two for family reasons. Attending a funeral.* The shoemaker put it more concisely. All he wrote next to his opening hours was *E.M.E.R.E.N.C.E.* Mournful music played in the distance. The urn was surrounded by countless tiny bouquets, but I couldn't bear to look at it. Józsi's boy and the Lieutenant Colonel led me to the family pews. I was worried that the minister might not come. He and I had spent a painful half hour in deep discussion. It was so like a dialogue from the time of the early church fathers, brought up to date by a contemporary problem, that it could have been published in a theological journal. The priest's position was this: how could anyone lay claim to a church funeral who had, at every step of the way, made it clear that she had turned her back on Heaven, who never visited the house of God, and who systematically outraged the faithful with her pronouncements? When I tried to make him understand what sort of person Emerence was, he looked at me coldly and replied that he had to consider the point of view of both God and the Church regarding a request for ecclesiastical services from an individual who did not practise their faith, was actively obstructive towards members of the religious community, lived an irregular life, and never took communion. "She's not asking for it," I replied. "I am. And so is every well-disposed person. It is appropriate, as a form of homage. She may have heaped expletives on the Church as an institution, but I've known few devout believers who were as good Christians as this old woman. What she said about predestination was that she didn't believe God was a lesser person than herself. When Viola did wrong she always took into consideration that he wasn't human, and didn't punish him for all eternity, so how could the Lord have been so unjust as to damn her before he had judged what she had done with her life? This woman wasn't one to practise Christianity in church between nine and ten on Sunday mornings, but she had lived by it all her life, in her own neighbourhood, with a pure love of humanity such as you find in the Bible, and if he didn't believe that he must be blind, because he'd seen enough of it himself. She'd been all around the neighbourhood with her christening bowl. The learned and rather severe young man neither consented nor refused. He asked when the funeral would take place and escorted me to the door very politely, but without any show of sympathy. As he did so, he let me know that it was a pity Emerence had never given him the opportunity to get to know her better qualities.

So when his gowned figure actually appeared, I was deeply moved. His address was intelligent and based on crystal-clear logic. He acknowledged the valuable contribution made by those who worked with their hands, but he also warned the congregation not to think only of the bread by which we all lived, and not to imagine that religion was a personal matter between ourselves and God, or that the life of faith could be lived in private, unconnected with the Mother Church. In an icily correct but effective speech he bade farewell to the old woman. His words were so utterly devoid of feeling it was impossible to reconstruct the real Emerence from them. As I listened I felt a dull numbness, like the effect of chloroform, rather than the primal, anarchic agony you usually feel when you encounter someone you have loved now turned to dust, in some object like a little bowl, and you are required to believe that it is still the same person who once smiled at you.

The crowd of mourners was now so great you would have thought Emerence had had twelve children, each of whom had a similar number of their own, and had worked all her life in somewhere large, such as a factory. The main thoroughfare and side streets were darkened by the flood of her "followers". Some stood near the priest, clinging to the words of his correct eulogy and its message of consolation, others had placed themselves further away and were luckier, in that they could weep. We made our way slowly towards the columbarium, where I placed a small bunch of flowers from our garden next to the urn. A prayer was intoned, then they cemented a plate over the opening. Sutu was choking on her tears, Adélka was all stiff attention. She had her eyes fixed on Sutu, not on Emerence in her urn.

If someone stabs you in the heart with a sharp knife you don't collapse immediately, and we all realised that the loss of Emerence hadn't yet made itself felt inside us, that it would hit us only later, that only later would we be struck down. That wouldn't happen here, where she was still to be found, if only in the impossible form of an urn. It would more likely take place in our street, where she would never sweep again, or in the garden, where injured cats with their velvet paws and stray dogs would prowl in vain, with no-one now to throw them scraps of food. Emerence took with her a part of all our lives. The Lieutenant Colonel held himself through to the end of the service as if called to be guard of honour; Jozsi's boy and his wife were weeping heartfelt tears; but as for me, I cannot cry where people can see me, nor did I feel that this was the time for tears. That would come later; they weren't to be given so easily.

When everything was over, most of the mourners stayed on. Since Emerence's death Adélka had become louder, more assertive and somehow more shrill, as if Emerence's forceful personality had restrained her and kept her in the background. Now she was popping up all over the place, apparently arranging some sort of post-burial get-together, perhaps over tea or a glass of beer, and her clientele continued to stand around chatting. Sutu remained an isolated figure and soon left. She'd been black-listed from the moment she made her offer.

We made our way home. The Lieutenant Colonel had asked the nephew if he wished to be present when he opened up the inner room for me. His team was coming that afternoon, we'd be clearing out the flat and he was going to check the inventory he'd promised the Health Department. Józsi's boy said he preferred to go straight home, since this part of Emerence's will didn't concern him. We should give the keys to the flat back to the tenants' committee, and I could take home whatever I could use and give away what I couldn't. His wife obviously wanted to come, if only to see what I had inherited, but he told her not to be so nosy. If anything had been meant for them, Emerence would have seen to it. What they had was quite enough, and for it they were inexpressibly grateful to the old woman. They went off home in their own car. The Lieutenant Colonel drove us back, as he had brought us. My husband got out at our apartment and we went on to Emerence's. The street was empty. I had read Adélka's mind well. She'd obviously organised a funeral meal somewhere near the cemetery.

The axe was still there on the porch, propped up in the corner, and with it the Lieutenant Colonel prised off the boarding his plain-clothes men had nailed over both the outer door and the inner one that had lost its key. He asked if I wanted him to go in with me. "Please do," I replied. Emerence was a mythological being and my inheritance might be anything. There was no priest now to wash away my tension with words of calm reason.

"What are you afraid of?" he asked. "Emerence loved you. Nothing bad could ever come to you from her hands. I went in once before, and everything was covered in sheets. She had a full set of furniture in there, and a very fine mirror. So come on."

We stepped in together. It was pitch black inside and at first we could make nothing out. Of course – the shutters. The Lieutenant Colonel felt along the wall. Near the door, some of the disinfectant smell had seeped through (the place hadn't been aired for God knows how long), and we began to cough in the choking fumes. Finally he located the switch. The instant the light came on he shoved me back into the outer room, the one now fully restored to order. He'd glimpsed me struggling with nausea, as if poisoned by gas. Only when he'd thrown every window open did he let me back in. But I'd already seen all I needed of Emerence's bequest.

You see this kind of thing in films, but even then the eye has difficulty believing. Dust inches deep covers the furniture; spiders' webs fly into the actors' faces and hair with every move they make. If she had once protected her things with sheets, they must have been taken off immediately after the police inspection, because they were nowhere to be seen. I stood in the most beautifully furnished room I had ever seen. I brushed the side of my hand along one of the armchairs, and a pale-pink velvet glowed in its gilded rococo frame. I was standing in a salon of the late-eighteenth century, a museum treasure, the *chef d'oeuvre* of some craftsman who supplied the aristocracy. For the house I had never bought I now possessed a drawing-room table with porcelain inlays on which shepherds chased after lambs, and a little couch with tiny gilded legs as slender as those of young kittens. As I patted the upholstery the dust billowed up and then drifted down again. But the blow had split the fabric, which tore as if killed by unkindness. A console mirror rose all the way to the ceiling. On a small table stood two porcelain figurines, and, between them, something at last alive, a perpetual clock, showing the days, the phases of the moon and revolutions of the stars. It was still working. I went to dust it off, but the Lieutenant Colonel stopped me.

"Don't touch a thing," he warned. "It's dangerous to move anything. The covers have perished, the furniture's dead. Everything here is dead, except the clock. Let me lift it down."

I wanted to take the figurines in my hands, or look to see what, if anything, there was in the console, and I didn't listen. I grasped the handle of a drawer. It didn't respond. I would have to play with it, to learn the special secret movement to which it would yield, which only the family would have known. What followed was very different. Suddenly everything around me became a vision out of Kafka, or a horror film: the console collapsed. Not with a brutal swiftness but gently, gradually, it began to disintegrate into a river of golden sawdust. The figurines tumbled down, along with the clock. The frame of the console and its table crumbled into nothing; the drawers and legs were no more than dust.

"Woodworm," the Lieutenant Colonel said. "You won't be able to take anything from here. It's all finished. Emerence hasn't opened the door since she let me in for the inspection. So, this was her reward for saving Eva Grossman. As it was, it would have been worth a fortune, but you can see it's ruined. Look."

He pressed the palm of his hand into an armchair and it too collapsed. I don't know why – it was an insane association of ideas – but images of the tank battle on the Hortobágy filled my mind. The chairs went down, the velvet splitting into strips and bursting from the wooden frames. The legs were turning to powder before our eyes, as if some secret chemical preparation had kept them alive only so long as they remained unseen by human eye. And I saw once again what I had seen as a girl, a herd of cattle machine-gunned by the Germans, the sky seemingly impaled on their horns, and the chair-covers, like the hides of those beasts, shredded into nothing.

"There's nothing here you could use," the Lieutenant Colonel said. "I'll have it cleared away. Will you take the clock? It's still ticking. The figurines, I'm sorry to say, were broken."

I didn't want the clock. It stayed there on the floor. I didn't want anything. I didn't even look back – that's how I left Emerence's home, still incapable of tears. The Lieutenant Colonel took his leave, but didn't bother to shut the door behind him. Adélka told me that when the team of cleaners arrived and looked in, neither the shattered porcelain nor the clock were there. There was nothing, only the pulverised furniture. But I was no longer interested.

THE SOLUTION

Back home, I found Viola passive, almost indifferent. I took him for a walk. We went past Emerence's door, where one of the tenants was doing duty sweeping the pavement, and we greeted one another warmly. I also saw Sutu, sitting in her stand again, not seeming in the least discouraged or sad about the fact that no-one was buying from her. She was eating some of her own fruit, and she greeted me politely. It was very quiet in the street; very few houses had the television on. Not quite knowing what to do with myself, I called on the priest to pay for the service. There was no-one in the office, but I found him out in the garden, reading, and he took the money for it. I offered him my thanks for his kindness, but he declined to accept them, rather stiffly. It was merely his duty, he told me. At this point we came closer to one another than at any time of our lives. He looked at me as if he'd suddenly noticed something that had escaped his attention all day, and said, "So few people are watching television."

"They're in mourning," I replied. "There are a lot of country people in Pest. This silence is a country custom. It's like Good Friday – it's considered wrong to listen to music."

"But she had only one relative, and he doesn't even live here. So who are these mourners?"

"Everyone. Catholics. Jews. Everyone owed her something."

I would never have thought him capable of this, but he accompanied me to the corner of our street, from where Emerence's former home could be seen. The lady engineer was silently sweeping the street. The priest looked at me again. This time he had no more questions.

On the Sunday following the funeral I went to church as usual. The congregation had never been so large. There were people there who never attended. The local greengrocer Elemér, from whose mouth you heard nothing but blasphemy, was there in black, along with the Evangelical doctor, the Catholic professor, the Jewish dry cleaner, the Unitarian furrier. The service was like an Ecumenical requiem; it would have been shameful to have stayed away. Only the handyman – who never missed his Evangelical meetings – was absent. But there had been a wild wind the previous night, leaves lay scattered everywhere and it was his turn to sweep the street. As he placed the wafer on my tongue, the priest looked me in the eye, and though I should have been keeping my eyes fixed on my three fingers that symbolised the Trinity, I returned his gaze, and he knew I was honouring him for his gesture of respect, paid to the people of the street at Emerence's funeral.

One other person was missing from the church: Sutu. We made our way home knowing ourselves without sin, and though we didn't talk about it we felt our superiority to her. So there! Nobody needed her. The street was united, and the tenants were fending for themselves. Even I had swept the leaves, once, though I was so incompetent Adélka had taken the broom from my hands, and I sneaked off, ashamed that I wasn't good for anything, probably not even my profession. Only Sutu took no part in the shared work, and we rarely saw her. She had closed her stall, and quite how she got by was a mystery. I had the feeling she was staying at home and waiting for something, but there was no indication whether she was still there or had gone away. It was summer, and no smoke was seen rising from her little house. Just what she was hoping and waiting for became apparent later.

The news was brought a couple of weeks later by Viola's old friend the handyman. Caressing the dog's ears to cover his embarrassment, he began by saying that Mr Brodarics had a message for me. The villa, it seemed, couldn't manage without Emerence after all. They could just about cope while the weather was fine, as now, but when autumn set in and the leaves came down, it would be beyond them. Few of them were young, and those who were worked from dawn till dusk.

"Say no more," I butted in. "Mr Brodarics is telling me the house can't manage without a full-time caretaker, so you're going to employ someone, if you haven't done so already. I see. Did you advertise?"

"As a matter of fact, no."

He looked away from me, his eyelashes quivering with anxiety. Viola suddenly lunged away from me. I hadn't meant to hurt him, but my fingers were so tense I had unwittingly squeezed his windpipe.

"Look," the handyman said, "we've known her a thousand years. She's clean, sober, hardworking, she doesn't drink and she's too old to chase after men. When Sutu made her offer, it was too soon, and we were upset. But since then we've all cooled down and begun to do some thinking. And finally, we've managed to agree."

"On Sutu," I said, bitterly.

"No, not Sutu. On Adélka. Mr Brodarics thought we should tell you, so it wouldn't come as a surprise."

But nothing surprised me any more. As soon as he left I went and stood out on the balcony. Emerence's porch was clearly visible, and there, at the table, sat Adélka. It was beautifully laid out, the way Emerence had liked it. She was hunched over a bowl, shelling or peeling something, and she wasn't alone. The shoemaker's wife was leaning over the bowl alongside her. At last there was no-one to see me, and I felt able to cry. My husband was unable to comfort me, though his eyes held nothing but compassion.

"The house can't manage without Emerence, nor can the people on the street," I heard him say. "Adélka isn't a bad woman, and it's true we all know her. She did well to bide her time. Sutu rushed it. So what are you grieving for now? It can't be for Emerence. The dead always win. Only the living lose."

"I'm grieving for us," I answered. "We are all traitors."

"Not traitors. Just too many things to do."

He stood up. The dog struggled to his feet, went to him and pressed his head against his knee. Since Emerence's death my husband had taken her place.

Once again, it wasn't me. All Emerence's miracles were oblique, never in a straight line.

"You're upsetting yourself, and once again you're not writing. You're behind with all your work. Why aren't you at the typewriter?"

"I can't," I replied. "I'm tired. And depressed. I hate everyone. I hate Adélka."

"You're tired because you're cooking, and cleaning, and doing the shopping. And you haven't been able to find anyone you can bear to have near you, because you aren't looking for just anyone, you're looking for the one person who will never be with you again. But Emerence has gone. Understand that, once and for all. You have binding contracts. You have to work. You should be getting on with your own work, and if you weren't so dead tired you would have known long ago what step to take. Everyone in the street can see it. The Brodaricses, the handyman. It's only you that can't. So do it now, for God's sake. The people in the villa have given you the message, in their own indirect way."

I covered my ears so as not hear. He waited until I had calmed down a bit, then he lifted Viola's lead off its hook.

"The handyman called because everyone here loves you, and they wanted to make it easier for you to do what you've already decided, only you don't have the courage to admit it. How long are you going to go on dithering? It's so senseless! You taught Emerence that nothing can rival the act of creation, so why should you feel ashamed of it before the person who succeeds her? She'll come to see it too."

Viola submitted passively as I fitted the leash on him. He showed no pleasure, and he made no protest. He was ready to go.

"Take the dog down, have a bit of a walk with him, and come to an agreement with her before anyone else gets her."

"I'm not going to make any agreement with Adélka. I don't want her. Emerence didn't much like her, she just felt sorry for her."

"Who's talking about Adélka? Adélka is mawkish, weak-minded and stupid. With Sutu. She looked after everything impeccably when we were in Athens. Sutu is straightforward, brave, unsentimental. She doesn't dither about, and as far as work is concerned, she's as pitiless as you are."

"Emerence." I uttered her name with a strength of voice that seemed to know, almost independently of me, that I would never be able to say that word aloud again, not to anyone.

"Emerence is dead, Sutu is alive. And she doesn't love you, or anyone else. She lacks that capacity, but her countless other qualities make up for it. Sutu, if you show her respect, will help you for the rest of your life, because you can never put her at risk. She has no secrets, no locked doors; and if she ever did have such a door, there are no siren songs that would induce her to open it to you — or anyone."

THE DOOR

My dreams are always the same, down to the finest detail, a vision that returns again and again. In this never-changing dream I am standing in our entrance hall at the foot of the stairs, facing the steel frame and reinforced shatterproof window of the outer door, and I am struggling to turn the lock. Outside in the street is an ambulance. Through the glass I can make out the shimmering silhouettes of the paramedics, distorted to unnatural size, their swollen faces haloed like moons.

The key turns.

My efforts are in vain.

www.vintage-books.co.uk